The Love Letters of Boaz Jackson

ANDI J. FERON

Ebook ISBN: 979-8-88736-162-8

Paperback ISBN: 979-8-88736-163-5

Hardback ISBN: 979-8-88736-226-7

Chapter One

Boaz Jackson was the epitome of evil in its purest form, and I'd never been surer of anything in my life. My biggest evidence to attest to this was the love letters he wrote to girls in our school. Joyful, beautiful romantic songs of devastation that wreaked havoc in their wake by restoring relationships, one hopeless couple at a time.

His disheveled brown hair leaned forward as he hunched over a notebook, moving his blue feather pen he had to use to devise his deceptive verses. He held his bottom lip between his teeth and stared down in concentration as thoughts flowed from his devious head into words formed without conscience.

The tall oak shading him from the sweltering afternoon sun inspired my imagination. A reverie took shape in my brain of dissolving the tree and holding a magnifying glass over his paper until the sun ignited his notebook into flames. The dramatics were beneath me, but since I didn't possess tree evaporating powers, they would remain in my mind where I placed all my most satisfying plots.

"You're staring at him again. No matter how much you try to burn holes into his notebook, I don't think your eyes are going to evolve and make it happen." My best friend Effie pulled her sandwich from its paper sack. She didn't trust food made in the cafeteria and had brought her lunch in a paper sack since kindergarten.

"Look at him, sitting there plotting to fix people's love lives. It's a terrible thing."

She snorted while lining her cookie up next to her chips and carefully removing her sandwich from its plastic encasement. "Yes, he's the devil for writing beautiful poetry that makes people feel loved."

"For sure. Exactly. He's the worst there is."

She rolled her eyes. "Ivy, you need a hobby. Live and let live is my motto."

"He should let people live their lives and not interfere, but he doesn't. He's what's wrong with this world."

Boaz gently folded his letter into a flat heart and placed it into one of his signature squared envelopes, tucking it into his black backpack. His eyes found mine across the school lawn, and he grinned as he had the nerve to wave at me.

Effie spread out her napkin, still in the process of arranging her lunch into perfect order. "See how friendly he is to you. How can you hate him?"

"He's grinning because he wants to rile me up. It's his favorite pastime." I kept my eyes locked on him.

He strode back toward the school, sent me one last wave, and laughed when I stuck my tongue out at him.

"You realize you look like a five-year-old when you do that." Effie used her plastic fork to inch all her food into a perfect row before grabbing her first carrot stick.

Only when Boaz disappeared could I relax enough to dig into the paste the cafeteria called mac and cheese. I knew firsthand the wickedness dealt out by Boaz Jackson, and someone needed to put a stop to his little charade. Effie didn't know

Boaz's cruelty like I did, and for now, I needed to keep it that way.

❧

Droolius Caesar jumped on me, nearly knocking me onto our grey wooden floor. His tongue continually dangled out the side of his mouth unless eating or drinking. He also had a lazy eye that took a few seconds to catch up with his normal one, the tip of his nose had fallen off at some point, and his left ear flopped over while his right stuck straight in the air.

All of his facial issues made him endearing. We'd gotten the white lab mix at a shelter a couple of years ago, hours before his death march. The lady said they hadn't expected anyone to choose him with the way he looked. We called him Droo for short. He panted, with his limp tongue bobbing against his cheek.

I scratched his ears and went back to my room to start my homework. When I reached my fifth algebra equation, a knock on my doorway startled me. I slid the headphones off and glanced up at my mom.

The messy bun holding her black wavy hair in place and the flour caking her cheeks told me she'd been baking again. That, along with her eye bags, told me today had stressed her out. My mother's stress fed us well.

"I need you to stay with Pop. Do you think you can handle it long enough for me to go to the store?" She leaned on the door as though her exhaustion didn't allow her to stay upright.

"Yeah, I can handle it."

I packed up my homework and headed into the den where Pop sat in his favorite blue recliner that had an enormous rip down the back. He stared at the off TV, mumbling about the media and gripping the silver walker in front of him. The small blue lamp on the end table lit up the small area around him.

I grabbed the black comb next to his Cubs baseball cap. "Pop, your hair needs some help here."

His white ring of hair laid down flat as I combed it and made sure not the scrape the bald front part of his head. His mouth moved rapidly, letting out incoherent sentences and grunts.

His eyes met mine. "Lilith. No eggs today."

I smoothed down the last bit of his hair and stood back to inspect him. Patchy grey stubble covered drooping cheeks, reminding me to write that he needed shaving on the care pad. "You look handsome today, Pop."

His eyes, blue as the sky, glazed over most of the time anymore as they did now. "Lilith! I said no eggs."

"I didn't pick eggs up at the store, so you don't have to worry about it."

"Good. Good." He pushed himself up on his walker and wobbled in place.

I steadied him as he shuffled. A few laps around the kitchen island usually wore him out enough to get him back in his chair. His mouth continued to move as he babbled about something I couldn't make out. He went to the kitchen and opened the cupboard, only to let it slam a few seconds later. He repeated this five more times before removing several cups from the cabinet. His eyes jerked to the neon blue marshmallow peeps sitting next to the toaster, and he removed them from their plastic baggy.

I went behind him, straightening everything he'd messed up. People always tried to stop him, but it irritated him. It seemed easier to fix things rather than fight with him over something he wouldn't remember he did in five minutes.

He slid his feet in tiny steps forward and made it to the pantry, where he found crackers to dump on the counter in front of the peeps. The crackers flew all directions as he emptied the box, so his fists could crush them.

I narrowed my eyes as he shoved the marshmallow candy into the crackers. "Pop, what are you doing?"

"Lilith! The birds need fed."

I grinned. "That's pretty smart."

"No eggs. Lilith, no eggs."

"Yep, I forgot them at the store. I have a present for you."

His eyes shifted from the floor to briefly meet mine. "No eggs."

I walked to a drawer, pulled out a soft red towel that had decorative bumps, and handed it to him. His face lit up. He draped it over his walker and started heading down the wrong hallway. I directed him until we made it back to his chair, where he sat, running the rag between his fingertips. His face rubbed against it, and when he tired of that, I threw him a pillowcase. Every ten minutes or so, I gave him a different material to feel.

"Lilith!"

"Yes, Pop?" I took his hands in mine and looked him in the eye.

"No eggs."

"The store is out of them for the next hundred years."

"That's a good thing. I love you, Lilith." His eyes cleared for a few seconds.

"I love you too, Pop."

"Ivy!" Mom stood in the doorway, watching me with a frown. "What's with the kitchen?"

"Pop needed to feed the birds." I smiled at her, but it didn't relax her tension.

"You can't let him do things like that."

I hugged my grandpa. "I'll see you later."

"Bye, Lilith. Can you buy eggs?"

I gave his hand one more squeeze. "Yep, next time I go to the store."

He smiled, and his eyes glazed back over.

♥

The bulletin board informed of many things, and it always became my first spot every morning, even before my locker. The overcrowded hallway contained the morning bustle of kids trying to make their first class before the bell. Lockers slamming and boisterous conversation made it difficult to concentrate as my eyes roamed over all the activities. Red in the far corner caught my eye, and I groaned. Business must have slowed for Hades. Boaz had put a flier up offering his services with a twenty-five percent discount for first-time buyers. I ripped his advertisement off the board, crumpled it up, and stomped on it.

"You owe me printing costs."

I whirled around, practically slamming into Boaz's chest. "I owe you no such thing. This is community service."

He raised an eyebrow. "Littering is community service? Someone is a backward thinker."

I picked up the paper and tossed it in the trash bin a little bit down the hall. "Where it belongs."

He unzipped his backpack and pinned another red paper to the board. With a salute, he hurried on down the hall. I marched over to the replacement flier, took out my sharpie, and wrote scam in giant letters across the front. Boaz had a lot of nerve doing what he did. It was my obligation to protect all the vulnerable hearts around me. The warning bell propelled me to science class that I unfortunately shared with Lucifer himself.

Boaz tipped back in his chair, resting it on the back legs. "Lovely, seeing you here today, Ivy. Been a minute."

I wadded up a piece of paper and threw it at his forehead. "Don't talk to me."

He folded it into an origami swan and set it on my desk. "All fixed. I'm great at turning ugly things beautiful. Feel free to stop by my house for a makeover." He winked and sat back down.

"That's convincing when you can't even help your own face."

He smirked and tipped his chair back as the teacher came in and wrote the topic on the chalkboard.

Mr. Lee wrote nature hike in big letters. "We are taking a field trip for our midterm exam in two weeks. It's going to be a scavenger hunt." Everyone groaned. "Don't get so excited, people. Contain your enthusiasm for the great outdoors. It'll be fun, and you get to compete against each other. The first team back will get extra credit, and then scores will lower with each team that returns. It'll be a blast. I promise." He laughed at the grumbles and started his lecture.

Chapter Two

I glanced at my phone for the tenth time and ran my fingers through my hair. Usually, by the middle of the week, I had six to seven requests for letters. It had become clear it was time to take things to the second high school across town.

I opened a new browser to check on Benson and scrolled through the comments, looking for an update. My fingers tapped my desk as the rhythm helped me concentrate. There had to be a way to bring in more money. Benson's life was an hourglass, dripping piece by piece into a pit he'd never escape unless something happened quickly.

I stared at the two pictures in shocking contrast to each other. His chubby, smiling cheeks and thick black hair showed happiness and health. The photo next to it showed a very different Benson, mere months after the first. His eyes were sunken, cheeks pale and scratched, and his mouth held not even a hint of a smile. His eyes had gone from vibrant to hollow, and it ripped me in two. How could the world allow this to happen? It happened every day, and no one cared.

Another glance at my silent phone showed I needed to step it up. Benson's sand spiraled too fast.

Noah clutched his teddy bear to him. "Bo, I need my bedtime story."

"Sure. Give me a minute." I closed out my browser tabs and put my phone on the charger.

Noah hurried to his room to climb under his Ninja Turtle comforter that rested on his race car bed. His room had shelves of books that he valued as much as his Elmo and Minion collections. They decorated his room in random spots throughout. He could tell you how many he had of each, and it became like where's Waldo to find them all.

I picked up the three books on his nightstand. "These the ones?"

"Yeah, I wanted a fourth, but that's okay."

"Which one did you want as the fourth?" I held up my finger. "I think I can guess this one. Was it Monster goes to cooking school?"

He laughed, and his soulful brown eyes with white speckles came alive. "Yeah, Cookie Monster origins. How he got his name."

I pulled it down from the shelf and started reading, throwing in voice alterations and dramatic hand gestures. My brother loved every minute of it and talked me into a fifth book.

"Maybe I could have a sixth, Bo? You think I could?"

I yawned and returned all his books to their proper locations. "It's a school night, bud. Maybe Friday night."

He nodded. "You'll leave the night light on?"

"Yeah, wouldn't dream of shutting it off." I hugged him goodnight and headed to my room.

My thirteen-year-old brother was my best friend, and I took him everywhere I could. Everywhere mom allowed anyway. People would ask me about him, and I would tell them he loved to cook and specialized in omelets. They'd scrunch their faces up in disbelief, as though someone with

Down Syndrome wouldn't be able to do that. Noah had spent his life showing what he could do instead of what he couldn't. His extra chromosome was an awesome fact about him that joined so many others.

I took one more look at Benson's pictures and turned out the lights.

Ivy Carter annoyed me to no end with her constant desire to sabotage my business. It wasn't my fault no one had ever paid me to write her a letter. That had to be the reason she hated me, right? It made the most sense, and her bitterness caused issues for me. I sat on her desk and waited for her to enter the room. The scowl she sent me made my entire day a success.

"Get off my desk!" Her nose twitched like a rabid bunny. Her green eyes swirled like a vortex, ready to toss me to the ground.

"We need to have a discussion."

Her brown ponytail swished behind her as she shook her head. "No." Such violent thoughts revealed themselves with her curled fists that covered her purple nail polish.

"Quit taking down my fliers."

She crossed her arms. "Go out of business."

"You're like an anti-cupid."

"I'm anti-you and your lies."

I rolled my eyes and opened my mouth when Mr. Lee walked in and shot me a glare. I jumped off Ivy's desk and sat down at my own. Several other students scrambled to their spots and drew out notebooks from their bags.

Mr. Lee sat his coffee on his desk and started up the projector for the lecture. He clasped his hands together with a loud pop that diverted the class's attention to him. "We are picking nature partners today. Two of you will work together to find the list in the hopes that you make it back fastest and receive the best grade."

A girl in the front flapped her hand around until Mr. Lee called on her. "Shouldn't it be about learning things and not about the speed at which we do?"

"No, you should have already learned things in my class, and finding these things is the test. When you take a test, are you learning or sharing what you have learned?"

"Both."

Mr. Lee shook his head, causing his gelled-down black hair to rise slightly in one stiff-looking sheet. "It was a rhetorical question. My assistant Ms. Donahue has randomly taped note cards to the bottom of your chairs. She used to be a poker dealer in Vegas, so they were well shuffled. Each one has a number on it. Your partner has the same one. You will pull out the card, write your name on it and hand it to me. I will announce who partners are on the day of the trip because I want no griping. It will be what it'll be. Che sarà sarà and all that."

We all grabbed our note cards and took them to the front. Mr. Lee went over the details of the hike and handed out permission slips. Those who couldn't get theirs signed or forgot would stay in the classroom with his assistant and do an essay-type exam. We'd get to skip the rest of the classes since the hike would take several hours. That seemed the better option to me.

🖤

I scowled at the bulletin board, took down the marked-up flier, and replaced it with a new one. The culprit wasn't a mystery. One person set out every day to make things harder on me, and part of me worried she'd succeeded. Business had dwindled at a time I couldn't afford for it to. I bolted for the parking lot and located Ivy's car, having the brief temptation to flatten all her tires. Letting the air out a little in a non-damaging way seemed appealing.

She marched toward me with her lips pressed and her eyes wide like the psychopath she clearly was. "Are you stalking me now?"

I snorted and broke into laughter. "Like you're anyone I'd want to spend time with."

"Why are you standing by my car?"

"The pavement is public property."

She crossed her arms, squinting from the bright sun overhead. "I'm getting a restraining order."

"I'm going to get one for my fliers! This is my freedom of expression you are infringing on."

"That's what I do when someone's expression hurts other people."

I threw my hands up. "What are you talking about? Do you even know what I do?"

"Yes, you write love letters that people give to other people that gives them false hope that they're loved. That's cruel."

"Who's to say they're not true?"

"If they can't write them themselves and mean it, it shouldn't be done." She stepped around me and opened her car door. "I would move out of the way if I were you."

"What are you going to run me over?"

"Don't tempt me!"

"Psycho!"

"Lucifer!" She got inside and slammed her door shut. She backed up onto the grass and zoomed around me.

I jumped back to save my feet and landed on my butt on the asphalt. She stuck her hand out her window and wiggled her fingers. Ivy Carter had issues. Her cold heart didn't want others to be happy. Who was against love letters? Ivy Carter's relentless pursuit to keep relationships in limbo bugged me to no end.

I got in my truck and drove to the middle school to pick up Noah. He jumped up and down, waving a paper. He hiked his backpack higher on his shoulders and charged toward me.

He flew into my car and wrapped his arms around me. "I'm so glad to see you!"

"I'm glad to see you, too. How was your day?"

"I got a good grade on my math test." He handed me the paper with a red smiley face by his name.

I gave him a high five. "You rock!"

"That reminds me. We should rock. Put some tunes on up in here, Bo!"

I laughed and turned it to his favorite station, watching him bob around in his seat.

"We should go to karaoke today!" He waved his hands back and forth.

"Karaoke is only on Fridays."

"You take me Friday?"

"Sure."

He pumped his fist in the air. "That's living, Bo! That's living!"

Whenever I got bored or down, I hung out with Noah because he never failed to liven up my life. We drove home and cooked dinner together. Mom walked through the door and stared at our spaghetti and homemade meatballs set out on plates, along with garlic bread and salad.

She set her purse on its hook and washed her hands at the sink. "This is amazing, boys! Thank you."

"I love cooking spaghetti because I get to make the sauce just right. It's like Goldilocks now." Noah set one of the plates in mom's spot.

She slid into the chair and used a spoon to lift some sauce and drip it onto the plate. "You got it, Noah. It's perfect."

Dad walked in from the hall. "I smell garlic bread." He gave my mom a kiss and sat down.

We talked about our days and worked together to clean everything up afterward. I slipped away to my room to do homework but got on my computer to check my favorite group. I scrolled down and put the pictures of a little boy named Charlie and a girl Esme in my save file. Five posts down, my heart stopped.

I'm sorry to inform everyone that Benson passed away today. He was twelve years old.

I blinked as tears pooled in my eyes and went over to my board, where I moved Benson's picture from one side to the other. I looked at all the others I'd had to move there and resisted the urge to punch the wall. Charlie and Esme's pictures went on the opposite side. Tomorrow I'd take fliers to the other high school and hope more jobs would start pouring in.

Chapter Three

Morgan's playhouse was one of the coolest places on Earth, and Friday nights were the best because they meant karaoke night. It was an awareness center that offered numerous programs to benefit individuals with Down Syndrome and their families. Their reading, writing, and math programs were unmatched. Noah had gone from being behind in school to catching up to his peers in most areas. They knew how the mind of someone with Down Syndrome usually learned best and taught them using one-on-one tutoring.

I aligned the chairs into neat rows on the grey carpet while Noah chatted with his friends. He stood with several kids around his age. These nights were his, so I always came along to help set up and tear down to ensure they had enough help to keep them going.

The open area was where most of the big events took place, but a hall to my left led to smaller rooms for classes and tutoring. The entrance had a welcome desk and an indoor toddler play area. A hall to my right led to a gym with a larger indoor playground. The windows were covered in posters of people with Down Syndrome who came to the playhouse. Noah's picture hung in the front window that faced the street. It made him very proud, and we had to get a picture with it every time we came.

Brenda tapped the mic but got no response. "Boaz, would you mind checking the sound system when you're done with chairs?"

"Yeah, no problem." I finished all the rows and went to the sound booth, where I found the mic system completely unplugged. "Try it now!" I shouted.

She tapped, and this time the mic released an echoing thud followed by a squeal. I moved on to the kitchen to see how refreshments were going.

Linda, another volunteer, pointed at a tray of crackers with cheeses and other assorted snacks that were arranged to look like a cat. "Your brother did those. I asked him to set some items on a tray, and he turned it into art."

"He wants to be a chef."

"He'll have to join our cooking classes when he's old enough."

I grabbed the tray to take to the snack table. "He's counting down to it. He can tell you how many days he has left. I helped him calculate it, and then every morning, he crosses one off and puts the new number. He drags me into his room to make sure he did it right even though he always does. I think he just wants me to see how much closer he is."

"I should talk to Brenda and see if we can do some junior classes."

I grabbed a second tray and balanced both on my palms. "You do that, and you'll be his hero. I'd be happy to help too."

"I'll let Brenda know."

I set out the trays, setting the cracker cat next to the bear and dog. Music poured from the speakers, and everyone chatting sprung to life, clapping their hands over their heads.

Brenda ran onto the stage and picked up the microphone

that let off another squeal. "Welcome! Who's ready for some karaoke!"

The kids went crazy, high fiving each other and chanting that they were ready. The first one got onto the stage and started hopping around to the music while shouting out the lyrics. Each person went until finally it was Noah's turn.

He jumped on the stage with his arms widespread. "Look at my Ninja Turtle shirt, everyone!"

The room clapped and roared about how awesome his shirt was.

Noah beamed as "Stand By Me" played from the machine. "This is to my brother Bo, everyone." He pointed the microphone at me. "That's him. There in the back."

Mandy, a girl in the front row, threw her hands out. "We know, Noah, you dedicate this song to him every week. Every single week."

"That's because he is the best big brother."

Noah joined the music a bit into the lyrics, and I waited for my part that would inevitably arrive.

My brother waved me onto the stage. "Bo, let's finish this together."

I made my way next to Noah and put my arm around him. We belted out the last few lyrics together. The night ended with a grand finale of everyone swaying on stage together to Noah's favorite song, "Boxes" by the Goo Goo Dolls. He liked how it talked about family being there for each other. Everyone left to get snacks, and I stayed behind to help tear down the stage and put chairs away.

Brenda gave me a hug. "Thank you for all your help with these events, Boaz. I don't know what we'd do around here without you."

I shrugged and finished winding up an orange extension cord. "It's no big deal. This place has helped Noah so much and will continue as he gets older. All the supports in place are amazing."

"Linda mentioned you'd be willing to help with a junior cooking class?"

"Yeah, I'd love to. That would make Noah's entire year, so whatever you need, let me know."

Once everything had been put away in the main room, I helped with cleaning the snack area and dishes. Noah stood with his friends, talking and laughing. I hung off to the side until he was ready, and we climbed into my black pickup truck. It had a balance of rust and paint and more dents than the surface of the moon, but it was my baby.

"Bo. Bo." Noah's eyes shifted to the floor, and he chewed on his lip.

"Yeah?"

"How do you get girls to like you?"

I chuckled and turned down the radio. The music still rolled out, but the lyrics muffled enough I could focus on our conversation. "It depends on the girl. Not all like the same things. That's why you need to get to know them. Ultimately, you should be yourself because if she doesn't like who you are, it won't work out, anyway."

"Oh." His shoulders slumped.

"Why? Is there a girl you like?"

He threw his hands forward and moved them up and down. "You can tell I do, Bo. I talk to her all the time. She sings karaoke like an angel. How could I not like her?"

I stared off for a second, running through all the girls at the event. Most were around Noah's age, and he talked to pretty much everyone. Apparently, he thought he talked to one more, and I should have noticed. I hadn't, but setup and tear down had kept me occupied.

I shook my head. "It's not coming to me, bud. I'm sorry."

He blew out an exasperated breath. "I will give you one

more hint. It's an easy one. She was the prettiest girl in the entire room tonight."

"They all seem like nice girls."

His jaw dropped. "One clearly stands out, Bo. It's Mandy." He smacked his forehead. "I can't believe I even had to say it to you."

"The girl who always yells at you about the songs you pick?"

"Yes! That's her. You finally got it! I think we could go on a date sometime."

"You never know unless you ask her," I said.

He sunk into the seat. "She may say no."

"She might. If she does, I'll take you out for chocolate fudge ice cream."

"Yes! Thanks, Bo." He turned the radio knob up. "Maybe we could have ice cream, anyway."

"Okay, sure." I stopped at Noah's favorite ice cream shop on the way home. We sat at a small round table, sharing our cones, while he told me all the reasons that he liked Mandy.

Back at home, I read Noah his bedtime stories and went to my room to check out the help wanted ads. I needed to do better, and with my letter-writing business dwindling, that would require something more traditional. I couldn't let another kid down the way I had Benson.

I clicked through the photos, trying to find a profile that only needed the thousand I'd saved up in my bank account. My hand paused the mouse when I came to Maisy, and I read her information.

Heart problems and needs surgery as soon as possible for the best outcome.

She needed a hundred more than I had, but I clicked the donate button and would work on getting the last hundred soon if no one else helped before I could. I printed off her picture and stuck it on my second board for those I was able to help. After staring at the photos for a while, I arranged them in priority and returned to my job search. A few applications later, I called it a night and went to bed.

♥

Arms shook me awake, and a bright light beamed straight into my eyes the second they opened. I resisted because, as foggy as my barely woken mind was, it still comprehended it was Saturday. That should have meant I slept for as long as I chose.

I stared up at my brother, glancing and groaning at my red, glowing alarm clock. "Noah, it's five in the morning on a Saturday. What could you possibly want?"

He grinned, showing his white teeth that had a slight gap between the two top front ones and an incisor that stuck slightly forward. His brown hair spread chaotically across his head like it had endured wind fury. "Bo! Mom leaves for work in an hour. We need to make her breakfast."

I sat up and squinted at my hot rod wall calendar. "It's not her birthday or Mother's Day."

"It's we make pancakes because we love her day."

"That's not a holiday."

He tugged on my arm. "I made it up. Come on. You're lazy."

Noah wore his flannel Ninja turtle pajamas, and I wore my boxers and a tank. He got all the ingredients while I set up our workspace on our large grey granite kitchen island.

I straddled a stool and opened the cookbook. "You're going to read the ingredients and then match the amount to the measuring cups."

He shook his head, making his chin and lower lip wobble. "You can. It's much easier as you show me."

"Who's being lazy now?"

"Pfft. You gotta play that card." He stuck his chubby finger on the first one and bent forward in concentration. "Flour is most important. It's first."

"They all are. Without any of these, the recipe will fail."

"It's first. That makes it most important." He took his time measuring each ingredient and leveling it off with a spoon to make sure it fit the exact right amount.

The griddle heated while he worked, and it hit the perfect temperature by the time we started pouring in the batter. It sizzled, and Noah hovered over it with a black spatula, waiting for the second I told him he could flip it.

He gave the first a big toss in the air. It flew out of control and landed dough side first onto our blue tiled floor. His mouth gaped.

"Maybe less enthusiasm on the next ones." I got a paper towel and cleaned up the rogue pancake mess.

We placed them on a big plate, and Noah set up a spot for our mom.

She came out of her bedroom in her business suit and hair in a bun. "Something smells good. I could get used to this."

Noah's eyes shifted to the floor. "Don't choose the bottom ones. They are black on one side."

She smiled and picked the top two. "They are fluffy and delicious. You did well."

Noah glanced at me while grinning and giving me a thumbs up. I returned his with my own. There would be no going back to sleep now. I decided today would be an excellent day to distribute my fliers. Once my mom left, and breakfast was cleaned up, Noah and I set off.

Chapter Four

The house had a lovely porch with flowerpots that held purple petunias and yellow daffodils. They added a splash of color to the grey chipping paint that covered the siding. I knocked and waited until the door creaked open, and Mrs. Hart smiled.

She waved me forward. "Ivy, it's great to see you. Come on in. Chloe is in her room. How have you been?"

"Alright. Sorry I haven't stopped by yet this week." I glanced at Mrs. Bowman's ceramic snow people collection that sat proudly in several glass cabinets in the living room. She seemed to have more every time I stopped in. "They sure make a lot of variations on the snow people."

Her face lit up, causing her weary eyes to rejuvenate for a moment. "Oh, yes, they make so many. People have no idea how extensive of a collection you can have of them. They add so much to our living room. Don't you think?"

"Yes, they accent your frosty blue couches well. It's like they have a frozen lake to look down on."

She clasped her hands together. "You're so perceptive, Ivy. The white rug is their snow too."

"That was a marvelous addition."

"This is why you're my favorite Chloe friend. You understand my snow babies' collection so well." Mrs. Bowman hummed her way out of the room.

I moved down the dark hallway that displayed visions of the perfect family in ornate brown frames. They smiled with their shoulders touching in poses instructed by the photographer. Chloe sat in the middle with her mom and dad in the back and her older brother Jimmy next to her. Pictures could hide so many things, but it was always the eyes that gave the truth away. Truth showed Chloe didn't buy this plastered happiness, as her irises contained a heaviness that seemed to break free from the mask she'd worn for a long time.

I knocked on her door and entered when she said. Her slumped shoulders and downcast gaze showed the mask had cracked and crumbled. I'd failed her by not seeing through it sooner. She'd showed signs for a while, but I'd missed them in my self-absorbed bubble. People never saw others' pain because they became too consumed with their own problems. When they did see, they didn't care—not enough, anyway. Not enough to spark any action. I'd paid the price for my lack of perceptive empathy.

I slid into the desk chair across the room. "How are you this morning?"

"Fine. You don't have to keep stopping by, Ivy. I'm not exactly fun to be around anymore." Her knees were peaked in front of her, where she rested her chin. It seemed as though she wanted to fold into herself and disappear. The way she pressed into the wall appeared to confirm this.

"I came because I miss you. Not because I want to be entertained."

She gave a swift, singular shake of her head to dismiss the notion. "Why would anyone miss me?"

My chest clenched as emotions flooded me in a way that I deemed too challenging to control. Because I loved my friend,

I would contain them. "How can I not miss you? We've been friends since we were two."

She laughed, a sharp sound. "Yet you never saw me. You never saw any of what was happening with me."

A tear regretfully escaped my eye. "I know, Chloe. For that, I'm so sorry." I set the plastic sack I'd brought on her desk. "Do you remember that choir concert? The one where we went to that bakery afterward, and we ate like ten of their lemon cupcakes?" I nodded toward the sack. "I brought some for you."

She chewed on her thumbnail as tears stained the pink comforter that rubbed against her throat. "Because a token from a better time will cure me. Right?"

"No, that's not what I meant by this."

She met my eyes. Hers looked fragile as they pooled with her pain. Her agony had set in so deep that it could locate no escape, not even through the windows in which she viewed everything. "Can you leave now? *Please*."

I nodded and headed to the door. I took one last look at my wilting friend and left.

♥

Effie sat across from me, unfolding napkins from a little baggy she kept in her purse. She reapplied hand sanitizer and flattened the napkins before lining up her fries in three perfect rows. She took the time to order them from largest to smallest and discarded any that looked burnt into a pile off to the side.

I watched shoppers move in and out of stores, gliding from one purchase to the next. A mother dragged her child onto the escalator, and he screamed while gripping the railing for dear life. She pried his fingers off, and they descended out of view.

"Chloe needs space, is all. It's tough when your mom makes you be home-schooled for your junior year. What kind of mom does that?" Effie had completed her arranging and swirled a fry in ketchup with two turns to the right, followed by two to the left.

I shrugged. "There could be lots of reasons for it. It's not necessarily her mom's fault."

"That makes no sense, Ivy. Chloe loves school. She always has. More so than you or I ever have."

A man bumped my chair as he tried to squeeze between tables with his tray full of pasta and pizza. "Sorry," he mumbled.

I nodded at the man and turned back to Effie. "Sometimes people change, and we don't always notice because we're busy staying the same ourselves. We think everyone stays stagnant, but not everyone does. Some people go backward. Okay. That's not the right term. Some people struggle, and they spiral."

Effie blinked and stared. "It's a struggle for her to be home-schooled. That would make anyone spiral."

I set my half-eaten pizza slice into its triangular box. "Yeah, that's the only possible reason."

We put our trash into the metal bin and set off to find me hiking boots for the science trip next week. I needed to ace the midterm and wanted to make sure I had the best odds. I found the size I needed in the sporting goods store and got a back-pack to place snacks and water.

I dropped Effie off at her house and drove home to find a strange black car in my driveway. My mom sat on our brown leather couches across from a woman holding a folder.

The woman handed the packet to my mom. "This should have everything you need in it. Let us know if you'd like one of the open spots as soon as possible. They fill up quick."

Mom shook the woman's hand, let her out the door, and

set the folder on the counter. I glanced at the words Crest Hill Nursing Home in disbelief.

I picked up one of the brochures and chased after my mom into the kitchen. "What's this?"

"Information on the nursing home I'm considering for Pop." She pulled a pan from a bottom cupboard, causing it to clang against several pots.

"We can't put him in a nursing home. This is his home."

She grabbed peppers and onions from the fridge, placed them on a cutting board, and set a knife next to them. "Slice up the vegetables while I take care of the meat. He's getting too much, Ivy. I get no sleep anymore and can't function. I've already had to quit my job, and it's too much."

I chopped into the vegetables with building fury. "He's your father. He lost sleep when you were a baby. We can't abandon him in one of those places."

She poured olive oil into the pan along with chicken chunks. "We may not have a choice. He's going downhill fast."

"So, we get him a night aide so you can sleep. He needs to stay here so we can have as much time with him as possible."

"We can visit him in the nursing home. It's too much. I've tried for the last several months, and it's only going to get worse."

My knife slashing into the vegetables soothed my tumultuous mind. "I'll help more. Take some night shifts."

She glanced over at my workspace. "We're not making baby food. I think they're done. Place them in the pan. You can't take any nights with him. You have high school to worry about and need your sleep."

I used the knife to scrape my almost pureed mess into the pan. They crackled and steamed next to the herb-covered meat, giving off a savory, spicy aroma. "It's worth it if I get to keep my grandpa close. We're going to lose him soon enough."

Mom pulled a loaf of bread out of the oven while I set the

table. We had everything ready to go when my dad walked in the door and placed his briefcase in its bin. He went to his room wearing his suit and returned with grey sweats on. My dad had an office job, but hated the attire it required. Mom got Pop, who mumbled something.

He sat down and glanced at my mom. "Lilith, I need my trousers sewn. I got an important meeting."

Mom filled his plate with pursed lips before pushing her stir-fry around with her fork.

Pop slammed his hand on the table. "Lilith! Do you have ears?"

Mom took a bite of her chicken, keeping her eyes latched onto her plate. Even downcast, I could see the worry over-flowing from her blue irises that matched the man next to her. The man who had raised her, but no longer knew he had a daughter.

Pop's face twisted in frustration, and I slid my chair closer to him, taking his rough, splotchy hand between my pale, smooth ones. "Pop, I will sew your trousers after we eat."

His face twitched as he narrowed his brows. "It's important, Lilith!"

I patted his hand. "I know. They will be done on time. I promise."

His face slowly untwisted, and he stared down at his plate that had extra small chicken pieces. "Okay. It's important."

I released his hand and nodded. "It will get done."

We ate the rest of the meal in silence. My mom kept her gaze lowered, but I still noticed the tears her napkin caught. Dad finished and went back to the bedroom. I talked my grandpa into returning to his chair to give my mom some space.

Cupboards slammed, dishes clanged, and metal scraped as my mother expelled her frustrations on our kitchen and its nonliving inhabitants. I sat on the couch watching Pop stare at the TV. A woman whipped her blinding hair around to show off the magnificent product commercialism begged consumers to buy.

"The media always tells us lies. Always lies, it tells us. Did we feed the cows yet? I can't remember." He squinted at the floor as he strained for recall.

"Yes, we did. They are all cozy in their barn."

"Good. A blizzard is coming tonight."

I glanced out at the clear fall sky. "Yep, I'm sure it's on the horizon."

It wasn't lost on me how difficult things were for my mom, but to the same magnitude, I couldn't let my grandpa go yet. How could we trust anyone else to care for him as well as we did? Couldn't my mom hold out a little longer? The ruckus in the kitchen seemed to say otherwise.

Chapter Five

Mr. Lee adjusted his wire-framed glasses, causing some of his black hair to stick out over his prominent ears. He wrote rules in big orange letters across the chalkboard. "Tomorrow is the big day, people. To give you as much time as possible on your hiking venture, I decided it would be best if we went over the rules now."

The front row girl waved her hand around like she needed to flag Mr. Lee down to change her tire.

"What is it this time, Becca?" Mr. Lee seemed on the verge of an eye roll.

"I think we should take a quiz on the rules before we leave in the morning. That way, you can make sure it sunk into everyone's brain overnight." Becca flinched as students pelted her head with paper balls and booed her.

Mr. Lee grabbed the yardstick held in the chalk tray and slammed it on his desk. "As annoying as Becca's suggestion is, we will respect her right to say it. We are leaving at six to give all of you the optimal time to complete the test. Do you really want to come even earlier or cut into your time?"

"I think we should because safety is everything, and rules keep people safe."

"Are your attention spans that corrupted by social media to not function enough to recall rules overnight?"

Becca slumped further as our classmates sent her glares. "It would be good to see if it consolidates into our brains."

The room mocked Becca again, which resulted in another ruler whack on the desk.

Mr. Lee wrote the first rule on the chalkboard and used his ruler to touch it. "One, you are to stay with your partner at all times. No matter what, your assigned person better be glued to you. If you lose your partner and return alone, you will get a zero."

Becca threw her hand around and waited until Mr. Lee sighed and called on her. "What happens if they abandon you, and it's not your fault that you have to return alone."

"You better stalk the heck out of them." He wrote out the second rule. "Rule two, there will be no going off trails, and you are to use the map that will be provided to you to mark the path you travel. All the items can be found without going into uncharted territory."

Becca waved her hand around. "What if the item we need is a foot off the trail? Are we allowed to step off and grab it?"

Mr. Lee's eyes became laser-focused, as though if his glasses could catch the sun just right from the classroom window, they might set Becca on fire. It was a look I knew well from Ivy watching me during lunch every day. I glanced at her, and her face twisted.

Ivy bent over her notebook and held the sheet toward me that made it look she was in the middle of flipping the page. *Keep your eyes to yourself.*

Like you're one to talk! I wrote back.

I have to watch you to make sure you don't destroy lives with your thoughtless words.

I shook my head and flipped the page of my notebook. *And calling me fifty different versions of Satan makes your words any better.*

She flipped to a different page in her notebook and rushed her pen over the paper. *The difference is I speak the truth, and you are full of lies. The names suit you. I have plenty of alternatives.*

I doubt you're that creative. Throw me your best Boaz adjectives and curses.

She set to work on the paper.

Mr. Lee brought his yardstick down on my desk. "Mr. Jackson and Ms. Carter, is there something more important than learning the rules that may save your life?"

We both shook our heads, and Mr. Lee returned to the front of the room. I glanced up to see all the rules had been erased and shrugged. The first two seemed like common sense, so the rest of them probably were too.

For the rest of the class, Mr. Lee went over the things we would have to find and bring back. Several of the assignments involved taking pictures with our phone that we would upload through an app to confirm we took the photo in the area, and it hadn't been uploaded from the internet. To further avoid cheating, each assignment involved a close-up of an object, and one zoomed out with our partner in the frame.

❧

"Boaz!" Phil slid down the hall, nearly plowing into the locker next to me. "I need your help!"

I sighed and shut my locker, starting down the hall. "Another one?"

"But this one will work. I know it. Seven is a lucky number."

"While that is true. If six girls stop dating you after a week of my letters, something is going wrong."

He ran to catch up next to me, using his socks to propel him on the smooth floor. "It's proof that your letters work, man. They make the girls give me a chance."

I stopped to stare down at his Llama covered in Christmas lights socks. "Where are your shoes?"

He flexed his arms in various muscleman poses. "Shoes are for the weak."

"Right. Look, I think it's become clear you need to get these girls to like you on your own. I can get them to date you, sure. But what does it matter if you don't keep them?"

"I'll pay you double."

I shook my head. "I don't think it's going to work and am not taking advantage of you."

"Triple, and you know I can afford it. You know what? Name your price, and it's yours."

Maisy's picture flashed through my mind. "Okay. A hundred and I will write you another letter that doesn't work."

"Deal!" He pumped his fist in the air. "Yes! Thank you, man. I owe you one."

I held out my hand. "You're right. You owe me a hundred."

He opened his wallet and placed the bill in my hand that went directly into the front zipper of my backpack.

I opened the middle pocket and handed him a form. "You know the drill. Fill this out with everything you know about her, and once it's complete, I'll start your letter."

His eyes shifted around. "I don't know much about her. I was hoping you could research this one for me."

"You know nothing about her, but you think she's worth spending that much money on for one of my letters?"

"She's gorgeous, and maybe she'll kiss me before deciding I'm not worth dating." He took out his pen, wrote against the locker, and handed me back the paper.

"At least we have a name. You could have told me that much and saved some paper."

"I thought it should be official."

I put the form back in my bag. "Normally, I charge more for the research, but I'll throw it in since you already paid so much."

He clasped my shoulder. "Yes! I appreciate this. You're the best!" He went sliding down the hall, using his socks as roller skates.

Phil was quirky, but there had to be a girl out there who'd appreciate that. He picked the wrong ones was the problem, and I couldn't convince him to alter his focus. He always chose the popular girls who knew they could get almost any guy they wanted. As I sat down in the library to research Wendy Williams, it became clear she was no exception. All her poses consisted of the infamous duck face, with the camera seeming to hang from the ceiling.

I flipped through each picture. Her other accounts didn't help me much either, which would make this challenging. Pictures of her in that same pose were all that made up her posts. Did she have a personality, or was she another shallow clone who surrendered individuality for acceptance into a social vortex that would never fill the void?

I got out my notebook and wrote out the first draft of a generic love letter with my go-to words that made the average girl swoon. Once the letter seemed good enough, I took out my blue feathered pen from its case and wrote on the weathered stationery that gave it an old-time feel. I penned each word with careful precision to ensure no mistakes were made and folded it into a heart. Lastly, it went into the square envelope, and I wrote Wendy in large flowing letters on the front, closing it with a wax seal that left behind a red rose.

I deposited the letter into a slit in Phil's locker and turned around to find Ivy glaring—her natural facial state.

She crossed her arms. "Ruining more lives, I see."

"According to you, it's what I do best, so I decided to stick with it."

"I should pry open that locker with a crowbar and save the poor recipient a lot of trouble."

My chin jerked toward the red light on the ceiling. "Go ahead. I'd find your suspension amusing."

"I finished it." She handed me a piece of notebook paper full of words. "The Boaz adjectives. Enjoy some contemplation."

"Snollygoster? That's a new one. I believe you have too much time on your hands." I started back toward the exit.

"It's derived from a beast who preys on the helpless. Seemed fitting."

I whirled around. "You know nothing about me anymore."

"I know enough to know you're not who you used to be. You don't care who you hurt or how you do it as long as you make some quick change."

"Like I said, you know nothing." I wadded up her note and tossed it on the floor.

"Who's littering now?"

I took larger strides out the door and into my truck. My truck door slammed, and I turned the dial on the radio to its highest volume. The music blared while I swerved out of the parking lot. Why did Ivy Carter get to me? She should have been easy to ignore. I took the long way to the middle school to calm myself down. I had to get through the midterm tomorrow. Then I would talk to my counselor into switching me to another science class for the rest of the semester.

How could Ivy get me so annoyed, angry, and upset so easily? It was the comment about hurting the helpless that bothered me. It was also how she hated me so much now, like everything from the past didn't matter because I did some big thing she refused to explain. Noah climbing into my truck snapped me from my thoughts, and I loosened my grip on the steering wheel.

My brother threw his arms around me. Hugging was his thing for pretty much every occasion. "Bo, you look mad. We should go get ice cream so you can feel better."

"I am a little mad, but you need dinner before ice cream."

"Why are you mad?"

"A girl at school isn't being very nice to me."

He released me and put his seat belt on. "Maybe we should take her ice cream."

"What?"

"When people are mean to you, you should be nice back. It makes them nice back to you."

I drove toward home, taking a few seconds to contemplate Noah's words. "I like the way you think, but I don't think that would help in this case."

It would probably get the ice cream smeared into my hair.

"We should try it. Just to be sure," Noah said.

"You still have to eat dinner before ice cream."

He flung his arms to the side. "Let's hurry and do that then."

I deposited the money I got from Phil and went home, where Noah convinced me to make more spaghetti for dinner. It was the third night in a row, but our parents smiled and thanked us, anyway. I settled into my room and paid the rest of Maisy's account in full. About an hour into my homework, I got a ping for an email. The Rodriguez family thanked me for my donation and gave me the link to follow their blog. I saved it in my favorites, excited I'd get to see how things would turn out long-term for Maisy.

Chapter Six

The autumn air had an unexpected chill to it that Mr. Lee looked angry about. He kept scowling at emptiness every time the wind picked up.

Becca stood outside the bus with a purple bin. "I checked the weather and planned ahead. Does anyone need a hoodie?"

Everyone sent her looks as they climbed aboard the bus, and she seemed to shrink into herself as her face fell further with each passing person.

I bent down in front of her bin. "I could always use an extra. How much?"

Her eyes lit up, and she waved her hand. "They are free. I enjoy helping people and thought this would." She glanced back at the open bus door and frowned. "I guess it was a stupid idea."

"No, not at all. This was very kind of you. If you want, I can help you load this. People might change their minds."

"That would be great. Thank you, Ivy!"

"No, thank you for your quick thinking."

Her smile grew as she grabbed one end of the tub, and I took the other. After placing the hoodies in the back, I took my seat next to it to avoid having to talk to anyone. I leaned to the side of the bus, putting my bag on the empty place next to me to avoid any company. I wanted to watch the scenery, not take on tedious conversation that would burn me out faster than running up the mountain we were traveling to.

The sun still hadn't risen in the sky, leaving the moon and stars to guide our journey out of town and onto the winding roads that grew steeper. Shadows from the mauve sky outlined the evergreen trees, transforming them from the night grey to the virescent of early morning. The blue swallowed the moon and stars as the sun took its stance.

As soon as we stopped, I helped Becca carry the tote of hoodies to a brown picnic table that had lost most of its white paint long ago. Cracks consumed the wood, and it looked easy to receive splinters from. The pine trees surrounded the area on three sides, with the fourth facing out to the parking lot and road. A log cabin visitor's center rested a few feet away from the picnic area.

Students talked and laughed in small little groups as they stretched from the two-hour bus ride. I closed my eyes and breathed in the crisp, chilly air, feeling it brush across my face. A whistle broke up my immersion in nature that I hoped to return to soon. I'd find all the objects as quickly as possible, then ask Mr. Lee if I could hike while we waited for everyone else to return. Hopefully, I got a partner as motivated as I was.

Mr. Lee held a clipboard and blew into the whistle again. "The moment has arrived! Fate will speak for us all. Remember, no matter how much you loathe the existence of your partner, you cannot kill them. There are rangers all over the place who will know what you have done. You must also always stay with them. Remember, for the next few hours, you are glued together. You have seven hours to complete the test, and there are thirty items you must find. Be sure to pick up your school-sponsored water bottles, sack lunches, and emergency kits. The rangers have assured me your cells should work as long as you stay on the trail, which you will do. Take out your phones." He waited for us all to do so and gave us his cell number.

We all got in line and grabbed the items he mentioned. I set my bag on the picnic table to rearrange everything to make the new items fit.

"Alright. When I call your name, you need to quickly make your way to my side, so I can introduce you to your new best friend. Any complaints about your partner that do not involve legitimate concerns like them trying to shove you off a cliff will result in ten percent off your grade. I will not tolerate petty whining. If you get a psychopath as a partner, there will be no penalties for complaints. Let's do this quickly. Hear your name, snap to my side." He began to call names.

People paired up and were sent to the side to make sure everyone got the same start time. I watched a squirrel scurry up a tree. Another joined it, and they battled over an acorn.

"Boaz Jackson, you are paired with Wyatt Leonard." Mr. Lee marked the clipboard and went on down the list.

I breathed a sigh of relief that I wouldn't have to put up with Boaz for the day. My mind drifted until Mr. Lee called my name and paired me with Becca. That seemed a good match because most people treated Becca poorly due to her need to express things that made her anxious. I recognized the worry and sometimes fear that poured from her face when she asked the questions she did.

"You are to meet back here no later than three. If you are late without just cause, you will get a zero. Do not make me hunt you down, people." Mr. Lee blew the whistle, signaling the race had begun.

The morning went well with Becca and I knocking through most of our list. We only had five items left to find when we sat down in a wildflower field to have lunch. It was the one spot we had found in the sun that helped warm us in the fall chill. I sat in the wildflowers while Becca stayed on the trail.

She turned her head all around. "I don't know what to do here, Ivy. Mr. Lee said I have to stay glued to you, but also not leave the trail. Which rule is more important?"

"You can still see me."

She chewed on her lip. "Okay. That's true."

"Well, unless I do this." I sunk down, burying myself in yellows, oranges, and pinks.

The grassy floral scent intertwined in the fresh air that brought the aroma of pine needles with it.

"Ivy! Please sit up. You need to be in my eye range!"

"Your eye range? You can still hear me."

"Keep talking then, so I know you haven't rolled away."

Not wanting to torture Becca too much, I moved next to her. She settled down, and we ate our lunch, taking in the blue and white backdrop of the towering mountain. We hurried up through the last five items and returned to the visitor's office.

Mr. Lee waved and marked his clipboard. "Your team is in sixth place. That puts you at an 88."

I glanced at the other students who were lounging around the picnic tables on their phones. "That's not going to work for me. We made it back with two hours to spare."

"Yes, and the rules were you lose points for every team that makes it back before you. There is an extra credit assignment if you would like to make use of it." He lifted the paper on the clipboard and pulled out a card. "If you can get a picture of a red-tailed hawk and a Glacier Lily, I will give you five points for each."

"Alright. I'll do it. Becca, are you ready?"

She glanced back toward the mountain and shook her head. "I think I'm going to keep my grade. There are too many scary things out there. We almost died like four times."

I scrunched my nose. "When did we almost die?"

She chewed her thumbnail and shrugged.

"Okay. I'll go myself."

Mr. Lee moved his finger back and forth. "You can't go alone."

"Is there someone else I can go with?"

"As a matter of fact, another student is waiting for another partner." He pointed over to where Boaz sat, writing at a table.

I stuck my hand up. "Oh, no! There has to be someone else. I can't work with him. I'll wait to see if any other students want to go with me."

"Suit yourself, but you only have two hours left."

I stared at my watch, and then at Boaz. The back and forth went on for twenty minutes. Two teams came back, and none wanted the extra credit.

"Fine! I'll go with Boaz." I controlled myself enough not to spit out his name.

Mr. Lee blew his whistle. "Good news, Mr. Jackson. I found you another partner."

Boaz stuffed everything in his bag and jogged over. "Who?"

"Ms. Carter."

He shook his head. "No, that can't be right."

"I assure you it is. You two better get going. You're down to an hour and a half."

Boaz glanced at his watch as though he didn't believe our teacher. "Fine. Let's go."

Mr. Lee handed us a sheet with pictures of the flower and bird. "Same rules apply to you two now. Glued to each other."

We both grunted and set out. I looked back at our fading classmates as Boaz and I made our way up the trail. "I'm laying some ground rules out right now. You are not to talk to me. Not a single word. Your voice is like a whale with a sore throat to me."

"And yours is like a dying penguin, so this goes both ways," he said.

"Deal." I stuck my tongue out at him for good measure.

He rolled his eyes, and we started up the trail. We found the glacier lily first and sent the pictures we needed to the app. Silence served us well until Boaz hummed some song.

I stopped to scowl. "We agreed to silence."

"What?"

"You're humming."

He scrunched his nose like he considered me the crazy one. "No, I wasn't."

"Yes, you were."

"You're hearing things. Your delusions are pretty grand, so that's not a huge surprise."

I snorted. "What delusions are those?"

"That I'm the Devil because I write letters to girls to help guys with their love life."

"That's not a delusion. That's the truth, and you know it."

He gave a short laugh and ran his fingers through his wild brown hair. "How does it feel to be out of your mind?"

"Better than being scum that tears girls' hearts apart. You have no heart yourself, so maybe you're jealous and want to ruin love for everyone else."

He stopped walking forward and parted his lips slightly as he took a minute to reflect on my comments. "Do you even hear how stupid you sound?"

"I'd rather be stupid than a snollygoster who preys on the helpless."

His jaw flinched. "Quit calling me that! I don't prey on the helpless."

"This isn't debatable. It's proven."

"How so?"

"The letters you write hurt people," I said.

"How can you even say that? They're innocent. You're so

vague. You shout generalizations at me with no examples as to how anything you say is true. Yet you claim I'm the one with the problem." His head snapped around. "I think we took a wrong turn somewhere."

We stood on a dirt trail close to a drop-off that descended into a valley with yellow grass and jagged rocks. There didn't seem to be any trail signs in sight.

I was about to suggest we turn around the way we came when a growl made me jump. My eyes grew, and Boaz paled as we backed away from the grizzly bear blocking our path back.

Chapter Seven

Many things flashed before my eyes as the bear stared at Ivy and me. I worried mainly about Noah mourning me and how he'd be able to keep going to karaoke and other things he loved at the playhouse. Thoughts of my brother were followed by those of the kids whose pictures hung on my wall. The world already lacked people willing to help. While I couldn't do nearly enough to make a huge impact, they couldn't afford one less donor.

I checked my cell, which revealed I had no bars, and neither did Ivy. The bear kept its eyes on us, and I tried to remember if we should or shouldn't play dead. Running seemed like a terrible idea, and Ivy looked seconds away from bolting as she took several steps backward.

I lifted my hands, ready to grab her if necessary. If it leaped at us, I'd jump on top of her. Only one of us needed to die a horrible, gruesome death. "Don't move. We don't need it to see us as prey."

"Are you kidding me? It already does. We probably seem like a great snack to it." She took a few more steps back.

"Snack! That's it. The lunches had jerky in them." I unzipped my bag and threw three pieces at it.

We backed away slowly as it sniffed the sticks and swallowed them, which took it about two seconds. It started moving toward us, and Ivy screamed. I threw my entire backpack far to the side, and the bear leaped after it. We took off running while it was distracted and rounded the bend to find the trail abruptly dropped to the valley below.

"This isn't a big deal. We hide here until it goes on its way." I peeked around to see the bear's nose deep in my backpack.

"Yeah, because it can't smell us."

"Do you have a better idea?"

"I'm smart enough to know not to feed it. It thinks we have yummy treats for it." She hopped up to a root hanging out from the dirt and gave it a tug.

"It provided a distraction."

"You're such a genius."

I chuckled. "Yeah, I think so too."

"Moron, it wasn't a compliment. We're about to be its main course after it whetted its appetite on your appetizer."

"At least I did something. You stood there looking like you were going to leap off the cliff."

"Falling to my death seems better than letting a bear toss me around in its mouth." She tried a second root by giving it a firm tug. It loosened, and she growled at it.

"Careful, the bear is going to think you're competition." I gripped the mountain wall as the bear shook my bag off its face and meandered toward us. "We have company!"

Ivy leaped for a higher root, and it pulled loose. "Give me a boost. Do something productive for once."

"I'm keeping bear watch. That's more useful than you grabbing at grass, thinking it can get you up the side of the mountain." I turned my attention to the bear that decided to lie down and view the valley below. Just our luck, we'd encountered a nature-loving bear.

"It's tree roots!"

I snickered. "More like flower roots. Either way, it's not the brightest idea to pull yourself up a mountain with materials that have broken all four times you've attempted to use them as rope."

"That's why I said to lift me so I can try to reach the rock. You apparently have no listening skills."

"I heard you, but I'm not going to agree to an idea that throws you off the mountain. We have to return together. Remember?" I shook my head at the bear and tried to think of options.

"If I fall, I'll just pull you with me. We're glued together after all."

"Unless we figure a way out of here in the next half an hour, we're failing the class, anyway. I don't think Mr. Lee will forgive having to hunt us down."

Ivy continued to pointlessly grab at flimsy roots while I kept my eye on the bear. Time ticked closer and closer to three O'clock until it flew by completely. By the time five rolled around, the bear hadn't budged. We were screwed in so many ways. Ivy and I had both given up and were slumped against the mountain wall.

"They'll send a helicopter or something. We'll be fine," I said.

Ivy twirled a blade of grass between her fingers. "I think we need to choose to climb or go into the valley before the sun sets and those dark clouds move in."

I glanced up at the black horizon that occasionally rippled with splotchy lightning. "Should we just roll on down the cliff like when we were five at the park? You know the giant hill that ended right at the slide."

"You always cheated. You would say ready, and then you'd start rolling before you even said set."

"You think you would have learned by the fifth time I did it."

"Your morals haven't improved with age," she said.

"So says the girl who used to pull the chair out from under me during musical chairs."

She shrugged. "A chair had to go."

"Not the one I was about to sit in."

She twisted her face, causing the shadows of the nearly setting sun to bounce around on her features. "You think you'd have learned by the fifth time I did it."

"You were my best friend, and I trusted you."

She pursed her lips. "We were five, and you have no right to talk about trust."

I threw my arms up. "What are you talking about? This is what I'm talking about. You never tell me what your issue is with me. You're mad we grew apart?"

She stiffened. "You really think that's it? You think I'm that petty?"

I kept my eyes on her, waiting for her to spill the truth. "Yeah, it seems so."

"The fact you can't figure it out makes it so much worse." She bit her lip and looked away.

Thunder boomed, and I glanced at our furry friend, who still blocked our path. The wind picked up, whistling around as a warning to seek shelter.

I stood up and looked down into the valley. "It's steep, but we might find a foothold and at least get to that ledge and away from that bear. I'll go first."

"What if I want to go first?"

"It was my idea, so I get to risk breaking my neck first."

She crossed her arms. "It was actually my idea. I suggested hours ago that we head down into the valley."

I took a deep breath. "You can do whatever you want, but I'm going down now. It would probably be best to go one at a time, so we don't both take the risk, but by all means, do what you think is best."

"I will."

"Okay, then."

"For sure." She picked up her bag and moved to the cliff.

"You always have to have the last word. Don't you?"

"I think you have me confused with yourself. Although, I do always win the last word."

"You basically just admitted you need the last word." I edged to the cliff and stretched my feet down to catch the ledge. I tested it before placing my other foot.

There was a slant to the cliff that grew more prominent about halfway down. It looked as though we could slide to safety if we made it that far. Thunder played louder in the background, which quickened my pace. We needed to be planted in the valley before things became muddy. Not to mention being high around lightning sounded like a terrible idea. Ivy had her feet swung over the ledge, but hadn't made a move.

I held my hand up to her. "Come on. I'll catch you."

"I'd rather plummet to my death."

"You can't be serious."

"Oh, I am." She turned herself around and inched down, trying to reach the ledge I stood on. She was around four inches shorter than me, which made her struggle more to reach me.

I kept my hands poised in case she slipped. She let go of the cliff and dropped a few inches, where she wobbled in place. I bumped her toward the mountain when she teetered on the edge. She stabilized enough to send me a glare. We took turns descending, and despite her protests, I made sure I stayed below her. We made it to the slanted part as the sky broke.

We scooted on our butts as the ground became mush and gave out from under us. We slid quickly to the bottom. As our momentum picked up, we spun and tumbled, finally coming to a rest at the base of the tree line. Mud caked our faces, hair, and clothes.

Ivy stuck her face toward the sky, letting the rain wash her clean. She'd always liked to be absorbed into the moment, especially when it involved nature. Her and the bear seemed kindred spirits.

I used the flashlight on my phone to lead us into the thick forest, where the canopy of pine branches caught most of the downpour. We trekked for a while to find signage or land-marks. An enormous fallen log had a shallow opening through the roots.

I shined my light at the trunk. "I think that may be our best bet for tonight."

She held her arms and shook. "We can't stay in the forest all night. This is crazy, Boaz. Even for you."

"Do you have a better idea?"

Her shoulders slumped. "No, but I think this means we failed the midterm."

"Yeah, summer school it is."

She walked over to the log and stared inside, shining her own phone on it. "Maybe they'll put us in different classes."

"Let's hope so."

She slid into the log, scooting far enough back she could still sit up but had protection from the crooked roots that had grown into each other.

I slid in next to her but kept myself as close to the opposite wall as possible. "Can we call a truce?"

"From what?"

I shifted on the scratchy, bumpy ground, not finding a

comfortable spot. "This war we're fighting. We need to get along to get out of this. Then we can go back to hating each other."

"I'll give it some effort for the sake of living." She unzipped her bag and pulled out her emergency kit. "This has two emergency blankets in it. That's a relief. We don't have to share."

"I'm surprised you're not keeping both."

"Don't push it. I might." She handed me one package and opened her own.

The blankets were made of some type of stiff foil rather than cloth. She handed me a hoodie and laid back on another.

"You don't have to give me this. I'll use my arm."

"It's extra. Becca gave me a few. Luckily, I had plenty of room because I bought a camping backpack last week. You sacrificed all your things to the beast. Stupid move, but you tried."

"It gave us a distraction." I adjusted the hoodie under my head and turned my back toward her.

"Sure. Whatever makes you feel better."

Ten minutes into our truce, and things weren't looking promising. I closed my eyes, hoping by morning, search and rescue would find us.

Chapter Eight

Birds chirping and the smell of pine and cedar greeted me to a morning in the forest. Boaz and I had unwillingly camped in the great outdoors for the night. My mom was probably baking enough to feed the entire continent of Africa. Soft snores came from the boy next to me. His forehead looked pressed into the bark as though he'd tried to sleep as far away from me as possible. I'd done the same on my side like saran wrap had separated us—flimsy but effective.

My phone had died hours ago, and we had no clue where we were. Sunlight made intricate patterns through the trees. Its rays created art open to interpretation. The branches served as lines and angles that drew pictures, which morphed at the will of the wind. Dry pine needles provided a blanket for the rich dirt that made up the forest floor. A red fox eyed me curiously with its head cocked before it scampered off in pursuit of some errand.

I wrapped the metallic blanket around my shoulders as the breeze picked up. The trees sheltered us from a lot of the wind, but to find help, we'd have to leave them behind at some point. I had five bottled waters, which gave us two and a half each. We could spread them over three to four days. Hopefully, help would find us long before then.

Boaz stirred and sat up next to me. "What's the plan?"

"What makes you think I know?"

"I figured anything I suggested you'd turn down. It's best to save time in these situations. We're in a truce, remember?"

I tossed him a water and energy bar. "Try to make this last today." I told him we could go three days, maybe four, if we pushed things.

"We'll be out of here before that. It can't be hard to find a trail in a national park." He nibbled on his bar and glanced at a squirrel balancing across a large branch.

"We walked pretty far from the trails last night. A few hours could have taken us anywhere." I sipped on my water. A little throughout the day would keep us alive.

"It feels warmer today, at least. Maybe we should stay put since this is the last place our cells died."

"We had no signal. Can they track our cells without that?"

He shrugged. "I guess I'm not sure. We could move into this log and make it our new home. Forge a life here."

"I'm not forging a life with you. I'd rather take my chances in inclement weather. This truce is temporary. It doesn't have a high shelf life. Spending this much time with you is awful enough."

"I'm sure frostbite and death are so much better than camping with me for a day or two."

I folded up my trash and put it in the front pocket of my bag. "It is. You finally understand something. I feel you need a gold star here."

"We could walk to the cliff and climb back up. That bear is probably gone."

"Do you even remember how to get to it?"

He held out his hand. "I'll carry your backpack."

I glowered. "Not happening. I don't need it contaminated."

"Fine. Whatever. It's your back."

"I'm aware of that. There's sun up ahead. We could see if it leads to anything and come back if nothing is promising." I secured my pack on my shoulders and started off in the direction I wanted, not caring if Boaz agreed.

He jogged to catch up to me. "We should go back the way we came. We know it is the direction of the visitor's center."

"Do we, though? We traveled pretty far last night. It would be easy to get turned around."

"What good is it to go farther away from where we need to be?"

I hopped over a large tree root that protruded from the ground and weaved around another. "Where exactly do we need to be? There's no one waiting for us at the visitor's center. They all left to go home."

His one eyelid twitched like it always did when he was trying to understand me, which happened almost hourly when we were together. "They probably have search and rescue all over the place, looking for us. They probably aren't going to expect us this far out. We should head back and meet them halfway."

"How do we even know we came that way?"

"Because we came upon the log root side facing us."

I picked up my pace, getting better at maneuvering around the extensive root system that seemed booby-trapped to kill us. "I want to see what's up at the light ahead. If it doesn't look promising, we can head back."

A bird squawked in the distance, joining the tiny black-birds and sparrows tweeting their songs. The light patterns spread out, forming more delicate shapes that molded form based on disturbances in forest movement. The crisp air blended with inviting green smells, making this a welcoming walk, despite the circumstances. Boaz kept pace with me but kept glancing behind him like he might turn around any second.

The forest broke apart into another field where yellow and purple flowers intertwined with a greenish-yellow grass that grew a few inches above our ankles. Several blue mountain peaks rose, peeking around each other like each one wanted to be seen for a group photo.

Rocks with sharp angles speckled the ground with black and blue formations of various sizes. The boulders backed up to the mountains where aspen and pine trees mingled. The aspens had taken on their brilliant golden autumn hues. Butterflies added even more vivid splashes to the already abundant color. A peace settled over me because we could have found ourselves lost somewhere less pleasant. I climbed onto a flat boulder, folded my legs under me, and straightened my posture as I took a deep breath.

Boaz sat next to me, resting his arm over his peaked knee. He let his other leg dangle over the edge. "What are you doing?"

"Get your own rock."

"We don't have time for this. We need to be rescued, which means we should go back the way we came."

I closed my eyes, absorbing the gentle breeze that rushed across my face. "This is the way we came from. I'm pretty sure. Doesn't it look familiar? I'm serious, though. Get on your own rock."

He let out a sharp breath and moved to one in front of me. "I'm not sure. It all looks the same, but it makes sense we arrived from the other direction because of the way we found the tree."

"I want to meditate longer, and then we'll try your way."

He gasped and cleared his throat, seeming to want to cover his surprise. "Really?"

"Yeah, don't sound so shocked."

"You agreed to my plan. I didn't expect that to happen."

"Keep talking, and I'll change my mind. Meditation needs silence." I straightened my shoulders and let relaxation flow through my muscles.

Boaz remained quiet, but his restless body shifts disturbed my concentration far too often, making me want to shove him off his stone chair. The dirt and grass would probably prevent any bodily harm from befalling him.

After his millionth sigh, I threw my hands up. "Well, so much for meditating. You make finding peace impossible."

"What? I didn't say anything."

"Your throat and lungs did as you heaved out your distaste as a whiff of air every three seconds." I untangled my legs from the boulder and took a sip from my water bottle.

"What?"

"You kept sighing. You can't give me a minute without showing how unhappy you are."

"I think that might be yourself, and I wasn't sighing," he said.

I leaped down into the grass and started marching in the direction he seemed dying to exert energy toward. "You're so unaware of yourself. First the humming and now the sighing."

"I have a lot on my mind."

"I do too. That's why I really needed the meditation. To free my mind of this stress."

Silence descended on us again, and I realized a lot of my stress involved Boaz being the one I had to survive this ordeal with. His face constantly reminded me of the terrible moments he'd caused. The moments he seemed blissfully ignorant to. I wanted to shout his transgressions at him and release all the emotions I'd bottled for weeks. Those emotions had clearly leaked out like a shaken pop bottle with a loose cap. My anger, sadness, and fear bubbled out through the small slits in my tattered heart. I needed to contain them, but the anger boiled too strong.

The desire to run and keep running until the pain stopped pulled strongly. I needed to flee the source of pain. This entire mess brought the predicament of needing Boaz while simultaneously wanting him far from me.

He should have known better.

We hiked past the fallen log, where the trees grew densely together, and the roots made it tough to avoid. At one point, the branches smothered the sun, and we inched through the darkness, stumbling over the natural debris. We came out the other side to another valley that looked the same as the last.

Boaz kicked a rock. "Dang it! This doesn't look familiar either. Maybe we took a wrong turn in the dark. You might as well meditate."

I rested my back against a boulder. "I'll do what I want." My tone took on the bitterness my thoughts had conjured.

"Right." He sat on the opposite side of the boulder, which removed him from my sight.

I rested my chin on my knees and watched a hawk dive for food. The hawk had a very distinct red tail that left me shaking my head. All this trouble for the creature meters away, diving for its dinner. The irony was that our phones were dead, and we'd never gain proof. That small token would have been nice to return with. While it wouldn't have saved our grades, it would have brought satisfaction in accomplishing the task that had caused so many problems.

Boaz gave me what seemed around an hour before he came back over to my side. "What are we going to do?"

"Maybe we should stay in one place. What's the point of expelling energy when this spot is as good as any?"

"Search and rescue is more likely to find us if we stay put." He pointed at the sky above the mountain. "Another storm might be brewing."

"We could always return to the log and wait it out." I walked into the field a little farther to inspect an interesting orange flower.

Sharp prickles pierced my skin, searing my flesh with burning sensations. My legs boiled like I'd stepped in lava, which ascended to my knees and kept going. I screamed as the agony signal rocked through my brain. I took off running until I couldn't take it anymore and writhed on the ground. Boaz shouted in the background, but the pain stole my thoughts. I couldn't concentrate on anything he said.

Chapter Nine

Ivy screamed and flailed in the grass as though something horrendous had latched onto her. I zoomed to her side to assess the situation. Tiny black specks scurried over her pants.

"Ivy, you're covered in ants. They're biting and stinging. I'll look away, but you need to get your pants off. I'll be right back." I bolted for the trees, broke off a pine branch, and ran it back to her. "Use this to brush them off. I'll go wait behind the boulder. Turn your pants inside out and shake them to make sure they're gone."

Her shaky hand held the branch, and I sat down behind a tree, relieved when her wails diminished.

I waited a while before I leaned my head to the side. "Can I come out now?"

"Yeah." Her words quivered.

I found her in a little trembling ball. "We need to find a river and get your legs wiped off."

She had her pant legs rolled up to her knees to reveal dozens of angry welts. "I need a minute."

I nodded and waited until she stood and limped toward the tree line. We traveled back through the forest and came out the other side. At least, I thought it might be a different place. Both open areas looked similar. Ivy said there was a difference, but I couldn't see it as easily as she could. She'd always had the talent for seeing the world differently than other people. It was like this war she'd started between us. She saw something awful about me I didn't see.

Which brought the fear that she could see me through a two-sided mirror. The ones that law enforcement used to watch criminals in confession rooms. They could see the accused, but the accused could only see themselves. When I looked, all I saw was the reflection familiar to me. The person I thought I was inside. But Ivy stood on the other side, looking in the window at me, and she knew the reflection was a sham. Only I couldn't tell because I sincerely thought I'd accurately interpreted reality, while my reflection remained an illusion she saw through. We walked with no direction and located no water source.

I stared up at the mountain. "Why don't I climb up the mountain and bring back snow. The cold will soothe your stings and wash them at the same time."

She closed her eyes and rested against a tree. "How are you going to do that?"

"I'll wrap it up in one of the metal blankets. They're waterproof. Maybe I can tell where we are if I go higher too."

"You might not find your way back. You aren't the best at navigation." She opened one eye to look at me, probably to see my reaction to her jab.

"You're the one that had to march off at the first sight of the sun, giving no logic to your hike. I'll make sure I take a straight shot up and back down again. This will give you more meditation time." I put on an extra hoodie to protect myself from the higher altitude chill.

I started up the incline, carrying the bunched-up emergency blanket and keeping my focus on the frigid white fluff that would bring Ivy relief. In some places, I had to search for good footholds. Trees blocked some of the path, but I always tried to move back over after going around obstacles.

The sun had moved close to the west by the time I made it to the top. The task had taken much longer than I'd anticipated, and I worried about leaving Ivy alone for the night. I reached the first bit of snow, used a branch to slide a good amount onto the blanket, and brought the corners into the middle, tying them all together.

The horizon stretched out to endless forest and mountains. Nothing resembling civilization appeared in any direction. How could that be? How could we have journeyed so far that no direction held any hope?

The trip down seemed easier, and I tried to make a straight line the best I could. The path steepened, and I used the trees to balance myself down. My legs gave out from under me as I slid on gravel. The blanket went one way, and I went the other. I shoved my sneakers into the ground to act as brakes. Blood dripped onto the dirt in the same spot my left pant leg had ripped. I twisted my calf around and turned my head sideways to see all the scrapes and cuts on my leg.

The blanket had come undone, and most of the snow had started to melt and seep into the soil. Back up the mountain I went, trying to stay optimistic about having less distance to travel this time. My muscles had stiffened by the time I started downward for the second time. I worked harder on finding more level ground, and in spots too steep, I placed the blanket on my lap and slid down on my butt.

An elk picked up its head to stare at me as I disturbed its evening meal with my strange ass scooting. My calves stung the few times I touched them against the dirt. When I made it to the bottom, my heart dropped when Ivy appeared nowhere around. I wanted to scream at how terrible I was about finding my way around in this place.

"Ivy! Ivy!" I called her a few more times with no success. "Ahhhhhhhh!" I yelled my frustrations to the empty field, and a collective of birds scattered into the sky.

"You don't have to be so loud. Some of us are trying to sleep," Ivy said.

I went around a large tree and found her leaning against it. "Ivy, how long have you been resting against that tree?"

She shrugged, keeping her eyes shut. "A while. Why?"

"You see the vines growing up the side? Have you ever heard of leaves of three let it be?"

She pulled back to look at the bright green plant weaving its way up the bark. "What is it?"

"You just found your namesake. Poison Ivy."

She scowled at the plant, followed by me. "If you hadn't moved at a snail's pace, you'd have been here to tell me that."

"I left to help you."

"I told you not to. Anything could have happened to you."

I untied the blanket to find about half of the snow melted. "You sound like you're worried about me."

"More like annoyed, you did another stupid thing."

I kept the blanket's corners together and tied it to a low-hanging branch while leaving enough space to get my hands into the top. "Do you want me to put the snow on your legs or hand it to you?"

She rolled her pant legs up, reached into the blanket, and pulled out snow she rubbed on her limbs and face. The cold water would help cleanse the stings and poison ivy. She mumbled something incoherent.

I filled my empty water bottle with the melted snow. "What?"

"Thank you!" She threw the words out so fast it took a minute for my brain to catch up.

"You're thanking me?"

"The snow helped. This doesn't mean all is forgiven, but this may extend our truce."

I held out my hand. "May I fill your empty water bottle? I'd accept knowing what I did wrong as a thank you."

She handed me the bottle and stared out at the sunset. Her green eyes that used to sparkle like emeralds had dulled in exhaustion. After a bit, she rolled down her pant legs and wrapped her metallic blanket around herself. "I don't have another blanket," she said.

"I'll be fine. It's warmer tonight, and I have an extra layer on." I pulled my hood up and stuck a second hoodie under my head.

She slid down, creating her own makeshift pillow. "Don't ask me again."

"What's that?"

"Don't ask me again to tell you why I hate you."

Though I'd already known she felt that way, hearing her spew her feelings so bluntly stung. "Why not?"

"Did it ever occur to you that maybe I can't tell you?"

"How is that fair?"

She rolled over to face me. Anger built tension in her jaw, and under the moonlight, half her face darkened, adding to her wrathful appearance. "Nothing about any of this is fair! Look at us. You're the last person I want to be stuck with, but the universe thought it would be funny. It's like fate is sitting up there in the clouds laughing at us. Nothing about the last few months has been fair. So don't talk to me about fairness because it doesn't exist." She scooted around a pine tree, which left only the bottom of her blanket in view.

She wasn't wrong. For a long time, the world hadn't seemed just to me. People made it that way with the things they allowed to continue. To Ivy, what did injustice have to do with me? Why couldn't she tell me? I picked up a rock, sent it flying into the field, and repeated with three more.

The stars looked clear, and all threat of a storm had floated away hours ago. My muscles ached, and soreness radiated from my calves. No ideas came to me about how to get out of this mess. It was as though we'd found ourselves in the Twilight Zone. Like we existed in a world no one else did. Either that or the world had forgotten us, and no cavalry was on its way.

I took one last look at the tree Ivy slept behind and decided to respect her request. She could keep this rift between us to herself, even though it would eat at me and cause me to doubt my reflection. The person who I thought I'd become was an illusion. Ivy could see that, and she left me with a distorted self-glimpse. My back faced her as I gave in to sleep for a second night in the wilderness.

Chapter Ten

I was a jumbled mess of itching, pain, and misery, crying myself silently to sleep. My parents had probably decided to ground me for the next year by now. Their perfect daughter had finally made a mistake. In a round about way, I found myself in this entire predicament because they insisted I keep flawless grades. That had driven me to take the extra credit.

At the same time, everything that happened after had been my fault or Boaz's—mainly Boaz's. I rolled my eyes at the part of my brain that demanded I cut him slack. He deserved none.

Hundreds of ants and a merciless plant had left burning welts all over my distressed body. Things kept getting worse, and not the slightest sign of rescue had appeared anywhere. We'd traveled too far and didn't know how to make our way back. We would die here. They'd find our skeletons months from now, and that would make Mr. Lee speak poorly about us to all his future students.

The sky sparkled with vivid stars forming the galaxy. It traced the atmosphere with dust that glittered into silver, purple, and blue brush strokes. The cosmos blurred in my teary vision, but watching them soothed my hysteria.

I tossed and turned, only occasionally nodding off through the night. When morning peaked over the horizon, I gave up the notion of sleep and climbed onto a rock to watch the sun as it colored the sky with unique beauty. The universe loved to paint, and each day it started with a fresh canvas. A visible reminder that new chances awaited humanity.

My stomach rumbled, and I drew out an energy bar, stuffing half back into my pack. I nibbled on what my desperate tongue perceived to be euphoria—a delusion derived from starving.

Boaz took a seat two rocks over, which showed he'd learned from yesterday. He sipped on his water. Thanks to him getting the snow, we could survive out here a few extra days before dehydration turned us insane and dead.

I pushed a hoodie under my legs as the roughness under me scraped against my puffy blisters. "What are we going to do, Boaz?"

He unwrapped part of his bar and popped the entire piece into his mouth. "I'm not sure. There wasn't anything promising when I climbed the mountain. It's all the same for miles. Not even any visible roads or trails. It's like we hiked way too far."

"We could stay put, but what if they never guess we went this far, and we die here?"

He turned to face me until our eyes met. A gentleness I missed poured from his golden-green irises. "We're not going to die. Worst case, we live here now and become mountain people. I'll even grow a shaggy beard for it." He chuckled.

I scrunched my nose at the thought of facial hair covering his squared jaw. "Winter won't hold off forever."

"We could build a shelter," he said.

"How? We have no tools."

He pushed his lips to the side and stared at the trees. "We'll figure something out. What else is in your emergency kit?"

I hopped off the rock, babying my descent to prevent the stone from cutting into my swollen skin. "We have matches, which will help if it gets cold. There are twenty."

"We could use them to make a signal, too. Maybe we should try that tonight."

"Shouldn't we save them to keep warm? Not only that, but don't most search and rescue teams go home at night?" I rifled through the emergency kit. "There are a few bandages, antiseptic, and a mirror. They must want us to see how terrible we look." I opened the package and cringed at the red blotches that consumed the entire right side of my face.

Boaz stood beside me and held out his hand. "Let me see that." He studied it, turning it over in his hand. "It's a camper's mirror."

"How is that for emergencies?"

He held it up, which caused the sun to reflect off it. "It's used for a signal. We flash it around, and if rescuers are anywhere around, they will hopefully see it." He played with it for a while longer, sending light into the clear blue sky.

Since we'd found the mirror, we stayed put for a few hours to see if it drew anyone to us. I retreated into the forest as the sun's warmth caused my skin reactions to intensify. Boaz remained in the open area, flashing the mirror around. By midday, no sign of rescue appeared.

Boaz stuck the mirror back into the emergency kit. "If we keep walking, we should come across something. We may have already messed ourselves up too much to be in the search party's targeted areas."

I drew lines in the dirt with a stick and kept my unfocused

eyes fixated ahead. "Where are we going to go? There are mountains on all sides."

"We could climb over one and see if the other side holds anything better. It could snow this time of year. We're stuck in that weird limbo where the weather can't decide which direction it should take things. Finding better shelter or signs of people seems like a good idea."

"Fine. The sooner we go our separate ways, the better."

He pressed his lips together and glanced away. "Yeah, my thoughts too."

We drank as much of the snow water as we could and made sure we refilled our bottles. I ran the chilly liquid over my damaged skin and closed my eyes to soak in the relief. Boaz dumped the rest and shook the blanket dry as much as possible. He folded it, and my eyes stayed locked on the way his fingers coordinated their efforts to fold the blanket into a small square again. Paper folding was his hidden talent few people knew about.

He handed it to me, and I placed it in the front pocket of my bag. Boaz led the way, and I followed. There seemed to be no method to his madness other than when things got too steep and dangerous, he altered our course. The problem with this was we were going more sideways than up. It also didn't help that he tried to take charge while also peering back at me every five seconds.

My stomach ached as it missed food with an intensity difficult to bear. One energy bar a day over the last three days didn't hold long. I loved nature, but never learned how to survive in it. Boaz didn't seem to have much of a clue either. He'd at least known what poison ivy looked like. My cheeks burned as they recalled the embarrassment. My parents had given me the name but never took the time to teach me about the dangerous kind.

We found level ground that didn't quite look like a man-made trail. Perhaps animals had blazed it for us. It opened into an enormous area that looked down into the valley we'd arrive from. We'd wrapped around the south side of the mountain, and I took in the stunning beauty of blue mountains and a clear sky.

Boaz stood at the edge and looked in all directions. "There's nothing. How did we get this lost? There are no campsites or trails. This place looks undisturbed."

"It's nice it exists. Something humans haven't ruined yet."

"Humans ruin a lot of things."

"Yeah." Bitter words stuck on the tip of my tongue. My muscles seethed as I clenched my response and prevented its escape. While we were under a truce, I'd try to contain myself. I laid back in the green grass, flinching as my legs rubbed against the ground.

Boaz sat down across from me but kept a vast distance between us. "How are your legs and everything else?"

"My skin feels like many cats are scratching me while also tickling me with their tails. Occasionally, they set me on fire."

"That's terrible. Do you think we should keep going or turn back?" He pushed his boot around in the dirt, creating spiral patterns.

"We might as well keep going and see the entire mountain range. The clouds are looking a bit grey in the west. If it snows, we're in trouble."

He nodded. "That's my thought too. If we can't find a civilization, we need a better shelter."

The fluffy clouds overhead spoke a different story than the wintry ones in the distance. They made the shapes that unfolded stories in my head, the way Boaz folded them with paper. Images of two flashlights pointed at a blue tent popped into my head. The light danced circles, which created silhouettes that spoke of things outside the realm we created under a sheet that became our fort. The adventures he built for us—a childhood of paper dragons, dancing swans, and flying horses.

His storytelling gift painted magical pictures and brought his origami to life. A sour taste settled in the back of my throat that six months ago, those memories became tainted. They lingered like ugly scars. A reminder of what he now used his talent for.

I studied his profile. His hair sat disheveled on his head in unplanned chaos. Its typical wild curls always had some control; like you could see, he planned for it to look crazy. In this wilderness, his hair did what it wanted. "Why love letters?"

He jerked his eyes to me, full of hesitancy to discuss this subject with me. "I'm good at it."

My arms tensed at his words. I'd asked; he'd answered. But the anger caused by his words seeped inside, taking hold like tar sticking to my vital organs. I stopped as my throat caught. My fury had to stop before it took over my voice box, and I screamed at him over this discussion I'd started. "So many other things you could write, and you choose that. You choose something that messes with people personally."

He turned his attention back to the mountain view. "Writing other things doesn't bring in money fast enough."

"Greed makes terrible things happen, Boaz. It corrupts hearts and changes people."

"It's not greed, Ivy! You judge so much you don't understand. You rip my fliers down and destroy my business, all based on what you assume are my motives. Assumptions cause problems too! They lead to terrible things."

"Maybe, but they don't come from a heartless place."

He let out a quick gasping laugh—a sound born of disbelief. "You think I write love letters from a heartless place?"

"Yeah, I do. There's no other explanation."

He stood up and sent a rock soaring over the cliff. "There's so much you don't know about me anymore, Ivy."

"I don't need to know more. Don't want to. What I do know is enough!"

"No, it's not. You don't even know what I do with the money."

I jumped up to match his stance. "I don't care what you spend it on. It doesn't matter. It really doesn't. Do the ends justify the means for you? Is playing with hearts all okay because of what you spend the money on?"

"You act like I'm murdering people or something."

"Maybe it's that bad, Boaz!"

He closed his eyes, taking slow breaths, as if trying to keep a hurricane inside. He turned and walked into the trees.

"Where are you going? You can't finish a conversation with me?" I screamed.

I plopped back down in front of the drop. The scenery that normally captivated me distorted in my vision as Boaz storming away played on repeat. I scooped up my bag in a split-second decision, removing Boaz's blanket and placing it on the ground with his bars and water. I marched away from him. I didn't need him and would be fine on my own.

Chapter Eleven

I paced back and forth between two enormous spruces, telling myself to breathe. Ivy Carter frustrated me more than any other person ever had. A lot of it had to do with all the half-truths she spewed. She told me halfway her problem with me, but never enough for me to understand. The half she revealed launched from her mouth, acidic and potent.

It melted my layers of control until anger became power-ful. That anger had nowhere to go other than into my legs, moving me forward to keep her words from choking me into a heap of loathing self-doubt.

I rested my forehead on a tree as I breathed slow, regulated breaths. The bark's scratchy surface kept me grounded until my emotions oozed from my chest to my feet, dispelling them-selves, which returned my focus. I sunk onto the ground that gave way slightly under me as the damp soil caked around my pants.

It took a little longer to get to where I could face Ivy again. I came out from the trees and glanced around, not seeing her anywhere.

"Ivy! Ivy!" I shouted as I spun in a circle. "I'm sorry and

shouldn't have run off like that." I moved in and out of the forest, and dread rolled down my spine. "Ivy! Ivy! Please! We don't have to talk or even be close, but let me know where you are."

Where would she have gone?

I looked between the way we'd walked this morning and the way we were headed.

Footprints!

The ground had slight dampness that had left visible footprints a lot of the way up. I ran back toward where we had gone and studied the markings. They seemed to go in one direction, so I checked out where we had been headed. Sure enough, one set of prints pointed that way. The sun caught the metallic emergency blanket, and I picked up everything she'd left me on the ground. The water bottles and energy bars went into my pockets, and the blanket tucked under my arm.

I held my head a minute to calm down because finding Ivy required a level mind. She couldn't have gotten too far ahead, and my stride was larger than hers. Distant memories drifted into my mind of another time I'd looked for Ivy.

"Ready or not, here I come!" I looked under the table, in the bathtub, and even the drier.

All her rooms were empty. I'd checked them all but her parent's room because it was forbidden. She wouldn't have gone in there. The backyard seemed the only option, and the slit in the sliding glass door seemed to indicate someone had stepped through it.

I kept to the left side of the yard, avoiding the right. The angry neighbor dog liked to smack the fence while barking and growling, which terrified me that he'd leap over and eat me.

"Ivy! I give up! Are you out here?"

"Boaz! Boaz!"

My head whipped to the right where Ivy's trembling voice had flowed from. "Come to this side of the yard."

"I can't. Boaz, I'm scared."

"Where are you?"

"In the tree. I climbed it and can't get down." She sobbed in a way that ripped my nine-year-old heart into tiny pieces.

I inched along the yard as my eyes stayed fastened on the fence. My body shook, and a tear rolled down my cheek. Ivy needed me, and that propelled me forward. The tree came into reach, and victory neared. With a loud thud, the dog smacked the fence. Its teeth scraped the wood as it snarled vicious sounds. The sun baked my eyes as they widened in terror.

"Boaz!"

I jerked my head upward to find Ivy clinging to the largest branch that spanned a good portion of her yard. The dog's fury slammed my heart into my chest, but I did the best I could to drown it out.

My arms stretched toward my best friend. *"Scoot back and slide down. I'll catch you."*

"I can't. I'm too scared." Her tears trickled into the grass.

"You trust me, don't you?"

She nodded.

"Then scoot back, and I'll catch ya."

She closed her eyes and slowly edged her way backward while throwing her legs over. Her body dropped, but she grabbed the branch as her feet dangled in the air.

"Let go! I got you!"

She plummeted straight at me, and I wrapped my arms around her. We fell back onto the grass and hugged. She continued to cry, so I grabbed her hand and led her to our blue tent.

"Tell me a story, Boaz."

I grabbed the blue construction paper because it reminded her of the sky. I folded a fox and a frog and told her about their biggest wish. Her smile returned the further I got into the story, *until she laughed at the way I altered my voice to suit each character. When the story ended, I folded a heart and gave it to her.*

"That's my favorite," she said.

I nodded. "That's why I made it. It makes me think of you."

My mind returned to the present, where I'd lost Ivy again. This time, the threats loomed bigger than a fenced-in dog and an oak tree branch. No, I had lost her long before this moment, and it hadn't even phased me. It happened so slowly, with time slipping away like sand on a beach. There were so many particles that you barely noticed when the wind carried some away. Ivy and I had so many connections that, little by little, they disappeared until we woke up one morning to a sandless beach. Everything that made our friendship had dwindled into nothing.

It didn't stop there. Something happened close to prom last school year that flipped something in Ivy. She'd gone from hanging out in a different circle to actively trying to sabotage my life. No matter how much I tried, I couldn't place why.

I shifted my focus back to finding Ivy in a hostile wilderness. The footprints led me forward until they abruptly vanished. The trail narrowed, and I went a little farther to locate them again. Panic overflowed in my chest, like a volcano erupting in my throat. I closed my eyes and peeked over the edge, bracing myself to see Ivy crushed on the jagged rocks below. My pulse slowed when I didn't spot her anywhere on the ground.

"Ivy! Where are you? Please!"

Above me, the mountain ascended at an almost straight angle, and no apparent footholds stuck out to me. Maybe the soft ground hardened here, which seemed the only explanation. I continued hiking while calling her name every so often until I'd made it to our goal. The other side of the mountain had an endless view of frosty white peaks. This would be our end. Tomorrow made day four, and I once read that most people who survived dilemmas like this were lost three days or less.

What chance did we have out here with no resources? What chance did we have alone, without each other?

Noah, sitting at home crying in his bed, popped into my head. His books sat untouched, with no one to read him a bedtime story. Tears itched my face, and I scratched them away as I slumped against a rock. Shock numbed me at the sheer length of the mountain range in front of me. Finally, I didn't stop the tears and let them pool onto the dusty path.

I pulled myself back together and continued. Hope returned when I spotted her shoe prints again. My muscles ached from walking all day, but I pressed on as the sun moved closer to plunging me into darkness. I had to find Ivy before the night stole my chance.

A muffled cry gave me a clear target, and I jogged despite my screaming calves. A silver blanket shook on the ground as intense sobs poured from under it. She laid in the middle of the path with her knees almost reaching her chin.

"Ivy!"

She flew forward and stared at me. Her right eye had swollen more from the poison ivy, giving her a winking appearance. Her hair rested in every direction, and tears streamed faster than I'd ever seen them fall from anyone. "Boaz? I'm so tired," she said.

"There's grass over there. Why don't we sleep on that?"

She picked herself up, limped over to the grass, and curled up under a tree. I chose one next to her. It put distance between us, but kept her in my view. For now, that would be enough. I stared at her tangled brown hair until my dry eyes closed for me.

Rain pelted my face, soaking my hair and snapping me awake. I jumped up to find Ivy on her feet. We both scooted farther back into the forest. Transparent sheets poured from the sky, and a few drops found their way through our canopy. Any other time watching the rain would have brought a calm, but this felt more like another trick mother nature played to drive us insane with misfortune.

Ivy's face contained no expression other than maybe defeat. Her one visible eye had glazed over, and her lips made a straight line, tipping slightly downward. "We're going to die out here, aren't we?"

My hand itched to take hers and offer comfort. Instead, I closed it around my water bottle. "Once there was a little fox, and her best friend was a frog. They both wanted to go to the moon, but everyone told them it couldn't be reached. The frog thought if he could jump high enough, he could land on the moon. He'd keep the rope in his mouth and pull the fox up to join him. He practiced and practiced until he gained enough confidence to try it.

"He announced his plan to his neighbors. Everyone in their town came to watch and mock the frog when he failed. The frog didn't care because the fox had the only opinion that mattered to him. The frog sat back on his legs and sprung with more force than he'd ever mustered before. Gravity, being such a possessive thing, threw him back to Earth. He hobbled away to sulk and hide from his friend. He'd failed her, after all. But what did she say when she found him?"

Ivy's eyes locked on mine. "That it was never about them going to the moon. It was always about the time they got to plan the adventure together."

A small smile broke through my heaviness. "You remember."

"It's not something I could ever forget. How many times

did I hear it? You always told me that story after scary or bad things happened, but I never knew why."

I shrugged one shoulder. "I think it was my way of saying we could get through anything as long as we stuck together. When we tried to do something on our own, it lost its magic. The moon went from being a possibility to something untouchable. Something we failed at."

She let out a hoarse sound that may have qualified as a laugh. "You thought that up at nine?"

"Yeah, but I don't think I understood it completely until I'd told it to you a thousand times."

She laid back down and closed her eyes. "I won't leave you again. Not until we're home and can safely go our separate ways."

My heart sunk a little, competing with the relief she'd stay with me in this place. I missed her, but the Ivy that was my best friend grew up to hate me. She hated me in an unfixable way for reasons she'd never share.

Chapter Twelve

Boaz watched me like I might disappear on him again. That was a fair conclusion on his part after I'd taken off on him like I had. It hadn't been the smartest thing I'd ever done, but it felt right in the moment with all the anger building inside. I needed to be away from him before I said something stupid that I regretted. Not something that would hurt him, but something that would hurt someone else.

The endless mountains had stunned us both and settled a deep melancholy into my chest. That I could deal with, but the hopelessness and confusing emotions bothered me because I struggled to sort them into understandable boxes. My emotions had always confused me as my mind sat at two extremes on almost every subject. Boaz proved no exception, but I hated him with more force than I loved him. That meant he got my anger. The part of me that loved him always would, but it had muffled over months of growing apart. Then fury over his actions severed a lot of it.

The small part left that loved him curled up in a tiny part of my heart. I refused to free it. I couldn't let old feelings return because what would that say about me? It would align me with him, and that was the last thing I wanted.

We spent most of the morning staring at snowy peaks. Grey and blue broke up the pristine white. The blanket of high altitude and frozen land. The sun made everything more beautiful as it did the snow when its rays turned frigid powder into crystals that spread rainbows across a desolate land. This high and away from civilization held forgotten things of humanity. The tranquil stillness had become lost in the scurrying to go from one place to the next. Our constant electronic connection voided the deep one buried in a primal part of cerebral hemispheres. A vital human element withered away.

We'd lost the art found in the way snow glided down a mountain and birds danced in the sky like the eagle above our heads. In all the heaviness his slumped shoulders revealed, Boaz found peace here, as I did. That meant something different for both of us and remained more vital to him. He often sought the stillness to exist among it while I wanted to be absorbed into it.

I grabbed my last bar and drew out my chewing. It tasted exceptionally well due to my lack of anything else to compare it to, as though my body wanted me to think the oats heaven and indulge in more.

Boaz set his last bar next to me. "Take this for tomorrow."

I shoved it back his way. "No, you're going to eat it because you're not going to die on me a day before I do. I don't want to smell your corpse."

"Why wouldn't you just leave me?"

I gave it another shove toward him. "Please eat it."

He grinned. "You're worried about me."

"I'm worried about having to be out here alone with you dead next to me. I don't handle dead bodies well."

"That's why it was always fun to watch horror movies with you."

"See, so take the bar because I don't want to deal with a real-life dead person."

He unwrapped it and took a small bite. "I doubt one granola bar is going to keep death away that long. Besides, humans can go without food for 3-4 weeks if they have to. Water is our primary concern."

I plopped back on the ground, sprawling my arms in the cool grass. "I hope we aren't out here that long, but it's looking more and more like this is our new life. My mom has probably made enough bread and cookies to replenish all the world's food pantries."

"I remember that time your dad was two hours late in the blizzard, and she made three pies and four dozen cookies."

I rolled over on my stomach to study a purple wildflower. The petals had tiny veins that brightened the flower in places to an almost indigo. "She'll probably put Pop in a nursing home while I'm gone. She knew I didn't want her to, but it would be easier with me out of sight."

"Why would she put Pop in a nursing home? How will he play Santa every year and share his fishing stories? He had some epic ones."

My finger ran over the petals to see if the veins added any texture. "He has RPD. Rapidly progressive dementia. It takes a person extremely quick from the onset. He went from playing Santa last Christmas to not remembering my mom by February. Dementia goes backward. It takes your latest memories first, so I left his mind even before that. They're saying at the rate he has progressed, he'll be lucky to make the year." Out of the corner of my eye, I caught Boaz's hand move toward mine.

He quickly pulled it back and looked out at the cliff. "I'm sorry, Ivy. He's a wonderful person."

I removed my fingers from the flower before I destroyed its beauty with my bitterness. "That's just it. He was the best Pop ever. He's done so much for us in his life, and my mom wants him to spend the last few months of his life with strangers. It's not right."

"It's got to be tough to watch your dad slowly lose all that makes him your dad."

My head whipped in his direction, and I bolted upright. "Of course it is. But he forgot most everything months ago. Why can't she stick it out?"

"Isn't it better for her to know her limit?'"

I got up and moved toward the cliff, taking in the drops of smaller peaks that looked like the tiny drums of a giant. Bright green patches broke up the grey, which gave the only sign that something existed below this mountain range. "Why can't she stick it out a little longer? I'm going to miss him enough when he leaves." I hugged my arms to ward off the chill not derived from the gentle wind.

What did it matter now if my mom put my grandfather in the nursing home, anyway? I'd probably arrive in heaven first at this point.

"I miss everything right now. What I wouldn't do for a cheeseburger."

I groaned. "Don't talk about food. My stomach does not believe the three-to-four-week timeline."

"I miss my brother."

I sat back facing him, playing with the long strands of grass. "How is Noah?"

"Good. He asks about you sometimes."

A sharp twinge struck my chest. "He does?"

"Yeah, especially at Halloween time."

I laughed, thinking about how much Noah loved Halloween. "Still a Ninja Turtle?"

"Yeah, five-year streak. He says it's not the same costume because he alternates which turtle he is."

"He always was pretty clever." That twinge grew into a stone bouncing in my stomach. At which point had Boaz, and I grown apart so much we stopped doing the things we'd done every year since we were toddlers? The stone heated into anger that I could consider that it mattered. We could never be friends again.

I jumped up. "We should probably get going for the day. I don't think search and rescue will travel this far out. It seems pretty abandoned."

He brushed off his knees as he stood. "That's probably a good idea. The grey clouds are back. My gut tells me we're being warned that winter isn't too far off. I think we should travel half the day, and if we find nothing promising, we build our own shelter. We at least have matches."

"How in the world are we going to build a shelter?"

"Branches, maybe. We have a lot of those."

I spun back around, looking around the area. "That's about all we have. There has to be a water source close. Forests usually have rivers or at least creeks."

"They do. We just have to be lucky to find one. We know the valley we came from had nothing, which leaves us with a few options. We could head back and cross the other mountain, or we could head down below and see what's there."

It constantly felt like Boaz and I stood blindfolded on an edge that fell into fate. The outcome of our lives depended on which side we chose to free fall into. The scary thought became that what if both sides held death for us? I'd told Boaz fate was sitting on a cloud laughing at us, but maybe she wanted to punish us.

I swallowed, thinking about deciding anything. "You pick. Your instincts are better than mine. Not when it comes to your business practices, but other things."

He gave a half-eye roll before his eyes popped back to mine. "You had to throw that in."

"It needed a disclaimer."

"There are so many mountains in both directions. It's like we're in the middle of the mountain range. Eventually, there is a way out, but for all we know, we're going in circles."

"Should we eenie meenie it?"

He ran his pointer finger across his chin. "Seems as good a choice as any at this point."

"We made it this far. Maybe we should keep going. If we head straight, there has to eventually be an end."

"Okay. Let's find a good place to climb down and do this."

We walked down the path until we came to a slope that angled less. Boaz went first because he seemed to think he needed to catch me if I fell, which annoyed me to no end. I kept quiet to reestablish our truce. We made it to the bottom and into the forest. The trees were less dense than in the other places we'd traveled. Moss covered rock formations and tree trunks. Yellow leaves crunched under our feet, adding to birds chirping and insects buzzing. A tree made a horseshoe shape over the path, creating a natural archway we ducked under. The air took on a dampness that pressed into my sinuses.

"Either it's going to rain, or there's a water source close," I said.

"I think you're right. The humidity level is up."

The ground turned softer, which made each step more work. We walked around a large rock, and a lake came into view.

Boaz jogged toward it, whipping his head around. "I don't see a lake house or road close. Maybe we should walk around it."

"That's probably a good idea."

"We can make a fire tonight and camp here close to the water."

I eyed the murky lake. "Is it safe to drink?"

"It would be better if we can boil it, but dehydration will kill us faster than anything else."

We made it to the other side of the lake, searching between the trees for signs of anything promising.

Boaz stopped dead in his tracks. "Look at that!"

My mouth hung open as I caught up to him.

Chapter Thirteen

I stared at the dilapidated shack as though I hadn't seen a building in years. All the paint had long ago abandoned the weathered wood that made up slanted walls. Two windows sat on either side of a partially open door, and it had a tiny, covered porch that at one time probably added a lot of aesthetic appeal.

Ivy's jaw looked like it might drop onto the marshy ground. "There have to be roads close. Sure, this looks like 19th-century pioneers built a life here, but they had to get here somehow."

The steps creaked under our feet as we pushed open the loose door to find a bed. A small area enough to stand and five cabinets running along the right wall made up the space. The bed had a patchwork quilt and two yellowing pillows.

Ivy climbed onto the bed and opened the cabinets. "Look, a rusted can opener without a can in sight." She pulled a black rectangle out. "I think it's a camping stove."

She set it on the counter and flipped the metal switch. Sparks flew out from the side, making Ivy back up, but the red burners turned orange.

I stuck my head under the bed. "Wow! Look at this. It's our lucky day."

"You found a satellite phone that will let us call for help?"

"Okay. Not that lucky, but fishing poles. Three of them and a tackle box." I pulled them out one at a time and leaned them against the side. "We can thank your grandpa for teaching us all about fishing."

"I'm not sure this camping stove is safe, but we could build a fire and cook the fish that way." Ivy shut it off and stuck it back in the cupboard. "The irony of tools for food that can't be used."

We went back to the lake, and I leaned the poles on a tree. The tackle box had a few promising forms of artificial bait, but earthworms always seemed to work best from my experience. I cupped my hands and scooped up some water to pour onto the ground. The rich soil smell struck my nose as I sifted through the mud that brought the worms to the surface. I placed them in a large section of the tackle box along with some dirt.

Ivy crinkled her nose. "I hate this part."

I chuckled, grabbed the first pole, and studied the hook. "You still can't watch?"

She shook her head. "It seems cruel."

"You may change your mind when we eat well tonight."

I sent the first line out into the lake, followed by the next two. The mud and some rocks held them all into place, and I leaned back against a tree to relax and watch. This seemed a great place to be. The shack behind us and the poles made it feel like Ivy and I were simply camping, like we would get to go home after a weekend of fun. It made the traumatic experience almost peaceful.

Ivy sat up straight. "Boaz! Look! One is moving!"

"So, reel it in."

"You're going to let me have glory after you did all the

work?" Ivy leaped over to the pole, which made me smile. She'd always hated the setup, but loved getting the fish. She yanked the rod back, reeled, and repeated the way her Pop had taught us. "This one is tough, Boaz."

I jumped up. "You want me to take over?"

"No! of course not! This monster is mine. Maybe help."

I hesitated. "Are you sure?"

"Yeah, hurry before I lose it."

I stood off to the side but helped her yank up on the pole. We took turns reeling while passing the pole back and forth with our shoulders touching. I gave one last tug, and the hefty bass flopped on the ground.

"Yes! Yes! Look what I caught!" Ivy twirled as she hopped her happy jig.

I grinned and shook my head. "Yep, after all that, you got that fish."

"I totally did because I did most of the work."

The poison ivy had diminished, and she could open both eyes again. Even with red splotches covering her face, I could clearly see how beautiful she looked when she was filled with joy. The way her green eyes became brighter than emeralds in the sun during happy moments had always been something I loved about her. I let her claim the fish victory because it sparked the first bit of hope I'd seen in her in a long time.

We caught two more fish, and Ivy's happy dance tempted me to catch more. We had no way to store them, and wasting them wasn't something either of us would do. The next project became making a basic fire pit. It took some searching, but we found enough large stones to make the circle three layers up. Mud between the stones held them together, and the afternoon ticked by as we completed our project.

Leaves and tiny sticks became our kindle. Our first couple of matches broke, which made me flinch each time. We needed as many as possible. The third time, baby flames nipped at the forest debris in our pit. When the fire grew large enough, I placed in bigger sticks until we had a full-blown fire going. Ivy rolled a log over for sitting as I sharpened the ends of two long sticks with rocks. A sharp stone worked to gut the fish, and we stuck each one on two sticks and dangled them over the fire. The silver bodies crackled and browned.

Ivy brought out the camping stove, and we used it as a plate and dug into our fish. We could barely eat an entire fish each, as our stomachs had shrunk over the last few days, but it tasted like heaven even without seasoning.

Since neither of us could eat the third, I released him from where he'd dangled in the water on a line. He swam away quickly, and I packed up the fishing gear. I dismantled the camping stove, leaving only the top for use.

Ivy turned her head. "You broke it?"

"You said it was unsafe, but it can withstand heat. It's now a bowl to boil the lake water."

The water rushed into the hollowed-out stove, and I brought it back out of the lake. It took some searching, but I found four forked sticks and two branches long enough to stretch over the fire. After soaking the sticks to keep them from catching fire easily, I stuck two forked ones on each side over the fire and balanced the stove over the long ones.

Ivy sat back down on the log and sipped on her last bottled water. "That's smart. You're useful for something."

"Big surprise."

"It is."

We let the water boil for a while, then each of us grabbed two of the sticks. We carefully lowered it to the ground, losing about half the water as we set it down to cool.

"Someone needs to be less shaky for this to work right," Ivy said.

I raised an eyebrow. "You mean yourself, right?"

She snorted. "You displaced most of the water."

"Yet I'm the one that thought of this."

"What good is it if you think of it but fail on the last step?"

I scowled, but for the sake of peace, I let it go. We sat back on the log, watching the fire until the water cooled, allowing us to refill our bottles. Grey clouds still threatened snow, but we had the shack. I still worried it wouldn't be warm enough to keep us alive in polar weather.

I sipped on my lake water that had a concerning metallic taste. "I think we should walk past the shack and see if we can find a road. It's like you said, it seems promising that if someone lived here, there is a path to civilization."

"That makes sense. Should we try in the morning?" She tipped her delicate chin toward the pinkish sky. "Night would make it tough to tell the difference in the forest ground."

"Yeah, first thing in the morning would be best. That means we're here for the night. We have the shack bed."

Her eyes popped to mine. "It's not like we can share it. It's a small bed."

"We shared a log."

"It had more space, and it wasn't a bed."

I scratched my nose and nodded. "Okay. You take the bed, and I'll sleep on the ground."

"That's not really fair either."

"Fine. You take it tonight, and if we spend another night here, I'll take it then. Does that solve the problem?"

She cringed as she gulped the water. "Sure. That seems fair. That's if we survive this water."

"True. We've made it through day four, which means we've already beaten a lot of odds." I told her the statistic.

"Yeah, but that means they weren't found. They could have lived a while beyond the third day, but were never found. We haven't been found either."

I added a log to the fire. "That's true. Thank you for pointing out that bleak fact, but we're still alive, which means there's hope. Tomorrow we'll find the trail or road that led people to the shack, and things will be good."

"I don't think anyone has been here in decades."

"Trails can last that long. There has to be a town or something close. I'm sure they left to get supplies when they needed."

Ivy stared into the fire as it danced across her face. Her familiar halfway smile faded with her lips pressing together. The expressions on her face and how they changed brought back the ache that kept randomly awakening when her presence summoned nostalgia from a childhood spent with her. How had I not missed her sooner? Maybe I always had, but I'd let days, weeks, and months demolish its power.

Her brows creased. "What?"

"What?"

"Why are you staring at me? You're enjoying my monstrous deformities."

I swallowed. "No, even through poison Ivy, you look the same."

She huffed out a breath. "Thanks! So, I'm ugly either way."

"Ugly wasn't the term that came to mind."

"Hideous?"

"The other direction."

Her nose twitched, and she turned her head to the sky. I avoided watching her too closely, though my eyes kept magnetizing to her.

After a bit, Ivy stood and hopped over the log. "I'm tired. See you in the morning." She laid my folded blanket and a hoodie next to me.

Even the way she moved toward the cabin brought back memories of all the other times I'd watched her walk away from me. Images of her flashed through my mind as she vanished behind the cabin door. I laid down in front of the flames, keeping far enough back not to set myself on fire during slumber. The stars shined overhead and joined the breeze to bring me a calm in this place we might die.

Chapter Fourteen

I pulled my silver emergency blanket to my chin and tried not to think about what lived in the mattress or pillows that I laid on. If I avoided thinking about that, the bed felt pleasant. It wouldn't take much after sleeping on the ground the last four nights.

The ceiling had wooden support beams that made two triangles on the peaked roof. I stared at the curves in the wood, trying to focus my mind on sleep. Boaz's face staring at me across the campfire wouldn't leave my mind. The ashy air had left me dizzy, making it tough to think. Had he called me beautiful?

What did it matter if he had? He tricked girls into romances for a living. He did worst things than that; I reminded myself. I couldn't let his hazel eyes trick me into believing he had good intentions. Despite my resistance to giving him thought, I wondered if he felt warm enough. I pulled myself out of bed, draping my metal blanket over my arm, and crept out to the fire.

He slept in a little ball that made him seem cold, and a brief flash of guilt flashed through me before I pushed it back down. I gently placed my blanket over him and tiptoed back to the shack. I cringed as I pulled back the musty blankets and climbed under them. It seemed best not to think about anything crawling around me. Since the ants, my skin had felt like something scurried over it, and it would be best for my sanity not to dwell on it.

At some point, my mind gave in to sleep until sunlight woke me. A savory aroma wafted through the cracked door. Boaz sat at the fire, roasting a fish with another already cooked on the hollow camping stove next to him.

I sat by him and took the bottle of water he gave me. "You boiled water on your own?"

"Yeah, the hoodie worked like an oven mitt so I could grab the container. Spilled less water that way, too. That fish should be cool enough by now if you want it."

I peeled off a piece of fish. "How long have you been up?"

"A few hours, maybe. I watched the sunrise while I fished. Somehow, I seemed to have gained an extra blanket."

"Hmmm... How strange." I chewed my bite to prevent further questions.

"I think we should head behind the cabin since the ground is more open in that direction."

I rubbed my arms. "That's as good as any. It's a little chillier this morning."

"Yeah, I think we should only walk a couple hours looking for a trail and then head back here to the shack. It's our only hope for shelter. I can sleep on the floor in there, so you're more comfortable."

"No, we'll stuff hoodies between us. It hit me last night we could do that, but you'd already gone to sleep."

"Alright. Sounds like a good plan," Boaz said.

We packed up the fishing supplies and put them back in the shack. The trees had changed from mainly aspens and pines to a few maples that added orange and red leaves to join the pine needles and yellow ones. A moose with enormous antlers meandered close, occasionally stopping to graze on tiny plants. Somewhere close, a woodpecker tapped its rhythm into the bark as twigs snapped under our feet, which seemed to be the only two things echoing around us.

Mist rolled out of my mouth. "That's not good. It's getting colder."

"We can go a little farther and turn back. Unless you're too cold." Boaz studied me, trying to make his own assessment.

"I'm fine. We should go a little more. There has to be a trail somewhere close. No one would make themselves that isolated on purpose."

"They might. Some people like the peace."

Nothing looking man-made appeared on our walk for the entire morning. The skies had taken on an almost black appearance, blocking out the sun. The air glistened as snow drifted in tiny specks practically too small to see. All around, the clouds had engulfed the blue.

Boaz stopped and glanced at the sky. "We're going to have to head back to the shack. We don't want to get caught in a blizzard."

My shoulders fell and hung loose in defeat. "It's like someone placed us in a snow globe."

Boaz turned around as he laughed. "Maybe Krampus got a head start on settling holiday disputes."

"That would make sense. Maybe the bear was his helper. You know how Santa has reindeer? Krampus has grizzly bears."

We'd walked a while, and the snow continued to pick up, which scared me we might experience white-out and get lost. Boaz blew out a breath as our new home appeared ahead. The snow had already reached the top of the first porch step. We got inside the shack, and Boaz stuffed hoodies under the doorway to cover the crack. We removed our shoes and socks because they had gotten soaked on the trek back, adding to our chill. I shoved my bag far under the bed to keep the water as thawed as possible.

Boaz spread out our two emergency blankets over the bed, and we climbed under three quilts, a comforter, and a sheet already on the bed. Boaz took the side closest to the window before I could protest. I buried my nose in the covers and shook, watching the snow fall. My temperature stabilized, and I drifted to sleep.

♥

I woke to warmth and a heart beating against my cheek. A familiar scent mixing with mud and pine caused me to take in a deep breath. My arms wrapped around something firmer than a pillow, and I noticed the weight around me. I clenched my eyes, trying to make sense of where I was. As my mind cleared, I became very aware that Boaz and I were snuggled extremely close together. I twisted out of his arms and backed against the cabin wall.

He bolted awake. "What happened?" He blinked while yawning.

My nose crinkled, joining my eyes in horrified disbelief. "We were cuddling, Boaz. As in, our bodies were pressed together with our arms holding each other."

"Really?" he mumbled and rubbed his eyes. "We were probably cold."

"We were touching, Boaz!"

"Nothing we haven't done before."

I gaped. "How can you say that?"

"It's true. I'm sorry if it made you uncomfortable. I didn't intentionally mean to hug you. Won't happen again." His voice trailed off. He turned his back toward me and settled in as though the incident didn't bother him in the slightest.

I climbed out of bed and removed the three remaining sweatshirts. The snow had continued to fall and nearly covered the bottom of the window. We were in so much trouble. The few seconds I found myself out of bed made my teeth chatter. I climbed back into warmth and stuffed all the hoodies in between us. My eyelids drooped, and I returned to sleep.

I awoke once more in Boaz's arms, but this time our legs were tangled together, and his chin rested on my head.

"Boaz!" I shoved him away.

He sat up and glanced around. "What?"

"We were cuddling again!"

"What do you mean again?" He rubbed his eyes then widened them to dislodge sleep.

"You know, like earlier when you told me it was nothing we hadn't done before."

His brows knitted. "I said that?"

"Yeah, along with we must have been cold. We must have been cold, Boaz? You think? We got super cozy there. This has to be a nightmare. When am I going to wake up?"

"Sorry, Ivy. I can sleep on the floor from now on."

"You'll freeze. We need a bigger barrier between us, is all."

He ran his finger through his hair. "I'm really sorry. I'd never want to make you uncomfortable." He glanced out the window. "This is great. We're snowed in."

I rested my chin on my knees and sobbed into them, which magnified into a wail. "How cruel is the universe to make it so I have to cuddle with you to stay alive!" I cried until my head pounded, and I sunk down on the bed.

Boaz kept to the corner away from me with his eyes pointed out the window. His profile blurred in my teary eyes, but I caught his tight jaw. He pulled himself out of bed and returned with a water bottle for each of us. We'd filled all six before we'd hiked, and the camping stove top had more in it that Boaz had placed under the bed before we'd left on the hike. We'd have about five days' worth.

I accepted the bottle and sipped on the water. The hunger no longer held so strongly, like my stomach had accepted the predicament better than my heart and head. He climbed back under the covers and pressed himself into the corner as far as he could get from me while still being able to wrap himself in blankets. I did the same to my corner, and we drank our waters in silence.

"This is going to be a fun few days," Boaz said.

I sniffled. "Absolutely terrible. The worst place we could find ourselves."

"And here I thought that was dead."

"This is pretty close." I pulled my blanket tighter. "It's so cold."

"I'm pretty sure that's the only reason we kept cuddling together. Our bodies are programmed to find warmth when we are too cold while sleeping."

"Did you make that up?"

"No, it's science. I promise. You can look it up when we get home."

"I will," I said.

He threw a lopsided grin at me. "You do that."

"I already said I will."

"There's that last word thing again."

I pursed my lips, wishing daggers could fly out of my eyes. "You have to have it too."

He burst into laughter. "I really don't, but this is fun to see how long this will keep going."

"Boaz Jackson! We are in a tiny space with no escape for who knows how long, and you want to rile me up!"

"Maybe I'm hoping you'll leap across this bed. I'm missing your warmth and all."

I pelted him with one of the loose hoodies. It had failed me as a barrier so it could suffer as a weapon. He grabbed his pillow and launched it at me, which made me grab mine and slam it into his face. With one swift sweep across the bed, he reached for his pillow and flung it into my jaw. The battle went back and forth, with all my frustrations pouring into pillow whacks.

I slammed into him, using my pillow as a shield. He flopped on the small ground and gasped out a grunt.

I covered my mouth. "Are you okay?"

"No, I think you're going to have to smell my corpse until the snow melts." He flung his arms and head to the side.

I slammed my pillow into his face, but he grabbed it, which caused me to fall on top of him. We both froze, staring at each other. His eyes transported me to a time I found safety in them. His hand brushed my hair behind my ear. The trance broke, and I leaped on the bed, shoving myself back into my corner.

How traitorous my emotions were that they could feel anything but anger toward Boaz Jackson. Tears flowed down my cheeks, and for the first time in months, I hated myself more than I did Boaz.

Chapter Fifteen

All there seemed to be to do was huddle under blankets and watch the snow fall out the window. Despite its crumbling appearance, the shack seemed insulated well. Our water hadn't frozen, and the blankets seemed enough to keep us alive. It felt chilly but not unbearable. It made sense, seeing as whoever built it probably wanted to survive the cold in it.

I tried not to glance at Ivy too much. She'd cried off and on most of the morning. Our ordeal hadn't been easy for either of us. The tension that had eased between us had returned since the pillow fight. She gave short answers to anything I asked her and slept a lot.

What we would do when the snow melted had weighed on me for the last few hours. I didn't know if search and rescue even looked for us anymore or if they had called off the search with the inclement weather. Either way, Ivy and I were probably on our own to find a way out of here. Whoever had built this probably wanted isolation and had gone far off-grid on purpose.

Ivy stirred and met my eyes with her puffy red ones. "Is the snow gone yet?"

"No, it's still going, but it's slowed a little. Can I get you anything?"

She sat up, bringing the blankets with her. "A story? I have paper in my bag."

I tried to mask my surprise while I jumped off the bed and took out her notebook. "How many should I use?"

"As many as you want. I have no plans for it."

I set to work folding a farmer, his two children, and a snake. Ivy studied my fingers as I made each one. She'd always appeared to enjoy watching me fold.

I lined up the characters in the order I needed. "One day, there was a snake who decided he wanted to make his nest in a farmer's barn. He lived there happily for some time and became great friends with the farmer. They did everything together for many years. The farmer's son was cruel and set out to harm the snake. The reptile bit the boy out of pain and fear, which cost the boy his life."

Ivy gasped and covered her mouth.

I smiled and brought back out the farmer. "The farmer became angry and chopped off the snake's tail out of vengeance."

"I'm surprised the farmer didn't kill him."

I shook my head. "Well, he didn't and only de-tailed the snake. The farmer's daughter had seen all the events and told her father of his son's cruelty. The father went to the snake to make amends, but the snake refused to forgive him."

"That seems turned around. The farmer lost his son and the snake only his tail."

"Well, the snake thought both were terrible because he told the farmer that there could be no restitution for either of them because the loss suffered by both was too grave. The farmer had to go away distraught because no peace could be found with one party unwilling to fix things." I folded three porcupines, taking my time to roll each quill between my finger while I ignored Ivy glowering.

She picked up the snake and frowned. "I think he was wise. He knew that there are things that can't be fixed."

I set the porcupines aside and moved on to two cows. "Once, there was a mom, dad, and a baby porcupine. The parents taught the baby to be afraid of the world and act quickly at any sign of a threat. When it came time for the baby to go out into the world, she was suspicious of everything, but she wanted to make some friends. She came across some cows and introduced herself. The cows seemed happy to meet her, but cows always greeted each other by sniffing. The cows lowered their heads, which startled the porcupine. She shot her quills at them, causing them to flee. Similar things happened everywhere she went until no one around wanted to be her friend."

"Those cows could have been hostile. She had no way of knowing. That's what it means, right?"

I laughed and shook my head. "Because of miscommunication, the porcupine found herself alone. She gave no one time to explain or explain herself before she attacked."

She jerked the paper away from me and started folding something unclear. She set the wadded paper ball in front of me. "I have one for you."

"What is it?"

"It's a rat."

I turned my head. "It could pass for a snowman. Maybe."

"It's clearly a rat!"

I stuck my hand up. "Okay. If you say so. Proceed."

"I will if you quit interrupting me with your judgment."

"By all means."

"Once there was a rat, and he had two friends."

I glanced at the paper. "Where are his friends?"

Ivy's jaw stiffened, and she ripped off two papers and

crushed them into little balls. "These were his friends. A cat and a songbird. Don't look at me that way. That's what they are! Anyway, the songbird had the most beautiful voice anyone had ever heard. The cat always tried to compare herself to the bird, but never came close. Still, they were good friends and sang at lots of shows together."

"Would you like me to make a cat and a little bird?"

She threw one of the paper balls at my forehead. "The cat says to be quiet because it's my turn now, and she's happy with the way she looks. Anyway, they had a rat as a friend. Only they didn't know he was a rat until he stabbed them both in the heart." She demonstrated by flattening the supposed cat and songbird with her fists. She held them up. "This is what he did to them."

"That's a pretty vague story. What does it mean?"

She laid down and turned her back on me. "It means you're the rat."

"Who are the cat and the songbird?"

"Figure that one out."

For the next three days, the snow level remained too high to leave the shack. Ivy and I still gravitated to each other when we slept, which resulted in her kicking me away each time she woke. I never woke first, so the only time I became aware was when her feet or hands shoved me back to my side. We placed items between us to prevent cuddling, but we somehow pushed them away in our sleep.

Ivy and I had been missing eight days, and it seemed safe to assume everyone thought us dead. We were missing much longer than average, and the blizzard would have increased the probability of our demise to rescuers. Finding a way home rested on our shoulders more than ever. As long-lasting as the storm had been, the weather had warmed again and started to melt things. The lake hadn't frozen entirely over, with patches of ice popping up here and there.

I started a fire and set up the fishing pole. We hadn't eaten since the morning we got trapped in the cabin. Instead of lake water, I melted snow over the fire to give us a fresher taste. By mid-morning, I'd caught a large trout, and we split him as neither of us could eat more than a few bites. I buried the leftover in the snow to preserve it.

When the snow melted, I set the stove top on the ground to cool, and Ivy refilled our bottles. I created another batch that I took back to the shack and slid under the bed in case we got stuck inside again. Origami animals covered the bed, as it was about all we'd had to do. We'd run out of paper quickly, but I'd folded each sheet several times over into different animals. Ivy had listened, but if I told a story she didn't like, she'd tell me her own with wadded-up balls she insisted looked like her story characters.

"Are we going to start looking for trails again?" Ivy asked when I returned.

"We'll have to unless we want to live here. The best thing would probably be to go out in all directions, but not too far from here unless we find something promising."

"What if there is nothing close?"

I rubbed the patchy stubble on my chin. "Eventually, we'll have to leave this place behind, but we should have an idea of which way we want to go first. The first few trips out can be scouting trips unless we find something obvious. After that, we can decide which looks the most promising and go that direction and keep going until we find something."

"That seems like a good plan. I just hope we don't get far out and hit another storm with no shelter." She looked at the cloudless sky as if searching for warning clouds.

"That's the problem. We either live here until spring or abandon our only known safety net. I mean, we could wait, but that would be months. That's not something either of us wants."

"Definitely not. That's the stuff of worst nightmares." She stood up and walked toward the denser trees. "I'll be right back."

"Where are you going?"

"To finally find a private place to use the bathroom. Having to share that plastic trashcan for the last few days is an experience I'd like to burn from my mind."

"At least we had the trash can," I shouted as she disappeared out of sight.

I packed up our things and made sure the lids fastened tight to our bottles before placing them back in Ivy's bag. The lake rippled in the light breeze, pushing fallen leaves to new destinations. We had a good setup. Suitable for the circumstances, anyway. It made me reluctant to give it up over uncertain possibilities. All my concerns became void when I thought through staying here through winter. We'd both most likely go mad by that point. It seemed mad that I even considered it. If it had been only me in this situation, it wouldn't have mattered so much. Ivy's life made it a more challenging decision.

A herd of five deer nibbled the ground and strolled in the distance. Now and then, one picked up their head, listening and observing for the group. I sat back on the log and took a sip of water. My body had accepted my lack of nourishment. Hunger no longer consumed my thoughts, which freed me up to ponder other things.

Hooves pounded the dirt as screams ricocheted off the trees. I jumped to my feet, tearing toward where Ivy let out another strangled cry.

Chapter Sixteen

I ducked between trees, making sure they concealed me from Boaz. We'd had to share a tiny trash can we'd found in a cabinet for our bathroom. Luckily, one of the windows proved easy to open, but restoring this privacy felt close to bliss.

We'd gotten lucky by the temperatures not dipping too low and the shed keeping us warmer than it looked like it would. A white fox balanced over a log with swift, graceful movements. We stared at each other for a moment before it leaped deeper into the woods.

Leaves blanketed the ground with bright autumn colors. Something glimmered in the sun, and I stepped closer. I squinted, trying to figure out what it was. Three steps forward, and the ground gave out, plunging me into the frigid water. I screamed right as my head went under.

I kicked my legs but found a sheet of ice halting my way to oxygen. Since the temperature hadn't dipped too low, it cracked as I beat on it. I found a slit and kicked my legs as I shoved partially through, screamed, and sunk back down. I pushed myself back to the slit as I tried to make my way to freedom. I tilted back so my nose and mouth could take in air while letting out another scream.

I swam sideways until I found an open spot. As I tried to climb out, the ice kept giving way. A thick branch plopped in front of me, and my eyes followed it to find Boaz lying on his stomach, stretching it out to me. He shouted something that muffled under the water pressure in my ears.

I grabbed the branch, and he yanked me onto the ground. He scooped me up as I shook against him. My muscles ached, and my teeth chattered all the way back to the shack.

He set me down. "You're going to have to take your clothes off, put on a hoodie, and wrap in the emergency blanket."

My fingers didn't want to bend to remove my shoes, so Boaz removed them. He left to put them by the fire, and I removed everything. The dry hoodie went over my head, and I swaddled myself in the silver blanket.

Boaz knocked on the door and came in when I told him to. "Can I carry you to the fire?"

"I can walk." My words shook with my trembling lip.

"I know, but it'll keep the blanket from getting dirty."

"Okay."

His arms went under me, and I rested my head against him. He set me by the fire and ran back to the cabin. When he returned, he wrung out my clothes and dangled them over branches to air dry.

He dropped to his knees in front of me, meeting my eyes. "Are you okay?"

I nodded, but my racing pulse disagreed. His tears falling down his cheeks ignited my own. He rested his forehead on mine, and I threw my arms around his neck. That was all it took for him to pull me onto his lap. His body heaved with mine on the dusty ground in front of the campfire. We clung to each other until I closed my eyes and slept.

I woke back in the shack under all the blankets, still cocooned in the one I'd wrapped around myself. Shadows bounced across Boaz's face as he shifted while looking out the dark window. I'd apparently slept the day away.

I wiggled my way upward. "Hey."

He whirled around and sent me a tight smile. "Hey. How are you feeling?"

"Tired, which is odd since I must have slept the entire day."

"Fighting a frozen lake is exhausting. Your clothes are dry if you want to put them on." He crawled into bed and stared at the wall while I got dressed.

My eyes stayed fastened to him, and he didn't sneak even a slight peek.

My emotions crested as I climbed back under the blankets. "Boaz?"

"Yeah?"

"Can you hold me? It's okay if you don't want to."

Arms pulled me against his t-shirt that smelled like sweat, forest, and him. His fingers ran through my hair, and we fell into sleep.

I awoke with my emotions all over the place like a ping pong ball caught in a cyclone. The funnel ripped at me, threatening to slam onto rocks and finish me. The water yanking me to the lake bottom rushed into my mind. Despair had taken hold at how close I came to dying. Boaz had rescued me, and

I'd needed his comfort. What kind of person did that make me? How could I let us go there?

Boaz smiled down at me. His eyes exuded warmth and kindness—a deception I couldn't believe. I squirmed away from his arms and ran out of the cabin, needing the fresh air to think. I wanted so badly to keep running until my legs gave out, but yesterday had proven the ground could kill me. Nothing here could be trusted to behave as it should—not even me.

We would never escape here because we deserved to die lonely deaths in the middle of nowhere. That had to be why there was no solution anywhere. Some force was angry at us.

"Ivy," Boaz said behind me.

"I can't right now, Boaz."

"Talk to me. *Please.* Let me know what's going on."

"We can't do that again. Even if I have to sleep outside, we can't get close."

He hopped off the porch and came around to face me. "You'd rather freeze to death than let your wall down."

"Yes! I actually would."

"That's stupid, Ivy! Completely stupid."

I jumped up and took a step away from him. "What's stupid was me asking you to hold me last night."

His face flinched, but he quickly tried to recover. "Why? We both needed it. That's right, I needed it too. You almost died, and we both needed the comfort!"

"I don't care what you need! I hate you, remember?"

He sputtered out a harsh laugh. "I remember you want to hate me. You want to hate me so badly and keep failing at it."

My fists clenched and took another step away from him. "I do hate you. I hate you so much, Boaz. More than I ever loved you!"

"Why? Tell me, Ivy! Why do you hate me? You can't tell me, which means it's nothing."

"It's everything!" I marched behind the cabin.

Boaz chased after me. "Where are you going?"

"Away from you!"

"You promised! You promised to stay until we were home."

"We're not going home. I can't be around you anymore. It's making me weak. And you promised a lot of things that you never kept. This seems fair." I picked up my pace.

"What promises didn't I keep?"

"That you'd always be there for me."

"You weren't there for me either!"

"I know. We deserve what we're getting here." I took off running, feeling the air blow through my hair, which restored a bit of calm to the chaos surging through my nerves.

Boaz appeared before me, blocking my path with his jaw set and eyes blazing with fury. "Let's do this, Ivy. Let's get this done with and then you can go off on your own and be an idiot who dies for no reason at all. Tell me your problem with me."

"I can't!"

"Yes, you can! That's a lie you tell yourself for protection."

I turned away from him. "It's not to protect me."

"Then who? Because you have the biggest walls up that I have ever seen, and that's to protect something. Talk to me, Ivy!" He stepped around to face me again.

"No!"

"Why not?"

"Because you're a traitor. Because you almost killed my best friend! *Your* best friend. You almost killed her, Boaz, and destroyed her life. What kind of friend does that make me if I don't hate you? What kind of person does that make me if I don't fight you and stop you from hurting more girls? Who am I if I let things continue when people are getting hurt in ways they don't recover from?"

His eyes widened, and he swallowed. "What are you talking about?"

I buried my face in my hands and rested them at my side so I could look him in the eye. "When did making a quick buck become so important to you it didn't matter what you put in your letters? It didn't matter how personal the information was or how someone gave you that information in confidence. You used it anyway. You used it because you knew it would work."

"You're not clearing up anything for me."

I closed my eyes and slid against the tree, barely registering the icy mud soaking into my pants. "I don't want to tell you and shouldn't tell because it's an invasion of privacy. It's not my story to tell, and yet it is. It puts me in this place of constant limbo where I need to stop you but can't come out and say why. I'm fighting our war with a cannon that doesn't have gunpowder."

He sat down one tree over and stared at the ground. "Ivy, please tell me. I can't fix anything if I don't understand what I've done. And I don't. I have no clue what I've done, and that scares me."

I nodded and kept my eyes closed, trying to lessen some of the sensory input to think clearly. "You think I'm just trying to sabotage you because I'm annoying and delusional."

"Yeah, that about sums it up."

I opened my eyes, shoved away the tears, and took a deep breath. "It was two weeks before prom. You know, your busy season."

"That was right before you started hating me."

"That's because that's when it happened. I mean, I thought about you now and then and wondered what happened that I could no longer go up and say hi to you. Somewhere along the way, it became weird to talk to you. Like we'd gone so long that suddenly talking would be awkward. Chloe and I were still close because of choir."

He squinted. "Chloe Hart?"

I pressed my lips. "What other Chloe would I mean? Have you really taken her that far out of your life that you have to ask her last name? Because I think you remembered her quite well when Todd Malone approached you."

Boaz's eyes seemed to search for something like a safe code locking into place, ready to open the vault on his sins he'd overlooked. "He had me write six letters for prom because he hoped one would stick. He's my biggest client other than Phil."

"Only one of those letters was a lot easier to write, wasn't it?"

"Chloe's. Yeah, because I personalize each letter to fit the girl based on research I do."

"Only you didn't have to do research for Chloe, did you?"

He swallowed again. "No, I already knew all about her."

"Even things she told you in confidence. Like how she likes to watch the sunrise because it was the last thing she did with her dad before he left."

His shoulders sank, and his breathing became shaky. "Where is this going, Ivy?"

"I didn't want to tell you because she didn't need any more private things brought to the light. But you're not going to get it. I'm never going to be able to stop you because you think I'm crazy."

"I've never thought you were crazy."

I jumped to my feet. "Don't. Not right now."

"What happened to Chloe, Ivy?"

"Two weeks before prom, I found her unresponsive with a note. I'm not going to tell you what the note said because Chloe deserves that privacy. But I found her and almost didn't get her back. Maybe you can piece the rest together from there. Perhaps you can see how writing a letter for a player who uses those letters to get girls to sleep with him and then dumps them might be a problem.

"Maybe you can see how putting in everything you knew Chloe loves would be a problem and make her think Todd loves her, so she does things she wouldn't have otherwise done with him. Can you see that, Boaz? Can you see how that might cause damage that takes an already hurting girl and pushes her over the edge?" My controlled sobs burst into a wail. I put my hand up as Boaz moved toward me. "Stop! I won't run off, but I need some time to be alone. Please give me that."

I left him standing there as the potent memory of Chloe lying on her bathroom floor haunted me.

Chapter Seventeen

Shame and guilt were restless and paralyzing. My skin buzzed with the energy of a thousand spiders scurrying in endless circles. The sensation brought a craving to run and hide from anyone who might see my exposed transgressions. While my muscles throbbed for movement, the heaviness kept me frozen, unable to make a move in any direction. I was bound in cords knotted by each terrible mistake I'd made. They held me captive with no hope of freedom.

I'd watched Ivy storm into the woods, unsure she'd return. My feet moved me back to the shed, where I stared at the water, sorting through everything Ivy had revealed. I didn't remember the letter I wrote to Chloe, but I apparently should have. It made sense I would have used the things I knew she loved. That's what I did, and it never crossed my mind it could be wrong.

The dirt blurred as my thoughts intensified. I'd crossed a line by making Chloe's letter so personal. I'd done it so thoughtlessly that when Ivy had mentioned Chloe, I still hadn't understood what I'd done. She'd had to spell it out for me, and now that I saw it, I hated myself too.

It wasn't about me, though. It was about Chloe and all the suffering my words had caused her. What was even the right thing to do here? The sun moved across the sky as I sat on the log, waiting for Ivy to return and a solution to come to me. Neither happened.

The restlessness propelled me to pace, and I fished the afternoon away. Everything happened automatically while my thoughts boomeranged on a continual track. When I thought of one thing, my mind hurtled something worse right back at me to ponder on.

Ivy appeared around sunset and went straight into the shed. The air had warmed enough I wouldn't freeze. I wrapped my blanket around myself and slept on the ground by the fire.

The sun had started to rise when I woke up to find a second blanket on me again. Even in her anger, Ivy didn't want me to be cold. I added more logs to the fire and roasted one of the fish I'd stuffed in the snow. I broke it in half and ate my piece. Ivy came out a short time later with her blanket wrapped around her shoulders.

She'd tied her hair in a knot, so it flopped in a loose, messy bun, revealing her thin neck. Her pouty lips were pressed as she'd always held a lot of tension in her mouth when upset. She took in the fire and the sunrise in a way she never seemed to lose awe over it. My heart longed to pull her into my arms, and I rubbed my chest where the ache settled.

She accepted the fish that I pushed her way and took a sip of water. "I know we need to talk."

"It can wait until you're ready, but I do have something to say when you're ready to hear it."

"And if I'm never ready to hear it?" She met my gaze and stiffened her jaw.

"Then I'll have to say it anyway, and after I've said it, you can go back to never talking to me again."

"Let's get it over with then," she said.

"We have over fifteen hundred students in our school. I wrote over five hundred letters the weeks leading up to prom."

Her face reddened. "That makes it okay! Because you were swamped and needed to cut corners."

"No, that wasn't what I was going to say. I have no excuse for what I did. I want you to know that I agree with you. Even with all those letters I had to write, I should have remembered Chloe's. It should have mattered to me. All of it should have. You were right this entire time. There's nothing I can do to fix what I've done, but I'm sorry. I hope someday you can forgive me. Chloe too."

She rested her chin on her knees. "What was so important, Boaz? What mattered so much that you had to play with the hearts of over five hundred people?"

I watched the water bob in the light breeze as I pondered the right words. "Orphans. I finished the accounts of twelve orphans with that money."

Her eyes widened. "Orphans? What accounts?"

"For people to adopt them. Adoption costs thousands of dollars internationally. People are willing to adopt, but they need help with the costs. It's a high upfront cost that if they get help allows families to get kids out in time."

"In time for what?"

I ran my fingers through my hair to think up the best explanation. "The orphans I help have disabilities. They vary greatly. The organization I donate through was originally set up to help adoptions for children with Down Syndrome. That's how I found out about them. A woman who went to Morgan's playhouse adopted a little girl through the program. I looked into it, and what I found out made me never the same. It made me desperate to do anything I could to get these kids out."

"Because they're on borrowed time? They need medical help."

I widened my eyes as tears pooled in them. "Some. But, Ivy, it varies by country, but there's an age at which these kids age out. Some before they are even teenagers. They are sent from orphanages to adult mental institutions. The ones that can't move very well. The kids with muscular dystrophy, cerebral palsy, and other similar conditions are tied to bed frames and poles. Same thing with kids who have Down Syndrome and are prone to wander. The institutions are where they are sent to waste away alone until they die." I let my tears fall freely as I looked up at Ivy. "So that's why I got desperate and took on so many letters and didn't think twice about what I did to Chloe. But you were right, Ivy. The ends don't justify the means."

Ivy gaped. "How is this allowed to happen?"

"It's legal in these countries, and not enough people care to help. There was this one named Benson. He had Down Syndrome, and he looked so much like Noah. He had thick dark hair, full cheeks, and the happiest smile. I followed him and donated to his account, but no one picked him on time. Once he was moved to the institution, his picture never looked the same. His eyes became hollow, they shaved his head, and his smile disappeared."

"What happened to him?" she whispered.

"He passed away alone, tied to a pole in a dirt pile."

Ivy and I sat in silence for a long time after that. It made me think of my wall with two bulletin boards. One for those I couldn't help in time, and the other for those that still needed to get out. I always chose the ones close to aging out or with the most medical needs. Having money already in their accounts made families more willing to choose them. Sometimes, as with Maisy, I paid off the last bit so their families could bring them home.

Letters were the fastest way I knew to gain money, but it had become apparent I needed to think up something else. Saving these kids shouldn't come at the expense of hurting others.

Ivy and I sat around the fire, lost in our own thoughts for the rest of the day. We needed to work on a plan, but a numbness had settled between us as all our revelations weighed heavy.

I slept by the fire again while Ivy took the shed. When morning arrived, I once again had a second blanket. We'd made it to day ten, but it felt more like months. So much had transpired, and not a fragment of my world remained untouched.

Ivy came out for breakfast and had braided her hair. It swept over her shoulder, which gave me another splendid view of her neck. Her delicate nose tipped to the dusky sky as the nearly dissipated moonlight traced her cheekbones and full lips. She was the most beautiful girl I'd ever seen and always had been. Though I'd never told her, I felt it at my core.

I used a hoodie to help move my latest batch of boiling water. "We should probably start our scouting trips today."

She blinked out of the trance the sky had placed her in. "Hmm... Oh, yeah, we should."

"Do you want to pick the direction?"

"No, you pick with your magic gut feelings."

I filled all our water bottles and started on the second batch. "I haven't led us anywhere great so far."

"You led us here, and it was exactly what we needed. We got ourselves so turned around that first night in the storm and dark that this was a pretty good find considering things," she said.

A crane dipped its nimble neck into the lake to grab a drink. It stretched its head toward the sky and walked forward on its stilt legs, that bent dramatically with each movement. I watched it until it flew away, and we set out to the left of the shack. The goal would be to keep as straight a line as possible to make sure we could find our way back to our camp. It would serve as a home base until we found something promising or had to move on.

Tension and silence filled the space between us as we hiked. We'd remained civil and kept conversation polite, but we were strings pulled tight enough to snap at a slight tug. I hoped soon we'd relax and maybe find a road back to at least remaining cordial. We broke through the forest and up a grassy hill. We trudged up the steep incline and made it to the top to find another forest.

Ivy gripped my arm. "Boaz. There's smoke!"

My head whipped around until, above the trees, smoke rose in the distance. We'd finally found a sign of someone else.

I took a step forward and stopped. "Let's hope they're not hostile."

"Let's hope they'll let us call our parents."

Chapter Eighteen

We stepped down the hill and toward the woods to find the smoke source. As we approached the tree line, growling pierced the silence. Boaz stepped in front of me as four wolves stepped out of the shadows. Their sharp teeth came into view as they snarled.

"We need to face them and back away slowly." He grabbed my hand and took a step back.

"Shouldn't we run?"

"No, they have a hierarchy, and we need to look like alphas to them. We need to face them." He took another step back, holding tight to my hand.

The wolves made a semicircle around us. Boaz boxed me in with his arms behind him like he'd jump in front of any that charged us. We continued taking steps back while the pack stayed in place, growling. We made it to the base of the hill, and all four of the beasts bolted back into the forest.

Boaz released his intense grip on my hand. "That was odd."

"They must have wanted us out of their territory."

"Yeah, I guess so. We could try to reach smoke from a different direction."

We circled around to the left, only to be greeted by the wolves when we hit the tree line. The same thing happened when we went to the other side. It seemed no one could get close to the smoke source without being attacked by wolves.

Boaz rested his arm across his peaked knee. "Either they are werewolves or highly trained."

I laughed at the thought of us finding paranormal circumstances. "Maybe they could turn us, and we could survive the winter then. Do you think they are protecting property?"

"Seems that way. A lot more likely than the werewolf theory."

The sun hung bright overhead but had slowly eased its way to the west. We had a long way back but took a minute to sit on the hill and take in the landscape. The treetops looked like a black blanket speckled with green and occasional browns. The smoke made a near-constant stream into the sky like something desperate breaking free from a stifling environment, only to evaporate once liberated.

It remained both within reach and inaccessible. The wolves wanted us nowhere near it. Unless we found an alternative, the vapor of hope would remain a dead end.

The ground on our walk back looked patchy, like winter had tried to dominate fall and failed. Snow still blotted the earth in segments, but colorful leaves smothered the white in most places. Green hung on the pine trees and stubborn pieces of grass, not surrendering to yellow. Silver and white clouds swirled together in a way that suggested winter wanted to once again break through autumn.

We returned to the shed as the blue sky had dimmed into indigo and a few stars dappled the sky. The rising moonlight caught the shimmers of sluggish tiny flakes melting into the still-warm ground. Boaz eyed our fire pit where he'd put out the fire this morning. We only had ten matches left, making them precious.

I paused in the shack doorway. "You better sleep in here tonight."

"Are you sure?"

"Yeah, I'd prefer to wake up to you still alive and without pneumonia," I said.

I stepped inside and left the door open to show the sincerity in my invitation. He glanced up at the sky as though trying to determine the storm's intensity.

After a few minutes, he followed me inside and set a fish on a crumpled paper he pressed flat. "It's cooked but cold. Probably won't taste the best."

I accepted the half a fish he handed me on another paper. "It's better than nothing. We have to eat and are not exactly in a place to be picky. How many do we have?"

"Twelve."

"Twelve!"

"Yeah, I may have over-fished yesterday, but the snow is keeping them fresh. We're covered for a while." He finished his meal, grabbed my trash, and set it outside the shack to keep the smell out.

The snow had picked up, but not as bad as last time. Boaz laid down facing the window, and I kept my eyes fixated on him. My emotions tumbled like rocks in a landslide. Everything I felt for Boaz shot through me, collided, and mixed. He shouldn't have even agreed to write a letter for Chloe from Todd in the first place. The fact he'd put so many personal things in it made it so much worse. It was the part I couldn't forgive him for.

She'd put it in her note about how personal Todd's letter was and how much she'd thought he loved her because of it. He'd dumped her the day after they slept together, and when she confronted him, he'd shouted to the entire hallway how easy and terrible she was. Someone recorded it and uploaded it to social media. People no longer had any decency or respect for others. Anything seemed worth ruining someone else's life. Anything for a few new followers had become mankind's mantra.

People made me sick over what they were willing to do for attention on a meaningless social media site, as though a stranger's praise was oxygen society needed to breathe. Instead, what it really did was suffocate us one thoughtless comment at a time. The video of Chloe crying in the hallway while Todd shattered her heart got half a million views. She dealt with it a week before she'd decided not existing was better than dealing with how all the kids looked at her and laughed. All of it spiraled from Boaz writing such a perfect letter.

My fault in this entire thing was laid out clearly in the letter Chloe had left for me. It detailed how I hadn't even noticed all the terrible things she'd gone through. I'd gone to choir practice with her every other day and hung out nearly every weekend but hadn't noticed my friend sinking further into depression. Her letter to me had taken hold in a way I couldn't suppress. I needed to protect others in the way I hadn't protected Chloe.

Boaz settled under the covers, bringing my thoughts back to the small cabin we shared. Moonlight lit up the still gliding snow. I didn't know what to do about him anymore. If I let go of his actions, I'd confirm what Chloe had written in the letter. I was a terrible person who pushed my closest friend to a cold bathroom floor.

I turned my back on Boaz and told my body not to drift to his as we slept. This time it obeyed, but I woke up in chills, unable to fend off the icy weather. It didn't feel enough to kill me, only make me miserable. I turned over to see Boaz awake. Our eyes met, and the gentleness they always held made it tough to hate him. They always had, which was why most of the time, I avoided eye contact. It became easier to hate him when I focused on his letters instead of the boy himself.

The dim room made it tough to entirely decipher what his irises conveyed, but something about the way he stared back at me made my chest bubble.

"Are you okay?" His sentence shook like he was driving down a gravel road.

"It's so cold. I think we better hold each other. You know to warm up."

His brows knitted. "Are you sure?"

"I hate being cold."

We scooted toward each other, and his arms brought peace to the mayhem inside my struggling brain. I buried my face in his chest and cried. We clung to each other out of necessity, but we fit together in a way that seemed natural. As I drifted to sleep, I didn't question it. On this night, I needed only this.

♥

The morning warmed enough that the snow mostly melted, proving autumn kept its reign. Even though muddy remnants lingered, fall had shoved winter back in its place. The two seasons competed like sisters battling for control over a shared bedroom.

Boaz had a system with the fish where he rotated the old forward. He kept them in a hole he layered with snow and placed leaves and sticks over the top. It had dwindled some with the rising temperature, but not enough to uncover the fish.

Boaz stretched and discarded our fish bones in another hole he used to place our food scraps. "I guess we go right today."

"It seems like as good an option as any."

He finished boiling our batches of water and put out the fire. We had nine more matches, and once they ran out, we'd have no means to cook fish. It appeared to be the biggest reason Boaz cooked fish and buried them in the snow hole. He was providing food for us for a long time. It occurred to me we'd both fallen into an acceptance. We actively looked for a way home, but it had lost some urgency. I didn't know exactly what it was. Perhaps it had become a coping mechanism to help us handle having lived in the wilderness for almost two weeks.

At what point would they declare us dead? Had they told our parents we probably already were? I pictured my mother baking as her anxiousness set in while they looked for me. Eventually, the baking would decrease, and she'd slip into her depression, where all she did was sleep and go to work on a repeat cycle. Except she didn't even have work anymore. It left her all day alone with Pop and without me. She didn't have me to focus on making sure her daughter stayed perfect, which would give her too much time to think about my loss.

Boaz took my hand to help me up a steep embankment, and I no longer resisted his assistance. It had become something I quit thinking about over the last few days. My thoughts had taken a different turn. When I didn't think about my parents coping with my assumed death, I thought of Chloe and Boaz. The place they held in my mind seemed like balancing on a log over a raging river. If I leaned too much to one side, I'd topple.

How did I balance Chloe against Boaz? How could I do the right thing as Chloe's friend when that meant hating a boy who spent a good portion of his free time saving the lives of orphans with special needs? That one weighed heavy on me. Boaz stopping his letters meant fewer kids could be saved, but not stopping his letter meant people might suffer.

The ground had mixed terrain in the direction we traveled for the morning. We trudged up a hill and stared at the mountain.

Boaz leaned forward. "Do you see that?"

I squinted, not making out anything but endless trees. "See what?"

He pointed ahead. "There's something there. An opening. It looks man made."

"Hmm... Yeah, something does look out of place."

With a goal for the rest of the day, we set off to check out Boaz's latest find.

Chapter Nineteen

We trekked up the mountain, finding less dangerous spots to climb, which took us a while. The ground flattened and led to an opening framed by wooden beams. As we approached, the environment changed from dirt and rocks to cement. The walls and ceiling were arched and made of smooth brown stone. The cavern receded into darkness several feet back, but we stepped forward to go as far as the light touched. A pathway formed where a track started, and a deteriorating wooden cart rested by the entrance.

Ivy leaned over the side of the cart. "Look at this!" She pulled out a golden lantern with a wire handle. "There are four of them." She turned the little knob on the front, and it flickered to life.

Three out of the four worked, and we left the dead one behind. Ivy stuck two in her pack, which filled the last of the main pocket. I held out the remaining lantern as we used it to proceed farther than planned. A door appeared on the right of the main cavern. I pulled it open, and we stepped inside an office. I ran around to check out the drawers of a metal desk, hoping for a map, compass, or anything else that might allow us to navigate. They all proved empty.

Ivy moved over to the bookshelves. "There are five cozy mystery books. These might be fun to read."

I joined her in looking the literature over. "Anything would be great to read at this point. Even *The Case of the Vengeful Pumpkin Pie.* I held up the book with the evil smiling pumpkin pouring a green liquid over a steaming orange pie."

She wiggled another book. "I don't know. *The Puppy's Fury* sounds pretty exciting to me."

I chuckled. "I bet the villain licks its victims to death."

"Tough way to go." She frowned and stared down at the black, panting puppy on the cover.

"What is it?"

"I miss Droolius Caesar," she said.

"I do too. He's the best dog ever. I remember when you picked him out, and your mom narrowed her eyes and asked if you were sure. You told her you'd never been surer of anything in your life. How is Droo?"

"As happy as ever." She stuffed the books in the front pocket of her bag.

"Why don't you let me take your pack for a while. It looks like it's getting heavy. It has stuff for both of us, so it seems fair."

She slid it off her shoulders. "Okay. That is fair."

I almost gaped as she handed it to me, but I was happy to ease her burden. She sunk into the desk chair and lowered her gaze.

I went around the other side and leaned back on the desk close to her. "What's wrong?"

"I miss home and school. Everyone and everything. Everyone probably thinks we're dead, and Mr. Lee is probably furious. It's going to make it tough to be in any of his classes in the future. He may flunk us automatically. My parents will love that. They're probably mad I failed the midterm and will have to go to summer school if we get out of here." She sunk in the chair as though her despair made her melt into the cushion.

"First, it's not if. It's when. Second, your parents and Mr. Lee are going to be thrilled you're alive. Mr. Lee acts tough, but he cares. Have you thought about the safety rules we missed arguing? Like maybe if we'd caught them all, this wouldn't have happened."

"I think one was warning us about the bear. Maybe what to do if we came across one."

I scrunched my face while turning it to the side. "What makes you say that?"

"When I glanced up, I saw him erasing the rules, and one included a picture of a bear. I didn't see the point of it at the time. We really messed things up with our arguing."

I hopped up on the desk and swung my legs. "We did, but maybe this was meant to happen."

Her eyes snapped to mine. "How can you say that?"

"You probably never would have told me why you hate me. I would have gone on for the rest of my life, not knowing what I'd done. How can I change my ways if I had no idea what needed fixed?"

"Maybe. This could be a cosmic punishment for our deeds. You for writing the letter and for me being an awful friend to Chloe."

"Ivy, you stalked me through my life, taking any chance you could get to sabotage my business because of how great of a friend you are to Chloe."

She fidgeted and shifted in her chair. "I wasn't before and missed everything going on with her. It never occurred to me how badly she was doing. Not one time. How could I not see her pain?"

"Some people are great at hiding it."

"Not with their eyes. You can have someone with the brightest smile, but their eyes always give it away. Let's not talk about this anymore."

I wanted to spend more time convincing her she wasn't the terrible friend her mind told her she was. Instead, I nodded. "Okay. This office is pretty warm. I think we can stay here if the temps drop too much. We can drink snow. I can head back to the lake and fish as needed."

"That's a long way to go."

"I'd only do it once in a while and store the ones we don't use right away in the snow."

We moved deeper into the mine to see if we could spot anything useful, but everything had been emptied. A rusted old pickax hung on the wall, serving, along with the cart, as a reminder of the old purpose here. Our hike to the mine had taken most of the morning, and we stepped outside to a sunny afternoon. I carried Ivy's pack while she held onto the third lantern. I walked around the side to gauge the best way down. Smoke caught my eye as it had yesterday, but at the height we were, I could make out a cabin. We needed to reach it somehow without wolves devouring our progress.

Ivy caught up to me and stared down at the unmistakable sign of other human life. "There has to be a trail or road up here, doesn't there?"

"There at least was at some time. It looks long abandoned, and the forest likes to take back anything left unbothered for a while."

"Maybe we should take the long way around to the front. That person has to get supplies somehow."

I started back toward the mine, so we could make it back to the shed before dark and think things through. "It could be the same deal as the shack. This person wants to be so far off-grid. We have to be careful, or we could get shot for trespassing. If those are their wolves, they clearly want to be left alone."

Our path grew steep in places, and I held Ivy's hands at the riskier parts. My larger palm covered her delicate one. In all we'd gone through the last couple of weeks, her skin felt like silk in mine, as though the harsh wilderness had left her untouched. I held it as close as wouldn't make things awkward, but this slight touch ignited two things in me. I wanted more connection, and I wanted to protect her with everything I had. Last night when I'd held her, I'd stayed awake a while, soaking her in. We'd lost so much time together, and now, because of my stupidity, I'd lose her as soon as we found our way home. That hurt and most likely would for a long time.

We made it back to the shed at sunset, and I lit a fire. We had eight matches left, which meant I needed to amp up fishing if we would move to the mine. I didn't want to waste the fish, which meant I would wait until we tried to get to the cabin the other way. Ivy had slipped off into the forest for some privacy while I added more wood and increased the flames. I sat on the log, watching the rippling lake.

She appeared in between the trees. She'd braided her hair, and a few strands framed her face. Something had lightened about her since she'd screamed at me in the woods. Tension remained between us, but releasing all the building turmoil had helped her while tormenting me. That was okay because I'd rather have had it go in those directions. I deserved the torment, and if any of her burden transferred to me, that was good.

She sat next to me by the fire with her knee edging up to mine. It surprised me, but I contained the shock not to spook her. The first time we'd shared this place, she'd sat far to the far end, almost to the point of falling off.

Ivy stared unfocused into the leaping flames. "Where did things go wrong for us?"

I stiffened. "I made an awful mistake."

"No, I mean, when did we stop being friends? What was the line?"

I used a stick to push the fire around to keep it going a little longer. "I'm not sure there was an exact time. Our line didn't disappear all at once. It faded little by little until we no longer spoke at all."

Ivy yawned and closed her eyes for a second. "I've thought about it a lot. I think it was when I went to choir camp with Chloe for the entire summer, where they only allowed us to use the office phone to call our parents once a week. When I got home, you were on your family trip to Europe. Then school started, and we joined different clubs that took our time away from each other. We got used to being apart until it no longer felt weird."

"I think you're right. It's weird that it stopped being weird. We used to do everything together."

She nodded. "I know."

I watched the fire glow move across her face, which made her features pop against the oncoming night. "I'm not sure how I could have ever forgotten how right it feels having you next to me."

Her head jerked toward me, and her wide eyes locked on mine. We stared, and my hand twitched to hold her face. My lips tingled, and I pressed them together to cool their excitement over her biting her lower one.

She blinked and took in a shaky breath. "I'm tired. Are you going to sleep in the shack tonight?"

I shrugged a shoulder. "It's not super cold. I can sleep out here tonight."

"Oh. Ummm... It might get colder."

I stifled a grin. "It might. I'll just expect that second blanket sometime after I fall asleep."

"I have no clue what you are talking about. Maybe as a precaution, you should sleep in the shack tonight."

"Are you sure?"

"Yeah, I mean, if you want." She started toward the shed but stopped in the doorway, giving me one last glance.

Chapter Twenty

I crawled into bed, watching the door. What did it matter if Boaz slept in the shed or outside? It was better to keep space between us. I turned over and closed my eyes. His face by the campfire a few minutes ago played in my head. His intense gaze seemed lit on fire, burning in my chest. The bed sunk down, notifying me Boaz had joined me after all.

I rolled over to look at him. "Hey."

"Hey. What you doing?"

"Here in this tiny room in the middle of nowhere, there are so many options available to me." My eyes adjusted to the darkness with the help of the surrounding moonlight.

A tiny smirk formed on his face, like mischievous thoughts had formed in his head. He opened his mouth, then laid back as though deciding to keep his ornery ideas inside. He stared at the wooden ceiling. "It's weird to think about missing so much school and our families going on without us."

"You're worried about Noah?"

He turned his head to the side with a raised eyebrow. "Yeah, I am. My parents are always busy and don't have much time for either of us. Since I got my license, I pick him up and take him from school."

"Do you still do karaoke and the buddy walk?"

"Yeah, and they were thinking about starting up junior cooking classes. Noah is really into that now. He's constantly trying to cook for our mom. I'm not sure if it's because he loves it or wants her attention. Maybe a little of both."

I nodded, watching his face shift between smiles and frowns as he talked about Noah and his parents. "Why are they so busy?"

"They've always been workaholics. It's like now that I'm old enough to do a lot for Noah, they leave me to it and can add more work to their plates and less family. They soothe their guilt by taking us on one vacation a year. We went to Hawaii this year. Noah and I spent most of it alone while they did their own thing or worked remotely. But hey, my college is paid for." He laughed, which turned a little bitter. "They want me to go east to ivy league, but it's not like I can do that."

"Why not?"

"Noah. How can I go over a thousand miles away from him?"

I glanced at the window, taking in the way it fogged over, dimming the room further. "My parents want me at ivy league too. That's why they are so strict about my grades. Like I couldn't get a decent job or build a life from community or state colleges."

"What do you want?"

"I don't know," I said.

"I always thought you'd sing."

I snickered and crinkled my face. "You can't be serious." I narrowed my eyes when I caught his expression. "You can't be. I'm not that good, and it's a field many want to enter, and few make it."

"That's true, but you being good enough isn't the issue."

I laughed. "You're delusional, but I've known that for a while."

"I love your songs. The way you love my stories. In that story you told me, you were the songbird."

I narrowed my eyes. "Boaz! I was the cat. Why would I say I sing better than Chloe?"

He rubbed his chin, and his eyes shifted to the side. "Oh, good point. You'd never brag like that. I guess I thought that because your voice is one of the best I've heard. Like I wouldn't mind if you wanted to sing now."

"Okay. But only because I'm going to prove you have a terrible memory. That and I'm out of practice, and I want to win a solo this year."

"Practice all you want around me. I won't complain."

I sat up, straightened my posture, and belted out "My Immortal" by Evanescence. When the last note concluded, I opened my eyes.

I squinted as the moonlight caught Boaz's tear streaks. "Are you crying?"

He wiped his cheeks, but a few more tears erased his effort. "That was beautiful, Ivy."

"I think mercury in the fish might be getting to your brain, but thank you."

"Sing another one." He got himself comfortable and propped his chin on his elbow.

I pressed my lips together to suppress a grin and sang "You Raise Me Up" by Josh Groban. After making Boaz cry again, I crawled back under the covers, facing the wall. "This isn't going to be a nightly thing."

"But you said you need to practice."

I smiled and closed my eyes.

The cabin seemed the best way home if we could access it, but Boaz had wanted to try hiking to the other side of the lake first.

"Why aren't we going to the cabin first thing?" I studied the contents of my bag to make sure I had everything we might need for the day.

"I'm not sure. Something tells me it's even more dangerous than it seems at first glance."

"One of your magic gut feelings?"

He shrugged as he refilled our water bottles, using a batch he'd saved under the bed. "I guess that's what you'd call it. I'm not sure how magic it is. Things feel off about the entire thing, and that doesn't make me the happiest about bringing you anywhere close to that."

"Me? What about yourself?"

"Not as much of a concern" He handed me the bottles to place in my pack.

"It is for me."

He stopped midway to the door to grin. "You're saying you're worried about me."

"I'm worried about being left out here alone."

"Sure. Okay."

I zipped up my bag and swung it over my shoulders. "You want me to be worried about you?"

"It's nice knowing you no longer want to send me flying over one of these mountains."

"I never wanted to send you flying over one of these mountains. Maybe give you a shove down a small hill with rose bushes at the bottom, but nothing that would end your life."

He smirked. "You do care."

We shared our morning fish, which seemed all either of us could eat anymore. Over the entire day, we ended up eating an entire one each, but split them over the morning and night. I no longer craved anything more. It seemed odd, but I guessed my body did what it could not to drive me mad with hunger.

We walked along the lake edge, which gave me two separate views each way I looked. On one side, the water bobbed in the breeze, providing food for several birds who dove into its depth. These creatures glided across the water surface with poised talons, snatching out prey. Fish jumped as though they wanted to break free from their captive barrier. They didn't know that action of desire brought their doom.

On the other side, the forest stretched with no end. It appeared more and more. Boaz and I had found ourselves inside a snow globe where we'd have to forge a life together. At least we had the shed and not the log from the first night. A few trees stood in a half state with leaves that fought against winter's arrival. The leaf patterns held a beauty, with none of them seeming to change the same way. Nature made a brief-lasting art in the way the leaves morphed their colors. The lake branched off from the trees, leaving an open area covered in massive leaf mounds.

Boaz leaped into an enormous pile. "Come on!"

"Are we five again?"

"Yeah, today we are."

He scooped up some orange leaves and ran toward me. "You need some motivation."

I shrieked and bolted away from him. "You're a crazy boy."

"And you're going to love every minute of it."

His longer legs reached me, and leaves flew over my head in a blurred orange tunnel. When my vision cleared, Boaz had disappeared.

I whipped around and spotted him running across the field. "You coward! You start a battle that you can't stay and fight."

"So, punish me for my cowardly ways."

"Oh, I will!" I clutched autumn debris and took off after him.

He slowed his pace and stopped.

"You're giving up," I said.

"Giving you a chance."

I threw the leaves at him. "Are you saying I can't catch you on my own?"

"That might be what I'm saying."

"Argh!" I threw the leaves at him.

He bent down and shoved some at me. We both plopped to the ground, tossing swirls of color at each other. We burst into laughter and buried ourselves. I stared at the wispy clouds, moving on to a new destination. A rustling sound broke my concentration, and I turned to find Boaz had disappeared. I sat up, but the number of leaves made it impossible to tell where a Boaz lump rested.

I stood up and screamed as he leaped from his hiding spot, yanking me back to the earth with him. We laid on our side facing each other while he burst into a fit of giggles.

His breathing became concerning as his amusement stole his oxygen. "You should have seen your face."

I crunched leaves in my hand and sprinkled the remnants over his head. "You'll be pulling nature pieces out of your hair for weeks."

"I feel like that's nothing new."

I smooshed them into his head. "Well, now they're extra stuck."

"I'll cherish them as souvenirs from you."

I stuck out my lower lip, which I quickly retracted when his eyes zoomed in on it. "You're not supposed to be happy about it."

"But I am," he said.

"It's punishment."

"Makes it even better." One side of his mouth tipped into a smile.

I shoved his shoulder. "That's not how punishment works."

"Maybe you should punish me some more and show me."

I rolled my eyes and plopped on my back. "So much for making a lot of progress today. We slept through the morning and got in a leaf fight like kindergartners."

"That was a good year to relive."

"Why is that?"

"It was the first time I got to see you every day."

My chest filled with an emotion that rose to my eyes but lessened in intensity as I avoided looking at his expression. Something about the wilderness made it difficult not to get weepy over nostalgia. We sat there a while staring at the sky until our eyes met long enough for more emotions to rise into my eyes, and I jumped up.

"We better do something with this day." I marched ahead like our infamous bear had peeked around a tree.

He caught up to me. "I don't know. The leaf war and your punishment made the day."

"Shut it, or you'll get more."

"I sure hope so."

I gave his shoulder another shove, and he laughed.

Chapter Twenty-One

Ivy and I hiked the next three days, but something had slowed about our search. We still carefully took in our surroundings, but it seemed more like fun nature walks than an attempt to find rescue. The angry Ivy hadn't appeared for the last few days. She smiled more often and even became playful at times.

Occasionally, her sadness and fear would return, but I mainly saw it in her eyes at night. She'd cuddle up to me for warmth, and I'd hold her to offer comfort. Her in my arms every night may have been part of what tapered my search efforts. Not that I didn't want us found, but she provided a big distraction as we grew close again.

I got up early to watch the sunrise and replenish our fish. After my fifth catch, Ivy still hadn't emerged, so I went to bring her breakfast. She laid still in the same position I'd left her.

"Hey. Are you ready to trudge through some wilderness?"

She groaned. "I'm not sure I can today."

"Yesterday wear you out? We went a little far."

"I don't feel so well."

I climbed onto the bed and found her almost ashen. Her forehead scorched my palm. "You're burning up," I said.

She drew her blankets to her chin. "I'm cold."

The next few hours were spent with me hovering over Ivy, trying to get her to drink. Her body went back and forth between sweating and shivering.

Her hands moved to her hair. "I need to braid it."

"I will if you're okay with it."

Her hand formed a point and plopped back on the bed. "My brush and ties are in my bag. Do you even remember how to do this?"

"Yeah, I couldn't forget. You liked playing hair salon way too much when we were seven."

"Yet you never let me cut your hair."

"That's a big mystery there." I rifled through her bag and grabbed the needed items.

She propped herself up, and I pulled her damp hair away from her face. I guided the brush through her thick brown locks and gave her two pigtails like she always asked for when we were kids. She drifted to sleep, and I got the water batches made. The rest of the day became a battle of getting Ivy to drink enough water. The fever and sweating made it so she needed more than ever, but she combatted my attempts, saying it hurt her stomach. She rested against my chest as I held the water bottle steady on her lips. She took a few sips before shoving it away. This repeated for hours, with me giving her long breaks.

She rested on me through the night, and I kept stirring to check on her. She remained still, worrying me enough to keep checking her breathing. By morning, my muscles ached, and I brushed it off as the stiff way I'd slept. I spent the morning stocking our water and getting Ivy to drink. A chill set into my arms, and a dull ache throbbed across my forehead. I sipped on water that sent sharp pangs through my gut. Ivy accepted the water I brought to her lips.

She opened her eyes as I climbed into bed. "You're sick too."

"How can you tell?"

"You look as white as you did that year that you trick or treated as a scary clown."

My stomach clenched in protest of the water I forced on it, but I smiled through the pain. "You kept eyeing me like I'd take you to the sewer any minute, but refused to leave my side. That's friendship."

"You had me on edge all night, but it would have been worse going without you." She cringed and moaned. "I feel like I'm dying. Everything hurts so bad."

"It's miserable, but it can't last forever." I helped her sit up and take in more water.

"What if it kills us?"

"Then we go together, and our suffering ends."

She let out a tiny sob, but too exhausted to cry, she drifted into sleep. I sunk down on the bed, and she soothed my aches with her presence. Ivy and I lost track of time in our disoriented states. Whenever I could muster a little strength, I made water batches and forced us both to drink. We didn't even bother trying to eat. It seemed to last days, but we slept so much it became difficult to tell.

We barely moved away from each other, and even when we found ourselves on different ends of the bed, we held hands. It was almost as though we wanted assurance that the other remained okay. After a long time, the aches eased, but weakness stayed. Time became easier to track again, and four days after we began to feel better, we took a short walk to rebuild our strength.

I held Ivy's hand and kept my eyes on her. "Are you doing okay?"

"Yeah, a little dizzy. Let's not do that sickness again. How long do you think that lasted?"

I led us under a maple tree. The red leaves provided a canopy from the drizzle. "I'm not sure. It seemed forever. We got out of bed four days ago, but I'm guessing the illness lasted a week, maybe."

"A week!"

"Yeah, maybe a little longer."

She shook her head. "If that's true, it means we've been out here almost a month."

"I think we have, but we've survived a lot thrown at us. We can go a little longer."

She picked up some white flowers and weaved them together. "What do you think we had?"

"E. coli or the flu. Something terrible I never want to live through again."

We hadn't made it too far out for the day because the weakness lingered in our muscles. We still had seven matches left from not building any fires while we were sick. The rainy day made it impossible to make a fire, but I'd fished yesterday, and we nibbled on my latest catch. We could only get a couple of bites down, but we ate more often.

My stomach quit twisting when I drank, so I tried to make up for lost time. The taste no longer struck my tongue as metallic and foreign. Everything we'd experienced proved how adaptable the human body could be when it had no other choice.

The rain dotted the window and ran in tiny streaks to the sill while we laid on our sides, watching its descent from our window. We spent the rest of the day lazily in bed to push recovery. The next few days went much the same way.

A deeper bond had formed during our illness, and Ivy talked more openly about how things used to be. She kept something between us, but it seemed more like a sheet than a wall. She left a barrier with clear boundaries, but I could sort of reach her behind it.

She no longer questioned snuggling. It had become a natural thing while we were sick and longed for relief. It helped with fall tipping closer to winter. We got the occasional snowfall, but it mainly stuck to rain.

The mornings contained short walks that we increased each day, and the afternoon held reading the cozy mystery books from the mine. We alternated them out and stopped halfway to discuss who the culprits were. After writing our answers, we'd finish the stories. Ivy guessed three correct while I got the other two.

From my estimate, five weeks had gone by since we'd gotten lost. The slate clouds and wind gusts increased each day, warning of winter in the woods if we didn't get serious. Our funerals had probably taken place, but if not, they most likely would happen by spring.

I pushed open the shack door and removed my hoodie to wring it out. Ivy had her face buried in her knees. Her loose hair fluttered around her as she shook.

I sat on my knees in front of her. "Ivy, what is it?"

She'd cried often when we'd first gotten lost, but it had tapered over the last couple of weeks.

Her puffy eyes met mine. "My Pop might be dead by now."

"They said he had a few more months, right?"

"Yeah, but he was going downhill so fast. What if I don't get to say goodbye?"

I slid next to her, taking her in my arms. Her cheek rested on my shoulder, and she sobbed.

I pushed her hair behind her ear and rested my chin on her head. "We're going to get out of this. Tomorrow we'll go back to the mine and check out the cabin."

"What about your gut feeling?"

"We need to try anyway and don't have many options. The matches are almost gone to cook fish, which means I'm going to have to freeze a lot to get us through the winter, or we need a way out. We could get completely snowed in like that first snowstorm and not even be able to reach the fish. We'll starve."

We took it easy the rest of the day and talked about our plan for the morning. Our strength had mostly returned, and we felt confident we'd be alright. Something sat unsettled in my gut about the cabin, but Ivy and I were out of options.

The following day, I got up early and restocked our food supply. Enough snow lingered that it didn't melt in the hole I'd made. Our fish would stay fresh for a while. When Ivy woke up, we set out toward the mine.

Chapter Twenty-Two

IVY

Boaz and I made it back to the mine about three weeks after we'd found it. Passing the five-week mark seemed like a milestone, like we'd survived the longest in a video game.

Boaz pointed down the mountain. "It looks safe this way, and it's a straight shot to the cabin."

Grass and rocks sporadically covered dirt like it may have once formed an intentional path. Boaz thought it might have been how the miners made it to work. We slid in some spots, and Boaz held my hand to assist me down the incline. We made it into the trees with no wolves showing. The small cabin appeared that had a rocking chair on the porch. Red curtains popped in the two front windows. The front door swung open, and a blast pierced the air.

Boaz let out a sharp cry, collapsing into a heap at my feet. I screamed and dropped next to him. He groaned and clutched his thigh as blood seeped between his fingers. I tied hoodie sleeves around his wound and helped him remove his belt. I cinched it over the sleeves to stop the bleeding.

"Stay where you are!" a gruff voice shouted from the porch.

"You shot him!" .

"That's what I do when I have uninvited guests." A burly man with a peppered beard and disheveled hair peered down at us with a brutish sneer.

"We only needed help! We're lost."

He thrust the gun forward. "Not my problem."

My eyes flipped between Boaz and the hostile man with crazy yellow eyes. Boaz whimpered and grimaced.

"You have to help us now. You shot him. He's going to bleed to death!"

Boaz gripped my hand and squeezed. "It's okay. I'll be fine."

The man lowered his gun. "I'll give you first aid, and that's it. Then I drive you to the edge of my property, and you'll be gone." He headed for the cabin.

I chased after him, ignoring Boaz's protests. "Can you drive us into town?"

"I don't go that far anywhere anymore. I'll get you to the edge of my property, and that's it."

"You're going to be a murderer."

He chuckled a raspy wheeze. "Your friend will be fine. I know how to hit the right spot."

I clenched my fists. "You're a horrible person."

"You think I care? You're trespassing, and that means the law is on my side. I live all the way out here for a reason. People aren't anything I care to interact with, and you better shut your trap, or I might hit you somewhere that *will* make me a murderer." He handed me a plastic box.

I gawked at the first aid kit. "You want me to put a Band-Aid on a bullet hole?"

He coughed and wheezed as he let out a stream of laughter. "That's a song, I'm pretty sure. Time for you to leave, or I'll put a bullet in his other leg." He grabbed his keys from a kitchen drawer and hurried out the door. He scooped up Boaz and threw him over his shoulder.

The man threw Boaz in the back of his jeep, which made the boy cry out. "What way do you want to go?"

I pointed toward the shed and climbed into the passenger side. The vehicle bobbed and slammed over rough terrain. Boaz's face twisted, and tears slid down his cheeks, making me want to punch the man next to me.

The man pulled the car over. "Get out!"

"He can't even walk. Don't you have any conscience at all?"

He hopped out and brought a large stick to me. "He can walk with this."

"You're kidding me!"

Boaz scooted himself out of the jeep and held out his hand. "Ivy, it's okay. I can do this."

I handed him the stick and steadied his other side as he stood. The jeep blanketed us in dust as the boorish man drove it away from us. Boaz tried to place most of his support on the stick, but it still required a lot of effort on my part to keep him upright. We made it back to the shack, and I helped him into bed, removing his shoes.

I paced the tiny entryway. "What are we going to do? We need to get out of here and get you help."

His jaw looked tight enough to crack. "The bleeding has stopped. I'll be okay." His body shook, and he released more whimpers.

"We can't sit here and wait for your leg to get worse or the bleeding to pick up."

"Ivy, can you please sing to me?"

I climbed onto the bed, leaned against the backboard, and brought his head to my lap. My fingers moved through his hair, and I sang "Somewhere Over the Rainbow" by Israel Kamakawio'ole. His face relaxed the further I got into my song.

"I love you, Ivy," he mumbled in a way that made me think he said it asleep.

I grabbed a lantern and lifted the blanket. The tourniquet appeared to have stopped the bleeding. I removed nearly everything from my pack and slipped out the door. The snow nipped at my hands as I dug through it and placed the fish in my bag. I swung it over my shoulders and clasped the lantern in my other hand. A trip to the mine provided me with a rusty pickaxe. I made it to the tree line beyond the large meadow and unzipped my bag. Four wolves surrounded me but bolted after the fish I threw into the forest.

I charged toward the cabin, throwing more fish behind me as I went. My foot caught on a leaf-covered root, which sent me flying down a hill. My body slammed down on my arm. A pop shot pain from my wrist to my shoulder. I bit my lip and used all my willpower to stop the scream. My arm hung at an unnatural angle, but Boaz counted on my success.

White curtains blocked the back windows, but a faded TV program played through the left. A shadow moved in the right, and I tiptoed around the side. I clutched my arm to my stomach and bit my lip with each step. Nausea and dizziness competed for most powerful sensation. I crept onto the porch and cringed at the creaking wooden beams under my feet. The door proved unlocked, and I edged along the wall. The hallway light turned on, causing me to hide behind the counter.

The old man hummed and stepped into the living room as I slid around the other side of the cabinet. Dishes clanged together, and a microwave whirled to life. After what seemed a thousand years, he returned to the back room. I inched around to the drawer and grabbed his keys.

My pulse slammed in my neck as I made my way to the exit. I got it open and slipped outside. My feet struck the muddy ground, and the pain in my arm dulled from my adrenaline surge. Dogs barked, growing close. The Jeep seemed a million miles away, as though I'd never reach it. A blast struck the air, and I flattened myself on the ground. My scream no longer stayed contained when I landed on my arm.

A second blast sounded. "You think you would have learned the first time!" He lunged toward me and grabbed hold of my shoe, dragging me to him.

I loosened the pickaxe from behind me and smashed it into his head. It didn't pierce the skin, but he released me. He blinked and swayed. I jumped up and gave all I had into reaching my goal. He fired a third time, but I made it next to the vehicle and threw the door open. My fingers fumbled with the keys, finally turning them in the ignition. I floored the gas and zoomed away from the cabin. Glass struck me in the neck, face, and arms. It took a moment for me to comprehend he'd shot out his own back window. My side mirror caught the mad man zooming toward me on some sort of recreational vehicle.

I wove around trees, paying attention to the ground to avoid getting stuck in a spot too closed-in to pass. Wolves blocked my path, and I backed up the jeep to go around them. They kept trying to lock me in, and I swerved, gunning the vehicle. One yelped, and my rear view mirror showed a crumpled grey body. Guilt surged through me, but it had been them or Boaz. The forest opened into a vast field and up a hill.

I headed in the shed's general direction. When the lake appeared, I knew I'd made it. My arm throbbed, and driving one-handed had its challenges on curves. The area in front of the trees had too many trees around it, and I had to get out and walk. The keys went into my pocket as a precaution.

Fear took hold as I ran into the shed, praying he hadn't bled to death on me. "Boaz!"

"Ivy? You left me," he said.

"Yeah, I stole the guy's jeep. We need to go now! He has some kind of vehicle to reach us."

He sat up and scooted to the end of the bed, and steadied himself on the walking stick. I let him lean on my right side and tried my best to hide my hurt arm. I helped him into the back seat, where he could stretch out his leg. One last sweep of our makeshift home allowed me to grab all our possessions and throw them in the back.

The only option was to head back the way I'd come until we hit the open ground. I sped through the field as fast as seemed safe over the rocky terrain. A red dot appeared up ahead, and I swerved to the left to alter our trajectory away from the man who gripped his steering wheel with one hand and his gun with the other. Gunshots echoed against the mountains, and another glance in my mirror showed him gaining on us. I floored the gas and flinched at Boaz's anguished cry.

We drove west as I tried to outrun the sun. Driving on uneven terrain in the dark seemed too dangerous, and I needed to get as far as I could before the night stole the light.

Chapter Twenty-Three

The orange and yellow horizon warned of the onslaught of indigo, which would consume the sky, leaving only darkness. We'd lost the psycho mountain man about twenty minutes ago, but time didn't appear on our side.

I glanced in the rear-view mirror at the boy, who had clenched eyes. Tremors rocked through him severely enough that I saw them clearly through the tiny reflection. "I took the blankets from the cabin. They're in the back. How are you?"

"Fine," he said.

"Boaz, your leg was shot. You're not fine."

"I am."

"Liar." I stopped the jeep and grabbed all the blankets from the back. "Put one over your head to keep out the chill.

He stared at my dangling arm, followed by my face. "You're hurt."

"Not really."

"Who's the liar now? You're cut up with a broken arm."

"You're shot, so you win most not alright." I tucked him in the best I could one-handed.

He shoved his top layer to me. "Put this around your shoulders."

I took it to settle him and got back in the front. One last glance at him helped me drive in peace. He'd covered his head with one of the blankets. We drove until the first star appeared for me to wish on for our safety. The ground leveled into a dirt road, and I refrained from shouting my happiness. It had to lead somewhere. I slipped on the car brights, driving cautiously around the sharp turns that backed up to high cliffs.

No cars appeared in either direction, but I kept driving. A ping alerted me to the dash, where low fuel lit up yellow. I groaned, but we could make it a little farther before running out completely. I drove until the car sputtered to a stop.

I glanced back over the seat. "Boaz, we're out of gas. I'm going to have to walk it." When he gave no response, I yanked back his blanket to find his head flopped to the side. "Boaz!"

He groaned and opened his eyes for about a second. "I'm tired."

"You sleep. I'm going to go get help." I grabbed my bags, kept one lantern out, and brought the last bottled water to Boaz. "You need to drink." I brought it to his lips as he had me when we were sick.

He sipped and nodded off again. The lantern light gave me a view of his legs, and my stomach churned as blood had seeped around the hoodie. It didn't look like a fast bleed, but he could die from a slow one left too long.

I covered him back up and kissed his head. "You stay alive. I'll be back." The top blanket covered him completely, and I headed down the road. I held my hurt arm as close to me as I could. It wouldn't bend properly, but I tried to give it as much support as possible. The dirt road turned into asphalt, and I spotted a bent road sign that let me know the dirt road was

Blueberry Road. The wind whipped my hair around as my teeth chattered.

Headlights made me squint, and I waved my lantern, stepping as close to the road as felt safe. They zoomed past, and I ran after them. My cheeks grew colder as the air struck my tears. I walked in the direction the car went but couldn't make out much around me. The lantern swung in and out over the line between asphalt and gravel. A few feet away, a grassy ditch formed. Three more cars ignored my light, and sharp pains in my chest spilled into more desperation.

I flinched as high beams came into view. A semi-truck barreled toward me, and I waved the lantern. It drove past but skidded to the shoulder. A tall man with a ball cap climbed out and strolled to me.

He studied my face and arm. "Are you okay, miss?"

A sob ripped from me, and it took a minute for me to calm. "My friend has been shot. He's in a jeep on Blueberry Road. We're lost. Please. Please help!"

"Come on. Let's get you warm in my truck and call for some help."

His cab smelled like cigarettes and sweat, but I'd never been more grateful to be somewhere. My muscles cramped, and my arm zapped pain through my shoulder and fingers. I leaned against the cool window to halt the dizziness settling in.

"I'm Dennis, by the way. I'm going to call someone on my radio." He picked up a black square connected to his dash and explained the situation to someone.

My eyes drooped until I could no longer resist unconsciousness.

❧

Movement, voices, and brightness woke me. Blurred

people in navy blue peered over me, doing things to me and talking. I closed my eyes and sunk back under. When I woke again, it seemed easier to stay awake. A warm blanket covered me in a small room contained by a blue curtain that wrapped around on three sides. My sore arm had some type of brace holding it still while the other had an IV pumping clear liquid into my veins. The room had a melting feel to it, as though I sat outside reality looking in.

A woman in blue scrubs walked in and widened her eyes. "Welcome back. I'm going to go get the doctor."

A short time later, a lady with red braided hair and a stethoscope dangling over her white jacket stepped behind my curtain. "It's good to see you awake." She checked me over and shined a light in my eyes. "Can you tell us your name and where you're from?"

"Ivy Carter. Glenwood. My friend Boaz Jackson. Is he okay? Did they find him?"

The doctor and nurse shared a strange look. With a nod from the doctor, the nurse hurried from the room.

"Yes, he's in surgery. I'm afraid I can't divulge much more than that," she said.

"Can I call my mom? Laura Carter."

"Yes, the police are taking care of contacting your parents. I'll let you know when we have an update."

Fog distorted my perception, and I drifted in and out of sleep. Three people got me for surgery on my arm, but much of what they said seemed more like it existed somewhere else. A mask went over my face, and I sunk into a tarry dream full of muffled voices and dark images.

The confusion receded, and I found myself in a big hospital room with two people in lavender scrubs talking.

"I can't believe it's them. After all this time, they're found. It's a genuine miracle," a voice said.

"It really is. They made it so far. It's unbelievable, really."

"They both have a long road ahead."

They finished messing with something in drawers and shuffled out of the room. An enormous, tinted window spread across one wall and gave a gorgeous view of a blue mountain with snow-capped peaks. A similar view to what I'd had for the last several weeks. Here I didn't feel submerged in it, but it gave it a transitional feeling like this hospital room was a go-between from the wilderness back into my life.

Nurses and techs came in and out of the room, checking me out and assuring my comfort. They wouldn't update me on Boaz, but one nurse took pity and told me he lived through surgery. I watched some television and picked at the food they got me. A small bowl of applesauce was all my stomach could handle.

"Ivy!" My mom stood in the doorway with her hand covering her mouth. She ran to my bedside. "My baby!"

"Mom!" Everything pent up inside burst out into deep sobs as my mother put her arms around me.

Her hug had weak force, as though she thought I might shatter. We shook in unison, not pulling apart until a doctor walked in. He gave my mom a report on my condition. The middle part of my arm bone had separated from the top and bottom sections. They had also started me on a nutritional supplement to gradually build me back to regular eating habits. They wanted to keep me for a few days. My dad arrived a short time later after parking the car.

He hugged me, and when he sat back in his chair, he shocked me with his tears. I'd never seen my father cry in my entire life. Both my parents remained weepy as they sat at my bedside, and I was no exception either. There was only a couch to sleep on, so my dad left for a hotel after it got late. He gave me a second hug before exiting the room, which made it maybe the fifth hug I remembered getting from him. He'd never been an affectionate man.

Mom made up the couch bed with bedding the nurse provided. "Are you comfortable enough? Let me know if you're in too much pain, and I'll call the nurse."

"I'm okay, Mom."

She nodded, looking unconvinced. "Are you warm enough?"

"Yeah, Mom?" I paused as my stomach jumbled into a swirling mess.

"What is it, sweetie?"

I slowed my breathing, that tried to fly out of control. "Is Pop... How is he?"

She shook the pillow into its case. "About the same as when you left."

I closed my eyes. "Okay. Good. That's good."

"Ivy, he's at a facility right now." She put her hand up at my gaping mouth. "Let me explain. He's there on a trial run. I needed someone to watch him while I came up here with you. They got him an emergency spot, but I think you're going to love the place I found."

I fiddled with my fingers and stared at my tan blanket. "I want him home."

"I know, but please keep an open mind. It's different than what you are thinking. Can you do that? Let me show it to you first?"

"Okay. That's fair."

Mom climbed under her covers. "Please wake me if you need anything through the night."

"Okay." I lowered my bed and drifted to sleep, hoping Pop wasn't scared at the new place.

Between all our walking and driving in the jeep, Boaz and I had traveled over two hundred and fifty miles from where we'd disappeared, which put us at almost three hundred miles from home. Over the next few days, mom stayed by my side, jumping in the second I needed anything. My mom tried to find info on Boaz for me, but his parents had him transported back to our local hospital. I thought about calling him until I realized his number wasn't in my phone. The last few months, he was my enemy and the last person I'd wanted to talk to. Now he felt like the only one I wanted a conversation with.

Acclimating into the real world again didn't prove a simple thing. They released me after a week in the hospital, and my room seemed distorted. I welcomed my bed more than pretty much anything else, but the adjustment didn't arrive as quickly as expected.

My mom wanted me home another week or two, and it gave me time to focus on missing schoolwork. Mom had been in contact with the school, and the teachers put a packet together. They said if I could get through it, I'd still pass my classes. The time at home would allow me to accomplish that and recover.

Not only that, but I didn't feel emotionally ready to return to school yet. I missed Boaz, but confusion had taken hold at what I had with him now—if I had anything at all. We'd agreed to go our separate ways once home. The thing with Chloe sat between us, and I didn't know if surrendering it was the right thing to do. Instead, I stayed in my room doing schoolwork and feeling miserable without him.

Chapter Twenty-Four

My leg burned like someone had placed hot coals across it and slammed a hammer on them, pressing the searing sensation deep into my muscles. Frigid air pelted from the shot-out windows, and the blankets provided the only protection. Every slight movement zapped pain through my nerves.

I shook, worrying about Ivy walking alone on a road at night. If anything happened to her, the pain would swell far more than my gunshot wound. I dozed, but the pain and cold kept yanking me awake. Sirens blared in the distance until they grew loud enough to pierce my ears with relief.

A police officer walked up to the car, pointing a flashlight my direction. "Are you injured?"

I lifted the blanket to show him my wounded leg. He ran back to his car and returned to tell me the ambulance was on its way. Before they arrived, I fell back asleep, and paramedics loading me into the ambulance brought me back.

A paramedic wiped my arm and stuck in an IV. "Can you tell us your name and age?"

"Boaz Jackson. Sixteen. Did you find a girl? Ivy Carter. Brown hair and pretty green eyes."

"I'm not sure. They'll probably know more at the hospital."

The ambulance bumping around on the gravel road lulled me back to sleep. When I woke again, my body barely had the strength to move. They rushed me through sliding glass doors on a gurney. People rushed over and got me on a bed. Information flew from all directions, making it difficult to latch onto anything concrete.

"Sixteen-year-old male. Gunshot wound to the upper right leg. No visible exit wound. Says his name is Boaz Jackson."

"The missing kid?"

The room spun, and the voices became warped as meds kicked in. I woke back up before I knew I'd fallen asleep. The same thing happened in spurts until each interval became longer. My pain level would magnify until I writhed and begged the nurses for relief. It kept me in a disoriented state, and both pain and numbness had disadvantages.

My nurse walked in, humming and smiling. "You're being transferred."

"To where?"

"Closer to your home at your parents' request." She flushed my IV and stuck the pump for it on a pole attached to my bed. "Transport will arrive soon to get you. I'm going to check your vitals before they take you."

"My parents aren't coming?"

"I'm told they will meet us at your local hospital."

I shoved away the emotions her words brought. "Has anyone gotten an update on Ivy Carter? I need to know how she is. I keep asking, but no one will tell me anything. Can I at least know she's okay?"

"We can't give out personal information on other patients, but between us, she's doing okay." She winked.

It wasn't nearly enough information, but it confirmed Ivy was at the hospital and alive. When transport arrived, I glanced in every room on the way, hoping to steal a glance at Ivy. I slept most of the way back, but in the few moments I stirred, anger toward my parents grew. They couldn't even be bothered to drive to the other hospital. Once again, they found me an inconvenience.

The room they delivered me to was much larger than my last one, with a bigger bed and TV. It looked more like a hotel than a hospital room. The medics got me situated and introduced me to my new nurse.

I straightened out my arm to allow her IV access. "Are my parents here?"

She gave me a tight smile. "I'm told they will be soon."

Soon didn't happen until the next day when my mother walked in with her sunglasses pushed back on her head.

She took the chair close to my bed. "How are you feeling?"

I gawked, waiting for emotion of any kind to tumble from her. "Not the greatest."

"I can imagine. Are they taking good care of you here? If not, we can transfer you to General."

"It's fine. Where's Dad?"

She shifted in the blue plastic chair. "They never make the furniture comfortable in hospitals. He's on a business trip and tried to get away but couldn't. He'll be home soon."

"I've been missing for thirty-eight days and been shot, and he couldn't get away?"

She shifted again and glanced at her phone. "I know that sounds terrible, but he really did try."

"Right. Trying is all that matters. Where's Noah?"

"He's with his respite provider."

"Respite?"

She nodded. "It gives caregivers a break."

"How can you need a break from something you never do?"

She narrowed her eyes. "What does that mean?"

"How can you need a break from Noah when you don't spend any time with him?"

She blinked and looked away. "Of course, I spend time with him. I know you're not feeling good right now. Why don't you get some rest?" She stood up and gave me a stiff hug. "I'm very relieved you're alright, Bo. You had us very worried."

"I'm sure I did."

"I'm going to go find your doctor and see if I can get an update" She slipped out of the room and hadn't returned by the time my night shift nurse came on duty.

The stout nurse had a massive grin as she got me an extra blanket. "Just in case you get cold. Can I get you anything?"

Better parents.

"No, thank you."

Over the next few days, my mom stopped by at least once a day for a brief time. She seemed even more absent than she'd been in the past. My dad stopped in after four days.

He waltzed into the room wearing a black suit and asked me how I was. An awkward silence descended on us before he gave up his trying and left. My room had filled with cards, balloons, and gifts from people at school and in the community. Most I only gave scant attention to. I tried to figure out how to contact Ivy, but no one seemed to have any information.

I groaned and turned over, moving my hands around the bed, trying to find Ivy. She must have shifted too far away as we slept. I sat up, scanning the room for her, only to find myself in a strange room away from her. The same thing happened almost anytime I fell asleep. I woke up searching for Ivy, missing the feel of her in my arms.

I ran my fingers through my hair and stared at the bobbing shapes of get-well balloons. My leg shot pain through my body due to nerve damage, but the ache for Ivy seemed so much worse in the middle of the night as I sat alone in my hospital room. Her sudden loss struck me with anxiety and grief. We'd spent five weeks together so close, and losing her brought an entrenched sadness. The abruptness carried an overbearing weight.

Two weeks in the hospital full of intense physical therapy allowed me to go home. I sat in a wheelchair, holding a homemade blanket the hospital had given me. All my gifts sat on a cart that a transport man had pushed out for me.

My parents finally arrived, and my dad jumped out to load everything. The nurse demonstrated the best way to get me into the car, and we rode home in silence. Dad pushed me into the house through a ramp they'd had made.

I searched every area as he took me to my room. "Where's Noah?"

"His provider will drop him off soon." Dad put on my chair brakes and assisted me into a new bed. "We got you a bed that can elevate the foot and head. It should make things easier for you."

"My old one was fine, but thank you."

He handed me the controls that looked self-explanatory. "I'm glad you're home, son." His mouth tightened, and for a moment, a flash of emotion clouded his face.

I turned on the TV and flipped through channels, not really watching anything.

"Bo! Bo!" Noah ran into the room. Tears fell from his eyes like a faucet turned on high.

I held out my arms for him, and he crashed into me. His deep cries tore me apart, and I brought him closer to me.

"Noah, I'm alright. I'm alright."

He didn't calm for a long time, so I held him, telling him over and over I was okay.

He pulled back and stared at me with gigantic eyes filled with a pain that had set in. One that lodged itself over time, and it beat at me that he'd gone through so much without me.

"Bo, it hurt here." He touched his chest. "It hurt here so bad."

I blinked out my tears. "The same for me. Exactly the same."

"Mom said you went to angels, and I kept telling them to bring you back. They don't need you as much."

"Mom told you I went to angels?"

He nodded and broke into a louder cry.

I drew him back into a hug. "It's okay. They listened. I'm back now."

My legs zapping pain woke me to search for Ivy to relieve it. Only emptiness greeted me. Noah slept in a sleeping bag next to my bed. He had for the last several nights. I didn't like him sleeping on the floor, but he refused to leave, and I had no ability to carry him to his bed like I used to.

My parents hired a live-in helper to make my meals and assist with anything I needed while they worked, which was pretty much all the time. Noah cried every time he had to leave me for school, and I had to promise him I wasn't going anywhere. He called me on his phone several times a day to make sure I hadn't disappeared. I paused my game at the knocking on my door.

Phil walked in with a large white envelope. "I have a present for you."

"You mean other than the amber energy stones?"

"You got those. Good. Use them. They can heal anything, and the world needs you better to write more letters for me." He set the pack on my nightstand. "That's all your missed classwork and stuff for the next few weeks. We have the same counselor, and she somehow knew I knew you."

"Probably saw all the times you chased me through the halls. However, I'm done writing letters."

Phil's mouth plopped to his collarbone. "You can't be serious. You mean while you're recovering?"

"No, I'm out of this business forever. You're going to have to win girls' hearts on your own."

His shoulders slumped. "You know I can't. They take one look at me and run the other way."

"That's because you're chasing after the wrong ones. You need to find one that appreciates exotic cheeses and troll doll collecting as much as you do."

"She doesn't exist. I need to keep pretending to be someone I'm not. It's been working great for me," he said.

"Really? How many girlfriends have you gained as a fraud?"

He chuckled. "You're a funny one. I'll give you some time to recover, and we can renegotiate terms."

"There's nothing to negotiate. I'm done."

"We'll see what your answer will be in a few weeks."

"I'll save you the time of investing in that mystery. My answer will be no."

He stepped to the door. "Get better, man. I cried at your memorial service and don't want to do that again."

After he left, I realized I should have seen if he could get Ivy's number for me. Phil's words brought a realization forward. Apparently, my parents had held a memorial service for me. Maybe that's why they pretended I barely existed. They'd already grieved me and moved on.

Chapter Twenty-Five

Fall rain showers had lingered all week, and I'd spent so much time watching the earth soak in the water until it drank all it could contain. The sun would claim anything unused and return it to clouds to nourish another spot that needed it more. I finished most of my overdue schoolwork the first week home, and the teachers had provided enough to finish out the semester at home. My parents told me I could go at whatever speed I wanted for the rest of the semester. Melancholy had sunk into my bones and made me mopey with emptiness. I didn't mind it and preferred it to the fake happiness many people lived.

Mom popped her head in for the seventh time in the last twenty minutes. "I want to make sure you're okay with me going."

"Yeah, we have to eat. Go get groceries. I can handle things here for a while. In fact, why don't you go to the salon or a movie?"

"No, I couldn't. You might need something."

"Mom, I have a broken arm. My legs and other arm work

just fine." I wiggled my phone. "Plus, we have instant communication."

She pressed her lips. "Okay. But if you need anything, let me know."

"I will. Mom, have some fun."

She frowned and left. With my mom gone, I could sink into despair. I turned up my music and got lost in the lyrics. My phone pinged, breaking my thoughts. I held my phone closer to my face to see if I read it correctly. Chloe wanted to know if she could come and see me.

I'd gone to visit her many times before getting lost, and she'd always cut things short. Not once since everything happened with Todd had she wanted to see me. I told her she could come over anytime, and she told me she'd be right over. I spent the time waiting for her, trying to process what was happening. She walked into my room and made a beeline for me.

She threw her arms around my neck. "Ivy, I got so scared. I thought I'd never get the chance to tell you I'm sorry."

I held onto her. "You have nothing to be sorry about. I'm the only one who should be sorry."

She scooted back on the bed until she reached the wall to lean on. "No, Ivy, I should have never written that letter to you. I hate I did that to you."

"You were in so much pain. I didn't notice. Your letter was right. If I had been a better friend, I would have noticed."

She shook her head. "Ivy, I hid it so well and then expected you to be a mind reader. These last few weeks, thinking you were dead gave me time to think about what you must have gone through finding me the way you did. Somehow, you kept your composure to save my life. Then I pushed you away for months. I was there when the rangers told everyone they were calling off the search because, with a snowstorm, the probability of you being alive was slim to none. I thought I'd never see you again. That's how you must have felt that day."

"My only concern was for you, Chloe. I wanted you to be okay but didn't know what the right thing was."

"You did all you could and stood by me. I've been going to counseling, and it's been helping. I still have times I struggle, and I think I will continue to, but talking to the counselor has helped."

We talked for a while longer, as Chloe shared even more with me.

She scooted directly in front of me until our knees touched. "What was it like being stuck in the wilderness for five weeks with Boaz Jackson? Did you guys finally kiss?"

"Why would you say that?"

"What do you mean? You've liked him since kindergarten."

My eyebrows shot up. "Yeah, as a friend, and then we stopped talking completely after the choir camp summer."

"I know, but you still looked at him like you had feelings."

"It's not like I could have anything to do with him now."

She scrunched her face. "Why not? Was it terrible in the wilderness with him?"

I leaned against my headboard. "The opposite, actually. It was like old times and more."

"More?"

I sighed. "Yeah, we had to cuddle together for warmth, and it became this natural thing."

Her face lit up. "You cuddled for warmth! I don't understand. What's the issue now?"

"How could I have anything to do with him when he writes letters that hurt people?"

She nodded and looked away. "Yeah, I got caught up in those words, thinking Todd had loved me enough to pay for a love letter. I always knew Boaz wrote it. Everyone does. All those girls who get a letter know it. They fall in love with Boaz because he's so easy to love. It's the feelings his letters create that make them work."

"Exactly. He creates the feelings that push girls to the wrong guys, and he made yours so personal like you said in your letter."

"He did because Boaz sees people. He really sees them, and he saw me. His letter showed me how well he did. He probably shouldn't have included personal things. He seals the letters, and sure the guys could read them, but that would break the rose seal."

Heat rose in me, not toward Chloe, but Boaz. All the anger toward him grew. "He started the chain of events that led to everything that happened with you."

"Ivy, that was Todd. Todd did that. Boaz wrote me a beautiful letter that made me feel seen."

I jumped up to look out my window, still trying to work through my emotions. "Yeah, that made you think Todd saw you."

"True, but I think only because I wanted to feel like he did. I really liked him, but in the end, I knew Boaz had written the letter. I knew that and still decided maybe it meant Todd felt that way." She picked at my quilt for a few seconds. "Even knowing who wrote the letter, I made the choice to do things with Todd."

"And that exempts Boaz?"

"Maybe not completely. In all my pain, I didn't see where the blame really belonged and that's what poured out in the notes I wrote. Out of everybody, Todd holds the most responsibility for what happened. Also, the people who recorded and posted it. Their motives seem a lot more malignant than anything Boaz ever did. His intention was to write letters that made people feel like they were seen and loved, and knowing Boaz's giant heart, I'm pretty sure that's all he thought would happen. I see that now that I've had time work through things.

Maybe it doesn't completely excuse it, but he's human. I think it makes him worth forgiveness."

"You think I should forgive him?"

She met my eyes. "Yes, because I already have."

My eyes released their emotions, and I scratched my tears away, only to have them replaced seconds later. "We can't pretend it never happened."

She hopped off the bed and yanked me into a hug. "Of course not, but we can realize Boaz is human, exactly like we are. He deserves not to be bound to this forever, and neither do you."

Chloe and I cried against each other until we had to sit on the bed in exhaustion. She was right. More than Boaz, I'd trapped myself in a cage. The bars consisted of everything that happened last spring. I'd lashed out at Boaz because I thought he stood on the outside holding the key to free me. Instead, the key had hung around my neck the entire time. More than anyone, I needed to forgive myself.

I sunk back on my bed and squeezed my pillow, thinking about everything. My head snapped to Chloe. "I haven't even gone to see him. He saved my life more than once and took care of me. No matter how much missing him hurt, I didn't make a move toward him. I haven't even gone to see him!"

Chloe grabbed my hand and pulled me off the bed. "We need to fix this. You need to go to him and work through this thing in a place you aren't forced. In a place you choose to. Let's go find your boy."

I wiped my tears, grabbed my phone, and stopped. "My mom won't be okay with me leaving."

"You never know until you ask."

I called my mom and convinced her to let me hang out with Chloe. She seemed reluctant, but relented when I promised to check-in. Part of me thought she was happy to see me moving forward to typical teenage things instead of lying in bed all day, as I had for the last few weeks.

I paused at the front door and ran to the kitchen. "It's raining, and I can't get my cast wet."

Chloe found the duct tape in the garage, where I told her to look while I located the trash bags. Together we wrapped my hand and arm in black plastic, and she drove me to Boaz's two-story brick house. White pillars accented the front, and his two green front doors made things pop more. His mom always placed wreaths to match the seasons to greet guests. The current one had red and orange maple leaves with welcome pumpkins in the center.

Everything looked perfect from the outside, as though no one flawed could ever live inside. It appeared like a life-size dollhouse where everything could be arranged precisely how someone desired. The illusion was one I'd seen through many times Boaz and I had hung out as children.

Chloe gave me a little shove. "Go get your boy!"

I bolted onto his porch with my fist poised to knock.

"Ivy?"

I jumped and turned to see Boaz sitting on his porch swing. "Hey!"

Indiscernible emotions flooded me and spilled out as our eyes stayed locked together. Any doubt, fear, or excuse sitting as boulders between us melted with everything Boaz conveyed as he stared back at me.

He jumped up with the support of a black boot on his injured side. "Hey."

"I need to tell you something. Show you something."

He grinned. "Okay."

Five fast steps and I found myself inches in front of him. He grabbed my waist, and I pressed him against the wall. I leaned my head forward, and he met me halfway. Our lips collided with desperate movements. I relaxed into him as he parted my mouth, deepening the kiss. His arms drew me closer in the way I'd craved all these weeks without him. We dissolved into each other with rain pattering behind us.

When the kiss broke, the world didn't return. Boaz's golden brown eyes mesmerized me, pulling me into a trance.

"I love you, Boaz." My tears released with my words.

He leaned into me and kissed my forehead. "I love you, Ivy."

We held each other, and for the first time in weeks, I felt pieced together.

Chapter Twenty-Six

Forget cloud nine. I'd sailed right up to cloud one hundred. Ivy's lips on mine lingered in my head, still shocking me with each replay. The memory helped make her absence easier than it had been. After our kiss, we had a long talk, and things seemed smoothed over. I'd gotten all my makeup work done and decided lying around my house all day held no appeal. Now that the doctor had switched me over to a boot, I had more mobility. The orthopedist had given me crutches and a scooter that removed all weight from my damaged leg.

On my first day back, I chose the scooter but discovered how inaccessible the school entrance clearly was. My lower leg bent over the seat of the scooter, and my booted foot hung over the edge. I stared up at the three sets of concrete steps in dismay.

Not enough of my strength had returned for me to manage hauling a scooter up the stairs. I stood there thinking through the dilemma and reciting all the other entrances into the school.

Wilbur Hanes rolled up in his wheelchair. "The truck entrance is what I use."

I looked around as though I could find what he meant. "The truck entrance?"

His curly red hair bobbed as he nodded. "Come on. I'll show you."

We journeyed until we reached the back of our enormous school. A large concrete ramp led to a yellow-painted platform. The incline took a lot of effort to get myself to the top.

Wilbur got himself to the entrance in half the time and pressed a red buzzer. "I have great arm muscles because of this."

"They make you do this every day?"

"Yeah, I can call the office to have help to push me up, but my arms work okay." He pressed the buzzer again. "Sometimes they take a while."

"Is this even legal?"

"School budgets aren't the greatest, and as long as they provide some way for us to get into school, it's considered acceptable, I guess."

Wilbur waved goodbye as we made it into the school. Everyone stared and whispered as I hobbled through the hall.

"He's been shot! That's so hot," a girl whispered and giggled.

"You're a celebrity now. Your letters are worth hundreds!" another shouted.

All around me, questions and snarky sayings bounced around as I hurried as fast as my injured leg allowed. I stopped at the bulletin board to see what I'd missed the last few weeks. The holiday formal was coming up with an added unique twist.

"Hey!"

I turned around and grinned at Ivy. Her eyes smiled in a way I hadn't seen in months. "Hey."

She glanced around me to look at the formal poster. "That's different."

"Yeah, I'm not sure I'm going to be able to ice skate in two weeks."

"I'll pull you and your scooter around."

"That'll look dignified."

She stepped forward, pinning me against the cork-board. "It'll be fun."

"This is fun. Feel free to trap me anytime."

"You want to be helpless in my arms?"

"You make that happen every time." I leaned in for a kiss.

We got a bit carried away for being in the school hallway and were broken apart by the whistles and hollers around us.

She rested her forehead on mine and laughed. "Why did we take so long to do that?"

"I can't tell right now. Maybe we should kiss again to figure it out."

"Good idea."

She pressed her lips against mine, and this time we ignored our audience.

"You're doing great," my physical therapist said.

I collapsed into the chair and rubbed my knee, wiping my sweat with a towel. "It doesn't feel like it."

"A gunshot wound with nerve damage isn't an easy injury to recover from. Trust me, you're doing great."

"What if I can't walk normally again?"

He typed something into his tablet. "Let's take it one day at a time."

The therapist left, and I hobbled into the shower, which was also frustrating because I had to remove the boot and use a shower chair. I reminded myself it was better than having to have more nurse help. When I went back into my room, Noah was playing with his Ninja Turtle toys at my desk.

He smashed two turtles together like they were in a brawl. "Bo, can we go to karaoke soon?"

"Yeah, sometime." I collapsed on my bed and clenched my eyes shut at the nerve pain and muscle fatigue.

"When?"

"I don't know."

"Why can't you tell me?"

"Because I can't. I'm not sure when my leg will be well enough to drive you and help."

His shoulders sagged. "Oh."

The knock at my door turned my mood instantly around. Ivy stepped into the room, and Noah leaped from his chair to throw his arms around her.

"You've stayed away so long, Ivy. Too long. I missed you." Noah grinned as he squeezed her.

She hugged him back. "I missed you too, Noah. How's life?"

He continued to hang onto her. "It's terrible."

"Oh, no. Why is that?"

He let go and picked up his Ninja Turtle toys. "Bo's leg is hurt, so he can't take me to karaoke."

She sat down in the chair next to my bed and slipped her hand in mine. "When is it? I'll take you."

He pumped his fist in the air. "Yes! That's perfect. It's Friday."

My mom knocked on the doorway. "Noah, let's go. It's time to go to day camp."

My brother ran over to Ivy and gave her Raphael. "You can borrow this. That way, you have to come back." He ran out of the room and shut the door behind him.

Ivy stuck the figurine in her purse and walked over to my board. "These are the kids?"

"Yeah, the current ones I'm trying to support on the left, and the ones I failed at in the middle. The far-right are the ones that are home with families."

"This is amazing, Boaz. Look, if you want to write letters again, to do this, I get it now. This is a really needed thing." She came back and sat next to me.

I lifted my blanket for her to climb in and kissed her head when she snuggled close. "No, my love letter-writing days are over. I'm not going to help jerks gain girls they don't deserve and are going to abuse."

"Your integrity is hot, you know."

I laughed. "What?"

"Let me show you."

Show me, she did with her mouth and hands. All my troubles faded as Ivy next to me washed away all my doubts and fears for the future. She rested on my chest as we both caught our breaths from our make-out session. Our legs tangled together and brought the sense of the home we'd created at the forest shack. That time had forged something vital between us.

She kissed my chest. "My mom is taking me to see Pop tomorrow. I'm not sure if I can handle seeing him in one of those places. It has to be so confusing. He's going to die with strangers around him. What if we can't get there on time?"

"You want me to go with you? I'd love to see Pop again."

"Are you sure? You probably shouldn't be on your leg too much."

"I won't be. I'll take my knee scooter."

Ivy and I took a nap together, and as we drifted to sleep, I didn't know how to live without this anymore. All of me was addicted to this being what sleep meant.

♥

My dad brought a large envelope into my room. "I think you got the early acceptance we applied for."

Mom walked in after him, and they both watched me as I studied the Yale label.

I opened it and read the letter, setting it on my stand. "I got in, but I'm not going."

My dad's brow furrowed. "Of course, you're going."

"No, I'm not. I'm staying here because if I leave my brother. You know, Noah. Do you remember his name? He won't have anyone if I go clear across the country to school."

"This isn't an optional thing. You're going and have no choice."

I stared at my blankets and nodded. "I get that not wanting me around is consistent with the two of you, but I'm not leaving Noah. Not with you two."

My mom gaped. "How dare you talk to us this way!"

I knocked the envelope into my trash. "It's difficult for me to talk to you either of you at all. I go missing for weeks, and you don't rush to get to me. You don't show an ounce of emotion at your son being found. You didn't even care if I was found alive, did you? Maybe you felt a twinge because I couldn't parent Noah for you anymore, but even that passed quickly when you discovered you could pawn him off on strangers."

"We got you the best possible room, doctors, and therapies, and this is how you show your gratitude? If you want college paid for, you will go to Yale," Dad said.

"That's fine. I'll figure it out on my own."

They lectured me for a while longer, but I tuned them out the way they continued to do to me. They finally left me alone, and I hopped on my computer to scroll through the orphan group. As the kids' faces peered back, I knew I needed to think of something to continue to help them.

Ivy texted me she was here, and I swished out of my house

on my scooter. My parents arguing about me played as background noise to my escape. Ivy hopped out of the passenger seat and helped me get my scooter into the trunk.

Her mom waved at me as I climbed into the back. "It's been too long, Boaz. It's good to see you."

"Good to see you too."

Ivy got in next to me and leaned her head on my shoulder. I wrapped my arms around her, hoping it settled her nerves. We pulled up to the nursing home, and she took a deep breath before climbing out to head inside.

Chapter Twenty-Seven

My stomach felt on fire, and it froze me in place. Mom got Boaz's scooter from the trunk and helped him out of the car.

He scooted over next to me. "It'll be okay. Whatever we find in there, I'm here. I got you on this."

I grabbed onto his scooter's handle and pulled him forward. "I can do this."

"Yeah, maybe slow down a little, though."

I turned around to see him trying to slide himself back on. "Oops. Maybe you should handle that."

The brick building looked nice on the outside, with white benches on each side of double glass doors. My imagination cycled through all the horror dwelling inside. Oldies Christmas music played against a buzzer that sounded as we entered. A cinnamon pine scent greeted us, along with a beaming stout woman.

She waved. "How may I help you?" Her cheekbones had to ache from the degree of her smile.

My mother wrote on a clipboard resting on a mahogany counter. "We're here to see William Reel. I'm his daughter."

"Oh, yes, it's nice to meet you." She picked up her phone. "Diane, Mr. Reel's family is here to see him."

We waited in the lobby that had five Christmas wreaths with red ribbons decorating an indoor balcony. Christmas lights, a decorated tree, and tinsel gave the entryway a festive look. A tall, slender woman with curly black hair led us through some doors after putting in a code. We went through a second set of doors, and my jaw dropped.

"Wow!" Boaz's eyes looked as wide as mine felt.

Shiny bricks made a path between two sidewalks that rested in front of little yards that had white picket fences. Small porches with rocking chairs created the entrances to tiny houses, complete with Christmas lights framing the windows and wreaths hung on each door. We strolled deeper into a holiday village with a large tree covered in colorful ornaments and candy canes. An animatronic Santa waved, and a model train circled around a glowing nativity. Shops, a movie theater, grocery store, post office, and several other businesses had residents entering and exiting them.

My awe subsided enough to allow me speech. "What is this place?"

The woman stopped and pointed at the buildings. "This is a little town where our residents can wander. It's built to look like a typical town set in the era that our average resident grew up in. We even have a theater they can watch movies from that time. Research has proven it has a calming effect and helps with the confusion."

"Is it all safe?"

"Yes, it's built with limited mobility in mind. Each resident has a monitor on their wrist, there are cameras that are constantly watched, and we have staff in every area." She pointed to several people in scrubs, helping the elderly do various tasks.

She took us down a street and stopped at a cheery yellow

house with blue curtains. We went inside a little living room where Pop sat in a large recliner, watching a black and white western on a tube TV. Open doors showed a bathroom and a bedroom. It looked comfortable and inviting. Pictures from his life were hung around the room, including a sketch I had drawn him when I was a little girl.

Boaz squeezed my hand. "Are you alright?"

I brushed away my tears. "Yeah, this is so much better than I imagined."

We sat on the couch visiting with Pop.

He pointed at the TV. "Nice show."

I reached over and patted his weathered hand. "It's a great show, Pop."

He met my eyes with slight clarity. "I missed you, Lilith."

"I missed you too."

His gaze locked on Boaz. "You too, boy."

A woman knocked on the door. "William, we wanted to know if you would like to see the therapy dogs and paint?"

I jumped up. "I do."

Pop hooked arms with me, and we walked to the town square where we got to pet puppies. A golden retriever sat in my lap and gave me a kiss.

"Droo needs a friend." I looked at my mother with a pouty lip.

She shook her head, but I'd continue to work on it. We moved onto the table, and Pop and I painted a picture together. His side had blurs of color that almost looked like a rainbow fish while mine had us fishing. Boaz assisted a woman with her art, and she asked him on a date to the movies, which was where we headed next.

After watching a musical called *White Christmas*, I walked my grandfather back to his tiny house. Boaz took his date to hers. I helped hang his painting on his wall and tucked him into a chair, using the knitted blanket I'd made as a home economics project in the eighth grade. It looked more like a trapezoid than a rectangle, but my grandpa had still loved it. I'd made it using green and red, his favorite colors, because they reminded him of Christmas. I sat across from him for a while and listened to him mumble about baseball.

He glanced up at me and stared. "Lilith, the Cubs lost again."

"That's what I heard too. What about those Cardinals?"

"They won. They won last week and the week before that." His eyes lowered to his blanket. He picked at it, unraveling some of the yarn. He'd done the same in a few places.

A woman in scrubs brought in his medication and another his food. The chicken noodle soup had a garlicky broth smell that rose from the steam.

I picked up the spoon from the pink plastic tray set on an end table. "I'll feed him if that's okay?"

She opened his straw and placed it through the slit in the plastic lid over his water. "Are you sure?"

"Yes, I'd love to."

She scooted the table on wheels close to me, and I got to work feeding him his soup. I waved the spoon gently in the air before each bite to cool it. He crinkled his nose as he chewed. His eyes seemed to search for an answer to the taste on his tongue. I kept branding all his expressions into memory, knowing each one could hold finality.

He swallowed his last bite. "The chicken is tough. I think it needs to marinate for longer, Lilith. The broth was good, though."

"You're right."

His brow furrowed. "Did we get the horses in the barn yet? I can't seem to remember if we did that yet."

"Yep, they are all safe."

He returned to mumbling, but I couldn't make out the

words. My attention stayed fixed on him until my mom got me to leave.

* * *

Over the next few weeks, Boaz and I visited my grandpa regularly, and we volunteered to help with the art projects. Christmas was two weeks away, and the winter formal was happening in a week.

Boaz continued to struggle with his leg and had grown increasingly frustrated with his mobility issues. He wanted to get a job to donate money to the kids again, but his leg pain made it too difficult to do much. It would strike him out of nowhere, and his therapist suggested he take a few months to recover before pursuing a job on top of school. For this reason, he decided to sell everything he could, including his extensive baseball card collection. I'd come over to help him clean out his closet.

He sat in front of his computer to appraise everything I brought him that he thought he could sell. "I should have done this sooner. Some of these cards are worth a few hundred. If I can sell them all, it might pay the entire accounts for a few kids. There are a couple who need it so badly. It might help a family pick them before it's too late."

"That'll be good." I climbed up the stepladder, stretched to the back corner of his closet shelf, and pulled down a white box. I brought it over to him. "Should I open it? It has my name on it."

His cheeks turned red. "Umm... Maybe. Let me think about it."

"Okay. What pile am I putting it in?"

He pointed over to his bed. "The keep one."

I set it down next to the other items he'd decided to keep. They were mainly a few outfits. Most everything else was going to the sell pile. Almost everything he owned would be gone if he had his way. He'd have nothing in hand to show for it.

The box called to me to open it. It screamed at me since it had my name on it, I had the right to open it. I placed a pair of shorts over it to distract my curiosity and returned to the closet. It didn't work. Every time I left the closet, my eyes zoomed right to it.

Boaz chuckled and shook his head. "You really want to open the box, don't you?"

"Why do you say that?"

"You keep staring at my shorts like they are the most interesting thing you've ever seen. It's really what you placed under them that you want." He used his phone to snap pictures of cards he'd lined up on his desk.

"It does have my name on it. What could be in there? Toys from our childhood?"

"It's a little corny."

"Now you have to show me." I set the latest cards next to him.

He avoided my gaze. "It's full of letters."

"Letters?"

"Yeah, I used to write you one every day. It's what inspired my business. Phil found them one time when he was over here. He said he'd pay me if I could write one like that to a girl he liked. I thought he was joking at first until he plopped down a twenty on my desk. After I found out about the kids, things clicked into place."

I removed the shorts from the box and ran my fingers over my name, written in wispy, lovely letters. "You always had the best handwriting. Chloe and I used to complain it wasn't fair for a guy with big fingers to write that gracefully. It's almost like you were destined to write beautiful handwritten notes."

"Yeah, to ruin people's lives." He chewed on his lip and went back to his work.

"I don't know, Boaz. It led to bad things for Chloe, but maybe it helped others more than we realize. Either way, are you going to let me read these?"

"You need more material to mock me with?"

I shrugged. "It's never a bad idea to store up ammunition."

"I'll think about it."

I piled the shorts and two shirts over the box and got back to work.

Chapter Twenty-Eight

I put on my coat and waited by the door until Ivy arrived to pick me up. The dress for the winter formal was flannel pajamas. The school had them for sale the week before in blue, red, and green. Ivy and I had coordinated in blue. A snowstorm had happened the day before, which made it so everyone had to put on outerwear over the unique clothing choice. The pajamas still worked well as a toasty bottom layer, so we decided to still wear them.

She ran out of her car, not able to wait for me to make it to her. Her white hat framed her face in a way that made her freckled mask pop more.

I paused my advance to look at her and how she smiled when she met my eyes. "You look beautiful," I said.

"You're not so bad yourself, handsome."

Her mom, staring at us, put a damper on moving in for a kiss. My leg had improved enough that all I had to use was my boot. The winter formal was taking place outside with winter activities, including ice skating. That would be an area I best avoided, but we would have to see how things went. When Ivy and I were little, we would pretend our sneakers were ice skates, and we'd slide across her driveway on cold winter mornings.

The pathway to the back of the school had been lit up with white icicle lights. They wrapped around old-fashioned lampposts that were spaced around four feet apart. The planning committee had transformed the backfield into a frosty North Pole. The famous red and white pole spun, blending the colors together. Students twirled and tumbled on the created rectangular ice rink. Holiday music blared from enormous speakers hung around the rink. Rows of booths with various activities had lines of students waiting to partake. Off to the side were winter games like snowman making and snow angels.

I hooked arms with Ivy in case the salt hadn't dissolved all the ice and pretended I could protect her from slipping. It hurt my pride to think the other way around, but with my bum leg, it was probably true. We walked through the archway and got our picture taken with a reindeer.

Ivy pointed her white mitten hand above our heads. "It's obligatory."

I grinned and tilted her back to place a kiss deep and long enough to warm the chilly air. I pulled back. "There's nothing obligatory about kissing you."

Her frosty breath heaved out. "People need to hang mistletoe more places."

"Agreed." We dissolved into another kiss.

"There's a line!" The photographer's shouting broke us apart.

We moved along to the hot chocolate booth and topped off our polar bear mugs with treats from a buffet table that contained chocolate chips, candy canes, marshmallows, whipped cream, and various other cocoa mix-ins. We snuggled up on a red bench decorated in silver tinsel to sip the steaming sweetness. Ivy leaned her head on my shoulder, and I kissed the top of her head, lingering to take in the tropical scent flowing from her hair. I could smell it through her hat and took a bit to absorb it into memory.

Ivy yanked me up from the bench, and we discarded our mugs in a bin. She dragged me after her, and I kept up the best I could, not wanting to thwart her enthusiasm she seemed determined to pursue. Ceramic figurines of all sorts were lined across a table where several students were in chairs working on their projects. A girl handed us a plastic globe with an open bottom and a black base.

We slid into chairs at the end and rifled through the figurines. I set to work following the instructions on the table and beamed proudly at my newly created snow globe. Ivy bit her bottom lip as she concentrated on perfecting hers.

She finished the final step on hers and frowned at mine. "A bluebird and a mouse, touching noses. Or umm... beak and nose?"

I slid it toward her. "It's us."

"What?"

"You know the songbird and the rat."

She glared while smiling. "You're not a rat, Boaz."

"I've immortalized your story forever. Merry Christmas."

She picked it up to inspect it closer. "First of all, I was never the songbird. I was the cat. Remember?"

"The author cannot always predict how the reader will interpret their story."

"Except, I literally told you how to interpret it."

I shrugged. "And I chose to disagree."

"You can't do that."

I nodded at my creation in her hands. "And, yet, I did."

She scowled. "Well, you can't, so there's that. I'll pretend to not be jealous about you being that close to someone else since I'm not the songbird."

I shook my head and picked up the sharpie and a sticker. When I finished, I smoothed it on the base of my masterpiece and handed it back to her.

"Boaz the rat and Ivy the songbird. Writing something doesn't make it true," she said.

"Everything I've written to you is true."

She stared at the sticker before meeting my eyes. "This time is the exception."

"You're cute when you're being stubborn."

"And you're hot when you finally decide to agree with me." She hovered her lips inches from mine.

"When does that ever happen?"

She shoved my shoulder. "You're impossible."

"It's why you love me."

She rolled her eyes. "Hardly."

I picked up her globe and stared at the nutcracker and the ballerina. "Second grade?"

Her eyebrows shot to the sky. "You remember?"

"Why wouldn't I? You made me dance with you for hours and promised sugar cookies but only gave me a stale candy cane."

"I couldn't help it that my mom was tired, and we couldn't use the oven." She set hers next to mine. "Mine is better than yours."

"Why can't they be equally as good?"

"I'm not sure because it didn't happen." She brought over tissue paper and little white boxes.

We wrapped them up well and left them on designated shelves to be picked up later. I waited until we made it out into the field and Ivy became distracted watching a bunny. It was fun using her fascination with nature against her. I scooped up two handfuls of snow and squished it against her cheek. She shrieked, and for a split second, I feared for my life.

I limped across the field, and she stood there, staring at me. Her eyes made it very clear I was going down. My head start proved futile when she launched at me, throwing snowball after snowball into my head.

"You can't chase an injured person! It's unethical." I screamed as the tenth snowball soaked through my clothes.

"Don't start a fight you can't finish, Jackson."

I held up my hands. "I surrender."

She continued slamming me with snow. "Coward!"

"Oh, yeah?"

"Yeah, you're worse than the cowardly lion. No wizard can help you."

I took off running the best my boot allowed, ignoring the stern looks my brain imagined my physical therapist would send me. Ivy stood her ground, pelting me with snowballs as I advanced toward her. I plowed into her but turned us to take the brunt of the fall.

She landed on top of me, and we rolled around as we tried to cover each other in snow. Screeches fled both of us until we were a shivering mess buried deep in frigid fluff.

Her teeth chattered. "You have to kiss me now before we freeze to death."

"Here we are. Close contact saving our lives again."

We warmed each other up with kisses and made our way over to the benches with heaters under them to finish the job. I stole a blanket from the sleigh when the driver left for a bathroom break and wrapped it around Ivy.

She scooted closer. "Remember, we're warmer if we share. It would be ironic that we survive weeks in the wilderness but die of hypothermia at the school winter formal."

"It sounds like something we would do."

"At least we go together."

Between the heaters and the blanket, our shivering subsided.

A girl climbed onto a stage that sat in the middle of the field and held a microphone to her mouth. The music cut out, and her voice broke through the speakers. "The tree lighting ceremony is about to begin. Head over to the east field if you want to watch."

Ivy and I meandered to where a giant pine tree rose above the others. It was the one student council decorated every year to boost morale around finals time. The principal held up the cord to the lights in one hand and the orange extension cord with the other.

"We are gathered here today to light this tree!" He lifted the cords higher in triumph.

"Turn it on! Turn it on!" the students chanted.

He plugged the two cords together, and the colorful bulbs hanging around the branches sparked to life. A girl handed us battery candles, and everyone broke into carols. I pulled Ivy against me, and our candles lit up her face with a flickering glow. We swayed as we sang "Silent Night" and stared at each other in a contentment that not even my icy soaked socks could ruin.

Five carols later, Ivy and I walked hand in hand to the cocoa booth to warm up some more. I returned the blanket to the sleigh man and thanked him with a sheepish grin. He shot me a stern look but said nothing. Most of our classmates had dispersed to their vehicles, and the chaperones were distracted with clean-up.

Ivy and I snuck onto the empty ice, ignoring the sign that said ice skates were required. My boot made that impossible, so instead, we recklessly slid around on our shoes. I twirled her in and out of my arms, and we glided together. After stumbling, we laid on our backs. The stars peeked through curtains of clouds that moved across the moon and painted morphing shadows on the trees and ground.

Ivy squeezed my hand and clenched her eyes closed. "A shooting star!"

"You're wasting it on chocolate wishes, aren't you?"

She gasped. "Chocolate wishes are never a waste."

Another one fell, and I closed my eyes. When I opened them again, I found Ivy staring at me. "What did you wish for?" she pressed.

"I can't tell you. It won't come true."

"You can tell your girlfriend."

I shook my head. "That's not an exception."

"It is."

"I wished for you to be happy because it's where my happiness lives."

"So, you're selfish."

I scrunched my face. "What?"

"You only wished for my happiness because it makes you happy."

I attacked her with tickles, and she squirmed and squealed. She curled against me and slammed her lips into mine. My arms relaxed around her, and she buried her nose against my collarbone. The music faded, and teachers shouted for us to get off the ice. We walked toward the parking lot, and Ivy took out her phone to call her mom.

"Mom, sorry. I didn't hear your calls over the music." She let out a whimper. "What?" Her hand went to her mouth. "No!"

Her legs gave out, and I caught her, bringing her over to a bench where she slumped against me. Her phone plopped into the grass, and she sobbed.

I rubbed her back. "What is it?"

She sucked in trembling breaths. "My grandpa died."

I held her until the ride her mom had called for us pulled

up to the curb. We went to her house, and I helped her inside. My leg didn't allow me to carry her like I wanted to, so I supported her as much as I could. I helped her out of her outwear and tucked her into bed.

She grabbed my hand. "Can you stay with me?"

I nodded, and we laid together in our flannel pajamas. She cried off and on through the night. I held her through the restless hours that led to dawn.

Chapter Twenty-Nine

When we were born, some things existed as absolutes. The people who came before us always lived and should continue to do so forever. It was only as we grew up and saw the world for what it was that we realized they can be taken from us.

Pop set his fishing pole down and patted the stump next to him. "Ivy, come here. Right now. We need to talk about this."

I crossed my arms and turned away from him. "No!"

"You can't go pushing people into the lake. They could drown."

"Boaz can swim."

"Ivy, come here."

I sighed but obeyed my grandfather because his words were truth and law. I sat on the stump but kept my eyes cast to the ground. "He said he was going to summer camp without me, but he would miss my eyes! Who says? And if he's going to miss them so much, why would he go without me." My nine-year-old mind was infuriated.

Pop let out a short laugh. "Maybe he doesn't have much of a choice. His parents could be making him, or he wants to do this on his own. It's okay for friends to have a little time apart."

"Not the whole summer! It's going to make things go bad. He needed to know that, so I yelled at him and ran away."

"You ran away after you pushed him into the lake. Now he's sitting in the cabin and won't fish with us. The last day we have here. The last day before he leaves for the entire summer. You know, Ivy, you'll catch more flies with honey."

I crinkled my nose. "Why would I want to catch a yucky fly?"

"Because sometimes that fly that you're mad at is really a butterfly in disguise that is going to add a lot of wonderful things to your life."

"Butterflies and flies look nothing alike."

"Sometimes, we just see them entirely wrong. Our perceptions are off."

"Well, Boaz isn't a butterfly. He's not that beautiful."

Pop's laughter flowed through the humid air, and the warmth evident in his grey eyes latched itself onto my memory.

The sunlight danced across Boaz's sleeping face. All this year, he'd seemed a terrible fly, buzzing around me and making everything terrible. He'd never been that at all. He'd always been my butterfly who added wonderful things to my life, and I'd always been wrong because his heart had always been beautiful. His gorgeous face, peaceful in sleep, was beautiful. I was too busy assuming flies to see the truth. Pop had known that all the time.

Boaz opened his eyes and met mine. His thumb wiped my latest tears. "Tell me what you need."

"Just walk through this with me."

"Always."

We laid in bed for most of the morning. My mom had arrangements to make, and my dad had gone to work to wrap some things up before he took leave to be there for my mom. Boaz and I watched tiny sparrows hop on the barren branches of the oak we'd climbed as children. We'd hidden in its green leaves in the spring and summer and jumped in the orange and red blanket its leaves provided the yellowing grass of autumn. In winter, the drippy icicles appeared as frigid and weeping as my soul felt on this tired morning where exhaustion found its way into my veins that left me only time to grieve.

Memories of Pop poured through my mind. The ones that a disease had turned to dust in his brain until he could no longer piece together the fragments to remember me at all. I'd lost him months ago, but the finality of his body lost too weighed on my chest and poured out my eyes. He'd been gone for months, but today death had collected the rest of him, leaving me with nothing more than memories he'd proven fragile.

And so, Boaz laid there with me as my soul ripped open and felt everything too massively to stay inside. He let me wail, sob, and tell him anything I needed to say. His soft kisses on my head, the breakfast he brought me, all the ways he took care of me on that sorrowful morning showed me he'd always been my butterfly that took me above all the terrible things the world would bring into my life. I woke today to find one of my absolutes crumbled, but next to me stayed a boy who showed me in my brokenness love could piece me together.

♥

Many people came to the funeral. My grandpa had served on the city council for many years and had a plethora of connections that he'd impacted enough for them to show up. Several staff members from the nursing home came as well.

The entire front of the room was covered in bouquets of vibrant flowers, as humans always tried to assign meaning to everything. Some way to make the cold seem more colorful and give life to the lifeless. Flowers showed life continued for those left behind and decorated the dead's exit in something that didn't seem so stiff. We gave flowers for the dead, and it seemed an illusion.

Chloe sang "Amazing Grace" at my mother's request. She'd asked me first, but I needed to sit in my sadness, not release it yet. I held it together until the graveside, and everyone left. I lingered, sitting in front of the open hole where a grey casket rested at the bottom. A blanket went around my shoulders before Boaz retreated a few feet away to give me these moments. Snow fell around me, but I stayed for a while, knowing this was the last time there wouldn't be six feet of dirt between Pop and me. I whispered my goodbyes to the soil.

♥

We ate dinner at the church Pop had gone to his entire life. It was Potluck style and served by two elderly women. People endlessly tried to feed the mourning when sorrow made appetites cease. Still, everyone had to continue eating, and it made it so you could mindlessly do so. My mind strayed a thousand miles away as I ate food that probably tasted amazing. Then we went home, and Boaz left to check on Noah. The solitude arrived, both welcoming and deafening. When I wobbled outside of my room the next morning, I heard sharp cries sputtering through a crack in my mother's bedroom door. I knocked, and she told me to enter. She clutched a shirt in her arms and sat up to wipe her eyes with the heel of her hand.

She lifted her blanket. "Come here."

I crawled in and cuddled against her as I had when I was

little and scared of the nightmare that broke through my dreams. "Are you okay, Mama?"

"No, but that's okay. You probably aren't either. It's been a rough few months for us both."

I nodded. "When I was lost in the wilderness, I was scared Pop would die before I made it back. I'm grateful I got more weeks with him because I knew he would pass soon."

"But you still weren't ready."

"No, I wasn't. It's like some part of me believed he would live forever. The people born before us seem immortal. Like they will always be, even though logic teaches us otherwise."

She pulled my hair behind my shoulders, then dropped her arm around my side. "Authorities told me you were dead, Ivy. Even though they hadn't found you or Boaz. They said the odds of you surviving after the blizzard and all that time were slim to none. Yet, I held onto that slim as though they'd told me they had spotted you alive and were on their way to get you. Boaz's family had a memorial service for him."

I sat up and stared at her. "They did?"

"Yeah, I guess they believed the none part, which I think maybe helped them cope. People encouraged me to do the same, but I couldn't. Not knowing is tough. I know that feeling you describe. It's even more powerful when you have children because as the world teaches you parents, grandparents, and all those before you will die, it teaches you your children won't until you have died yourself. There's no way to cope with that. In my sorrow for never seeing my father again, there is a happiness that I have my daughter next to me. Life is bittersweet. Happiness and sorrow weave their ways through everything in varying intensities. We somehow keep going because the grief makes the joy more abundant. We'll forever miss your Pop, but we still have each other to remember him together."

Mom pulled a box from under her bed full of pictures, and we spent the afternoon reliving the moments we still had my grandpa. We laughed, cried, and started a process toward healing that would never completely be finished.

Chapter Thirty

I gritted my teeth and slammed my hand into my healing gunshot wound. If you looked at it, you would think it had gotten completely better, leaving only a scar behind. It buzzed with pain and a crawling sensation that zapped my hip and leg at random intervals. Today was the worst it had been in a while. Luckily, school was on winter break, but I had another problem.

Noah ran into my room to argue his point for the third time since he'd woken me up. "Bo, why can't Ivy still take me? It's the Christmas one. They'll have Santa there. *Santa.* When else can I tell him what I want?"

I closed my eyes and leaned against my headboard. "Her grandpa just died. She needs time with her family right now. Besides, didn't you write Santa a letter?"

"Yeah, but he never got it because no one took me to mail it. See, that's the big problem I have."

"I think Santa will know what you want. He's pretty perceptive."

"This is too important to risk it. I need to go to karaoke, Bo. Can't you understand?"

I rubbed my leg and grimaced. "I do understand, but there's not much I can do at the moment."

"Can't you drive me? You barely wear your boot anymore."

"Not today. My pain is worse, and it's too risky to drive."

He slumped down on my desk chair. "It's super important. I need Mandy to be my girlfriend."

"You're wishing for Mandy for Christmas?"

"Yeah, maybe they'll put mistletoe up too, and she'll come over to tell me I have bad music. Then she has to kiss me."

"That's not the best plan. You should want a girl to want to kiss you, not feel like she has to."

He threw his hands up and down in front of him. "How is she supposed to want to kiss me if I never see her?"

"You're going to have to have patience. I can't drive you, and neither can Ivy."

"She said she would."

"She didn't know her grandpa would die."

Our mom knocked on my door frame. "Come on, Noah, it's time for day camp."

"It's Christmas Eve," I said.

Mom's eyes snapped to me. "Yeah, and he can go to day camp."

"Or you could take the day off."

She crossed her arms. "Let's go, Noah."

Noah ran and gave me a hug. "Have a good day, Bo."

"You, too. I'll see when you get home," I said.

I'd have offered to watch him myself, but with my leg hurting like it was, I was pretty sure today would be a pain med day, and I couldn't take care of Noah on those. They left, and I pulled myself out of bed, hobbling into Noah's room. I located his letter to Santa and arranged a pickup. Before placing it into the envelope, my name on the paper caught my attention, and I read it.

Dear Santa,

My brother Bo needs a new leg this year so he can spend time with me again. I told him I wanted Mandy to be my girlfriend, and that was my Christmas wish. But I want Bo back as my real wish. If you give me two presents, I'll take Mandy. Thank you. I've been good. I promise.

-Noah Jackson.

My heart sank as guilt trickled through me. The postal man came to our door, and I printed off the receipt before wrapping it in a box. I'd been working on Ivy's present for a while and hoped I'd have it done in time for tomorrow.

I worked about an hour before the pain in my leg got too much, and I had to take my meds. I fell asleep and woke up several hours later to my phone ringing. Sleep had set in deep, and I mumbled a greeting into the phone.

"Is this Boaz Jackson?" the woman on the other end said.

I yawned and clenched my eyes to dislodge the heaviness. "This is him."

"This is Juniper Hills Day Camp. We have you as an emergency contact for Noah Jackson."

I sat up, no longer having issues with drowsiness. "That's my brother. What's going on?"

"He has eloped?"

"What?"

"He walked out of our building, and we have been unable to locate him."

I jumped out of bed and threw my pants on while holding the phone between my ear and shoulder. "You lost him! Don't you have people watching?"

"He said he was going to the bathroom, which isn't usually a problem. He went out the back door we had opened for a delivery man. Otherwise, it would have alarmed."

"Did you call my parents?"

"Yes, they aren't answering."

I huffed out a breath. "Okay. I'll be right there."

I grabbed my keys, and for the first time since my accident, I got in my truck. The entire way, I yelled at myself for not getting it together enough to watch Noah for the day. It was Christmas Eve, and he should have been home with me. I dialed my parents over and over, pouring my anger into several voicemails. For years, I'd said nothing to them and let all of it slide to avoid conflict. My breaking point had arrived, and I was done.

I bolted for the day camp door, and the director showed me my brother leaving on the camera. I got back in my truck to comb the streets for Noah. Four blocks in, my head and chest were nearing hysterics, hindering my breathing and delivering a pounding headache.

Karaoke!

I called the playhouse. Brenda told me Noah hadn't shown up, but they would keep an eye out for him and call if he arrived.

I dialed Ivy through the speakers in my truck and heaved out words when she picked up. "Noah is missing. He walked out of his day camp. I can't find him."

"Where are you?"

"Driving my truck all around the blocks surrounding the camp. He's never done this before."

"Alright. Let me get my shoes on, and I'll be right there. Send me the address."

I pulled into a parking lot. "I'm at Darla's café." I ran my fingers through my hair. "He probably tried to go to karaoke and is lost. It's like twelve degrees, Ivy."

"I'm on my way. We'll find him, Boaz."

She hung up, and I slammed my head into the steering wheel a few times. Ivy met me about fifteen minutes later, and we split up driving directions. It would be dark soon, and the fear kept increasing. My phone rang, and I put it through my speaker.

"I'm trying to reach a Bo," a man said.

"I'm Boaz."

"I have a Noah here. He had your phone number in his coat pocket."

I slammed my brakes, causing several cars behind me to honk. "He's my brother. Where is he?"

"He showed up at our church. He said if he couldn't find Santa, he needed someone to pray for him." The man gave me the address.

I sped and called Ivy on the way to fill her in. A white church with a grey steeple and stained-glass windows appeared. The parking lot was full, and music streamed out from inside. Ivy pulled in right after me, and we bolted up a set of concrete steps.

A man stood on the other side of the red doors and handed us a pamphlet. "Welcome. The pageant has already started. We're on song five."

I took the paper and stuck it in my coat pocket. "I got a call from a Dan Stephens. He said my brother Noah was here."

"That's our pastor. He's in his office right over there." He pointed to a brown door.

We knocked, but when he told us to come in, I didn't see Noah anywhere. Fear gripped me that he'd run off again.

After our introductions, Dan stared out the indoor window that looked into the auditorium. "Noah is out there singing. Our director is keeping an eye on him."

"Thank you! I really appreciate you looking out for him and calling me."

"I'm glad we reached you. The other two numbers on his card don't seem to work."

"The problem is, all they do is work," I grumbled.

Ivy held my hand as we slipped into a packed auditorium, and an usher found us a spot in the fifth row back. Red carpet ran down the middle between two sets of pews and continued onto a stage where people in white robes sang "Silent Night".

Noah stood out in his blue winter coat, but he clapped in rhythm to the music as he swayed back and forth. They sang five more songs, and the pastor went to the front. Dan put a microphone to his mouth and spoke for a while.

When he got to the conclusion, he gestured to the back of the church. "Be sure to check out the Christmas cards from our missionaries on your way out. Some have specific needs you can pray for or donate to."

Ivy and I made our way to Noah as the church was dismissed.

My brother jumped up and down as he saw me. "You found me!"

I threw my arms around him. "You can't run off like that, Noah. Anything could have happened to you."

"I needed to get my Christmas wish."

I pulled back and kept my hands on his shoulders to keep his attention. "You still can't, Noah. It's freezing outside, and you don't know where you're going!"

He flinched and looked at the ground. "I'm sorry, Bo." Tears streamed down his face, and his lip trembled.

I yanked him back into a hug. "I'm sorry. You scared me. I'm sorry."

He cried against me for a little while, then wiped his eyes. "Can we look at the Christmas cards?"

"Only if you promise to never leave by yourself again."

He nodded. "Okay. I promise."

We went back to the bulletin board, where Bo asked me to read all of the cards to him. I read most of them and had him do the last three. We stared at the cards for a while longer, and as I stood there, an idea popped into my head.

Ivy's gaze burned into my neck. "What are you thinking?"

"I think I know how to help the orphans."

"That's awesome. How?"

I shook my head. "I need to think it through a little more."

The wheels in my head turned as we exited the church and returned home. Ivy left to hers, but promised to come over tomorrow afternoon.

Noah plopped onto the stool in front of the kitchen island. "We need to make cookies for Santa."

I hung up both our coats and pulled all the ingredients out. Despite his usual protests, I had Noah measure all the ingredients again. It took a lot longer than if I'd done it myself, but the more skills I could teach him, the better he'd be in the long run. It was what big brothers were supposed to do.

He stuck his nose in the fridge. "We have no carrots for the reindeer. Santa is going to think we are bad planners."

I reached around him and grabbed several oranges. "I heard reindeer love oranges even better."

He squinted one eye. "You sure?"

"Yeah." I peeled the oranges while we waited for the cookies to bake.

With the time we had left, I helped Noah get ready for bed. Once the cookies were cool enough, we decorated them and set them on a table by the fireplace with a hand-drawn card from Noah and the oranges. I read him four stories, and he fell asleep before I finished the last one. I went to wait in the oversized chair next to my front door for my parents to get home. My cell phone showed they still hadn't called me back. I'd finally had enough.

Chapter Thirty-One

My mother walked through the door first. She removed her shoes and hung up her coat before she saw me sitting in the chair, staring at her.

Her arm went to her chest. "Goodness, Boaz. You startled me."

"Do you ever check your voicemails?"

"Yes, as a matter of fact, I did, and I don't appreciate the ones you left."

My jaw tightened. "I don't appreciate having a mother who doesn't care about my brother and me."

Her eyes looked set on fire. "I've had enough of your attitude and disrespect. It's not going to continue in this house."

"That's fine, because I'm moving out."

"No, you're not. You're sixteen."

My dad walked in and stomped snow off his boots. He glanced between my mom and me. "What's going on?"

"Our son thinks he's moving out at sixteen." My mother crossed her arms the way she always did. The way she continually closed herself off to me and everything around her.

My eyes met theirs. "Do either of you realize Noah walked

out of day camp today because he didn't want to be there? He wanted to see Santa. Are either of you aware of that?"

"Yes, we're aware. I called the camp as soon as I got out of my meeting and got the messages. They said you found him and were taking him home."

Dad nodded. "Same. He was found, so the crisis was averted."

I stared at the floor, trying to focus my mind. "It was twelve degrees out, and Noah walked out of his day camp because he wanted to do Christmas things on Christmas Eve. You couldn't even mail his letter to Santa. I did that. I did that like I do everything for him. "

My mother scowled. "Yes, you do everything for him. That's why all you've done since you returned is lay in bed. You really have done so much for your brother. We have to work, Boaz. How do you think you have a roof over your head and all the nice things you have? Noah gets to go to the best day camp in the city because we work."

"They let him walk out the door! Are you both out of your minds? If you didn't work so much, he wouldn't have to go to day camp at all! You're missing out on his life. On my life. But that doesn't matter, does it? You already buried me. I'm dead to you. I don't exist, so you can keep working like that will matter when you get old and retire. You'll sit around doing nothing and realize you are alone because you never made any time for your kids. It was so easy for you to have a memorial service for me because you basically stopped noticing my existence years ago. I'm done with both of you. I'm moving out, and as soon as I have a stable job and place, I'm coming for Noah."

My parents gaped. My dad's eyes were wide while my mother's narrowed.

She put her keys in the bowl by the door and stepped into her slippers. "Go ahead and move out. Maybe it'll give you some gratitude for all we've done for you. You're not taking Noah."

"Why do you even care? You shove him off on others the first chance you get. He makes you food because he wants you to notice him. You say one or two sentences about how lovely it is, and then you go on your way. Like that made you a good mom. You're a terrible mom." My gaze shot to my dad. "You're a terrible dad. I don't want your money. I never did. I'll spend Christmas with Noah, and then I'm gone. That won't be much of a loss to either of you. Merry Christmas." I stormed out of the room, ignoring my parents' yells.

I gave my leg its morning rub as though I thought it would truly ebb the pain. It felt a little better than yesterday. The sun hadn't made an appearance yet, and to my surprise, neither had Noah. I checked on him first and found him sleeping peacefully, clutching his Ninja Turtle doll close. He deserved so much better than he got. His room was decked out from floor to ceiling, but he really needed people.

The glow of the television bounced off the walls in dull-colored shapes. My dad sat in his chair watching the screen that displayed my seventh birthday.

He glanced over and paused the TV. "Hey, could you come here a minute?"

I shut the fridge but stayed planted. "I think I'm good. Someone needs to make Christmas breakfast for Noah."

He came over and got a pan and bowl from the cupboard. "You're right. Why don't we do it together."

"Like I said, I'm good." I reopened the fridge and gathered the ingredients to make an omelet and pancakes.

My dad grabbed the measuring cups and utensils. "Somewhere along the way, I lost sight of what's important."

"You think?"

"Yes, I do."

"Why did you guys even have Noah and me?" I pulled out the griddle from a bottom cupboard and let it warm.

"The day you were born, it was a blizzard. A late spring one, right before summer. It was unexpected. I was stuck at work."

I mixed the pancake batter together and shook my head. "Big surprise there."

"Yeah, I deserved that, but back then, I ended up taking three buses and walking six blocks in blinding snow to reach the hospital to be there." He cracked some eggs into a bowl and stirred.

"I guess I must have been a disappointment for you never to make that kind of effort again."

He sprinkled cheese, seasoning, and milk as he seemed to ponder his next words for a few minutes. "You're right. Somewhere along the way, it became normal not to fight everything to get there when you needed me. You've always seemed so independent, Boaz. We never had to worry about you getting in trouble or struggling in school. You've always done everything you were supposed to, and then Noah came along, and you jumped right in and helped. That continued. You seemed to enjoy hanging out with him. Day after day, I grew to think you could handle things, and I could work more."

I poured the first of the batter onto the griddle. "That doesn't explain why you didn't care I was lost for weeks. It doesn't explain why you guys were so quick to throw a memorial service for me."

He stopped his movement, holding the large pan above the burner. "That's what you think? You think we didn't care?"

"I know you didn't. It took you days to see me when I came back. You dropped nothing. You buried me with no body after a month. A month was how long you held out hope I'd come back. Noah goes missing too, and you don't even rush home to see with your own eyes that he's okay. Yeah, that's exactly what I think."

He poured the egg mixture into the pan and stared off as he stirred. We fixed the rest of breakfast in silence. I made Noah's pancake into a reindeer by putting a small one on top of a larger one to make the snout. Whip cream and chocolate chips created the face, and bacon made the antlers. I tore off smaller pancake pieces and shaped ears.

Noah ran out from the living room. "Santa came! Bo! Santa came!"

"I know. Look what he left for breakfast."

His eyes widened at my creation. "Take a picture of me with it."

I grabbed my cellphone from my back pocket and snapped several pictures of Noah posing with his pancake. Mom walked out in her pink bathrobe and poured herself some of the coffee my dad had just finished making. She retreated to the living room to scroll through her phone and sip her mug.

Noah took her a plate. "Mom, you need breakfast."

She set her phone next to her and accepted the food. "Thank you, honey. This looks delicious."

"Bo made it. Can we open presents now?"

Dad had disappeared, and I figured he was on a business call in his study. I brought in the little box I'd wrapped yesterday and handed it to Noah.

He ripped up the paper and scrunched his nose. "You got me a piece of paper. Oh... Thanks, Bo. I will hang it on my wall."

"I overnighted your letter to Santa. That's the receipt that shows I did."

Noah's confused eyes lit up, and he ran to hug me. "Thank you, Bo! Thank you! This is the best present ever. I'm going to go get tape and stick it on my wall." He ran off, leaving me alone with our mother.

The tension seeped into the room, filling the space between my mother and me with an awkward heaviness that I'd never noticed before but thought had existed much longer than today. It was as though my mother had pretended well to love and want me, but when I went missing, that was too much of an effort to keep up her performance. How she treated me was all I had ever known, and it didn't seem strange until something as giant as my disappearance happened.

Noah came out from the back. "Dad said I could open presents without him."

I kept my mouth shut as Noah dashed under the tree and ripped open all the gifts with his name on them. He lifted each one to show me, and I snapped pictures with my phone as he posed. Mom sipped her coffee with a stiff expression. She kept glancing at her phone like she expected an important call any second.

Noah jiggled a small box with blue penguin wrapping paper. "This one is for you, Bo. It's the only one. Santa must have put you on the wrong list. Be careful; it might be coal."

I opened it and glanced up at my mother. "An Ikea gift card?"

"Yes, for your dorm room in the fall. You can go pick up whatever you want. They have them on the east coast too. This is what us working affords you," she said.

"Except. You didn't listen. I'm not going east to school."

She opened her mouth, but my dad stepping into the room made her close it again.

He handed Mom, Noah, and me pieces of paper with an itinerary to Miami. "It's time we go on a trip as a family."

Mom set the paper on the end table next to her. "We go on a trip every year."

"We're going to amusement parks. Together. We're going to stick with the boys this time."

"This is for March. They have school. We have work."

"It's two weeks. One of which will be their Spring break."

Mom stood up and walked toward the hall. "Can I speak with you?"

My parents went to their bedroom while Noah played with his new remote-control car. Their shouting volume carried all the way to the living room, but the words were muffled. I moved into the hall to hear their conversation. Normally, when they argued, I ignored it, but today I wanted to hear my mom's reasoning for not going on the trip.

"I've tried for almost seventeen years. It's too much anymore!" Mom shouted.

"They're your sons!"

"That *you* wanted. I wanted a career."

"It took both of us! You should have never agreed," Dad snapped.

"You threatened to leave me!"

"Because I wanted kids. If you didn't want them that badly, you should have let me leave!"

"Like you want them either! You work just as much as me." Mom's voice had gone high-pitched, almost to a screech.

"We've failed."

I went back to find Noah, no longer wanting to hear the rest of the conversation. Hearing my mother never wanted me didn't sit in my head as I'd expected. I felt numb. Probably because I'd processed it years ago. My dad had said I was so independent. The more I thought about it, the more I realized I'd always tried to do what I thought they wanted because maybe then they'd spend time with me. It had never worked, and eventually, it just became who I was. Someone who stayed out of the way and did what they were supposed to.

Chapter Thirty-Two

My mom dropped me off at Boaz's house after we opened presents and had Christmas dinner. I texted him my arrival, and he met me on the porch.

His arms went around my waist, and he buried his nose in my hair. "I've missed you."

"I'm not convinced. You're going to have to prove it."

"Am I now?"

"Yeah."

His lips froze less than an inch from mine, making me tingle as he teased me. Excitement buzzed through me as he showed me mercy and pressed his lips to mine. He drew things out, soft and slow while he ran his hand under my coat. I deepened our kiss and hurried our movements along. He caught up to my rhythm until we became breathless.

He rested his forehead against mine. "Told you I missed you."

"You can remind me anytime."

He grabbed my hand and led me inside, where Noah bounded for me, nearly knocking me over.

He hugged me tightly. "You came back!"

"Yep, I couldn't miss Christmas with you." I pulled out the present I'd wrapped with the Ninja Turtles wearing Santa hats.

He ripped it open and pumped his fist in the air. "A Ninja Turtle hoodie! I can wear this all the time. You see this, Bo. Ivy knew what to get me."

Boaz squeezed my hand. "She's pretty smart."

"You are the smartest, Ivy! Thank you!" He put the hoodie over his green Christmas pajamas. "Are you going to show her the surprise now? It's pretty, but I didn't touch it. Bo worked hard on it."

"Then I need to see it right now. I can't take it anymore."

Noah ran off to his room, and Boaz led me to his basement, where we used to make forts as children. The place he folded paper and told me stories. White icicle lights illuminated the basement. There appeared to be hundreds strewn across the ceiling, like stars in a cloudless sky. White sheets were propped up across the room. Little shadows swung back and forth behind the white canopies.

I soaked in the enchanting sight and caught Boaz's eyes that somehow looked bright in the low lighting. "You're going to tell me a story."

He shrugged, not giving me confirmation. "You'll have to find out."

He lifted a flap, and I stepped inside where folded paper dangled from clothespins attached to colorful yarn. There was space that weaved a path between the twirling shapes. I stopped at the first one. It had a school bus, and a boy held a girl's hand. Boaz had even folded tiny backpacks to hang on their backs and lunch boxes clutched in their palms. The bus had a folded red heart jammed in the door.

Boaz kissed my temple. "Open all the hearts."

I took the first note and opened it.

Dear Ivy,

Remember our first day of kindergarten? I was scared to get on the bus. Tommy Barth said I was a coward, and you shoved him in a mud puddle. You screamed at him and said everyone was scared of something. People who say they aren't are liars. I fell in love with you that day. You held my hand the entire time we were on the bus. I miss riding the bus with you.

A dog stood with its mouth open. Boaz had folded the tiny detail of its sharp teeth. The dog had his paws on a fence, and on the other side was a tree with a gaping girl. A boy had his arms reaching for her. On one branch hung the heart.

Dear Ivy,

Like you said, everyone is afraid of something, and your fear got you stuck up a tree. That was the day I realized I not only loved you but wanted to protect you. Why did I stop keeping my promise to keep you safe? Will we ever talk to each other again?

A fox and a frog sat with their arms around each other, staring up at the moon. A rocket sat next to them that balanced a heart on top.

Dear Ivy,

The moon is full tonight, and I can't stop thinking of all those stories I used to tell you. Your favorite was always the fox and the frog. Two very different friends who stayed loyal through everything. I expected that to be us. I miss you.

A birthday cake and a teddy bear hung side by side. Two kids fishing, watching the stars on a hill and catching grasshoppers in a field made the next section. Remnants of our childhood hung as paper shapes. Each had its own note and was followed up by ones from being lost in the wilderness. A mountain, bear, shack, a campfire, and forest created scene after scene with their own notes. Toward the back were us kissing on the porch, throwing snowballs, and cuddling with mugs on a bench. I moved through time with the letters, not always in order, but I read each one.

Dear Ivy,

I heard you sing for the first time today, and I'm pretty sure that's what the angels sounded like when they were happy about baby Jesus being born. Mrs. Brown looked happy about it, too. I don't think you're supposed to sing that well when you're eight.

Dear Ivy,

Today I picked dandelions for you behind my house and was going to ride my bike to your house. But my mom told me they were weeds. I threw them away and rode to your house, anyway. Your mom didn't like me cutting the roses off her bushes, but it was worth it to see your face.

Dear Ivy,

You're prettier than my dad's new car. Don't tell him I said that. It's true, but he really loves his car. I have to go to camp for the summer because my mom said so. I'm scared to tell you. Pop said I should give you a compliment before I tell you. I think telling you you're pretty might scare you. I think I'll tell you I'll miss your eyes because it's the thing I see the most when we talk.

Dear Ivy,

I woke up to you in my arms last night. We're stuck out in this wilderness, and I keep thinking back to you, stuck in that tree and how I promised to protect you. I'm scared I can't do that here, but I'll keep you as warm as I can in this freeze.

Dear Ivy,

You spinning in your pink dress does things to my chest and makes it so I can't breathe right. I'm not sure that's supposed to happen when I look at my best friend, but it did. You cried when Howard spilled punch on your dress, but it was still one of the most beautiful things I'd ever seen. Second only to your smile and happy eyes. That's why I told you a stupid joke. I wanted to make you smile.

Dear Ivy,

I sat in the back row during your concert because your singing always makes me cry. I couldn't let the guys see that. Don't be mad at me. I'm not ashamed of you like you thought.

I'm ashamed of myself. Well, I was until Pop told me music makes him cry, too. That must mean I'm like him, and I like that. He's not my grandpa, but he spends more time with me than any of my family. It feels like he's my grandpa and lets me call him Pop. He's also wise. Your voice is a good reason to cry. That sounds wrong, but I think you know what I mean.

Dear Ivy,

Sometimes it feels like nothing will be right again with you gone. We go to the same school. I still write you a letter every day, but you hate me. I'm not sure why, and I can't wrap my head around why we stopped talking.

Dear Ivy,

You infuriate me! I've never been so angry in my life and thought about slashing your tires. I know I would have just bought you new ones and changed them for you. It was a nice daydream. Despite everything, I wouldn't be disappointed if we got to be partners on the nature trip. Maybe you'll finally tell me what I did to earn you sabotaging me at every turn.

Dear Ivy,

I kept the dumbest promise I've ever made. The one where I said I would stay away from you when we were rescued. My bed feels so empty now. I'd never known I was completely alone until I lost you again. I love the way your nose scrunches when you're angry at me and the way you shove me away and pull me back in the same breath. Not having you close feels like insanity. The frigid forest showed me what it was like to have you back, and I sit here, alone, keeping the dumbest promise I've ever made. In a world that's much too loud, I can't find peace away from you.

Dear Ivy,

Do you know how people always say they could die happy? I finally understand that after you kissed me. I'd given up hoping we could patch things up, and you barreled in like gasoline set on fire. We lost all control as we fell, and it was the best thing that could have happened. For all the times I wished to kiss you, you blew my imagination away. You always make everything better than I expect it to be.

Dear Ivy,

My heart is broken because yours is. That's what happens when the person you love is in pain. I wish death hadn't taken Pop. As I watched over you while you grieved by his grave, I was overwhelmed with the need to shield you from everything that would make you hurt that bad. While that is not possible, I will do my best to always walk through the sad, scary, dark things of life with you. While I can't protect you from pain, you won't have to face it alone. That feels like what love is. Facing monsters, grief, cold, and darkness together. It feels like in the good and bad, we stick together. We hold each other, and we live with all we have. I love you, Ivy. I've never stopped. I've loved you every day since you held my hand on a bus. That love had nowhere to go, so I wrote you a letter a day to let you know. I wrote them long before I understood why. My feelings for you have never been able to stay inside.

At the end of all his origami artwork rested five more boxes full of red heart letters. My tears slid down my face, and I left them because my emotions needed to pour out at this moment.

I sat down and removed all the lids to take in the large amount of letters, all folded with my name written on each one. "Did you really write me a letter every day?"

He dropped to his knees next to me. "I did for the most part. I couldn't while we were lost until we found that paper. I kept them in my pocket until I got home. Some during our feud were pretty angry, but it was clear I still loved you through all of it. Only it wasn't apparent until I looked back over them."

I launched at him, knocking him back onto the carpet. He held me as we fell together, surrounded by our paper memories.

Chapter Thirty-Three

For Christmas evening, we went to a festival. An extensive park had been transformed by thousands of colorful lights. Fairy tale, Christmas, and other familiar characters comprised wooden cutouts framed in lights. Many blinked off and on in a way that made them look animated.

Ivy snuggled next to me as I drove past each one, and Noah had his eyes glued out his window. He gasped every so often at a display. The main reason I'd brought him along happened at the end, where Santa waited with a present for all the kids.

Noah barely waited for me to stop before he hopped out of my truck. "Santa! Bo, I can't believe this! He's still working after last night."

I helped Ivy to the ground and locked our fingers together. "He got all his work done, so he wanted to get some pictures with people who appreciated the things he brought them."

We got in line, and Noah couldn't sit still. He bounced around and swayed until we got to the front. He put his arm around Santa, and I took pictures of them side by side.

Noah grinned and patted Santa's back. "Thank you for all

the presents and helping my brother's leg feel better so he could drive me here today."

Ivy disappeared and returned with hot cocoa for our trek home. When we got back, she read Noah his stories while I went to rest my leg. I'd done a good job of hiding my pain from Noah, so he would think Santa granted his wish.

Ivy came back into the room and crawled up next to me. Her head rested against my chest, and I ran my fingers over her back. We laid there, doing nothing for a while.

"Do you want your present?" she asked.

I kissed her head. "I already have my present in my arms."

She kissed me, deepening it until it snapped me wide awake. I slid up to sit and pulled her onto my lap.

I kissed down her neck. "I like this present."

She laughed and got off my bed. "It's not your present."

I groaned. "It's the only one I need."

"You can have more of that later, but for now, here's this? It's not even close to the level your gift to me was, but it has a point to it." She handed me a blue present.

I opened it up to find a leather journal with an intricate design etched along the edges. Next to it rested old-fashioned pens and inks. "Wow! This is amazing."

"You told me you quit writing after we got back from the wilderness. Now I know you still wrote a few love letters to me, but I hope you can start writing things again for yourself like you used to. It's so much of who you are. You said your feelings for me were too much to keep inside, but I don't think that stops at me. I got you a journal because even if you can't write for anyone else, I hope you can for yourself."

"I love it. This is perfect. You're right. There's been a lot I've kept inside. That I always keep inside, but this will help keep the pressure off. I can write my thoughts without anything getting in the way." I set the journal on my nightstand and gave her a drawn-out kiss to thank her.

When our kiss concluded, she sunk back down onto my chest, putting her legs between mine. "Are you ever going to tell me your plan for the orphans?"

"I'm still working on typing out the idea and thinking it through. There's something I want you to know. I think that even though I personalized all those love letters for people to give to those they liked, I was writing the words to you. I think that's why they worked because it was my feelings for you. People could feel they were genuine, and I made the mistake of letting others think they were meant for them."

"Boaz..."

"No, it's okay because I realize it now, and that means I can do something about it. I've figured exactly what I need to do to help the orphans the right way."

"Okay. What is it? I can't handle the suspense." She sat up and stared at me.

"Well, I don't think my idea was too off from what I need to do. The problem was the personalization. I got really good at making people think that the one who gave them the letter wrote it. It was too handmade. Too personal. The person giving them should have been the one to make it real."

"Okay. I agree that was the biggest problem with it. How are you going to modify it?"

I brought over my laptop and turned the screen toward her. "The greeting card industry makes eight to nine billion dollars a year. I want to keep writing love notes but print them and sell them premade. I can add my origami into it for fancier cards. We get a website, sell in local stores and even around school. Everyone knows what's printed on the card is created by the store. People can write what they want in them, but the words in pen will be theirs."

"I love it, Boaz. What if we talked to Principal Reynolds about doing a Valentine's banquet for startup costs?"

"If not, I bet we'll sell a ton around that time."

"I can't fold paper like you, but I can help you with whatever else you need," I said.

I laid back down and pulled her with me. "You want to do this with me?"

"I do. Your big heart is going to do amazing things, and I want to be there to watch things happen."

We sunk under my blanket and kissed awhile.

I ran my fingers over her upper arm, making her shudder. "I'm moving out."

"What? When?"

"This week."

She propped herself up to meet my eyes. "Where are you going to go? How is this even possible?"

"I talked to Phil. He's going to let me stay at his house until I can get on my feet." I told her everything that had happened since I'd gotten back.

Her face flew through varying emotions, but she remained silent to the end.

She snuggled in closer and kissed my chest. "I don't even know what to say. I'm so sorry, Boaz."

I shrugged. "It is what it is."

She held me, and I played with her hair. We spent most of the evening in bed, cuddling. Her mom arrived, and she left. I packed my bags. In the morning, I would tell Noah, which would be the toughest part.

I woke up extra early and got everything for pancakes ready before getting Noah up. He bounded out to make breakfast with me and measured all the ingredients as I directed him.

I flipped the first pancake. "There's something I need to tell you, Noah."

He lined up four plates on the counter. "What is it?"

"I'm leaving."

"Okay. I'm going to camp today. I'm leaving too."

"No, I'm going to live somewhere else." I took the first set of pancakes off the grill.

"You can't do that. You're my brother. We have to live together. That's what brothers do. Mom and dad won't like that either."

We finished getting breakfast ready, and Noah continued to tell me reasons I couldn't move out. My parents came out of their room in their business attire. The day after Christmas, it was back to work.

Noah slid a plate to our mom. "Mom. Dad. Bo says he's moving out. "

My dad's head snapped up. "You're not still thinking that, are you?"

I nodded. "I'm packed and have a place to stay."

Mom scrolled through her phone. "You'll be back in a week with an apology. This will be a good lesson for you. Don't expect your cell phone to be paid for. I'll be calling today to take you off. That'll give you about a week before it shuts off. I'll expect you back then."

Dad's fork dropped to his plate. "Let's talk this through."

Mom sent Dad an icy glare. "This will be an excellent lesson for him."

I cleaned up breakfast and got my suitcase from my room.

Noah clung to me as we hugged goodbye. "Don't leave, Bo! Don't leave me!"

"We'll still see each other. For now, I need to do this," I said.

My mom looked in the mirror as she put her earrings in. "Let's go, Noah!"

My brother's lip trembled. "Bo."

"I'll see you soon." I watched as he slipped out the door and sent me one last look that dissolved my composure.

I limped to my truck and drove to Phil's.

Phil was a little too happy I'd moved into his house. He had plenty of room, and his dad said I could stay if I helped in his glass shop. He'd pay me hourly and deduct rent from my paychecks. The only downside was Phil constantly wanted to play chess or Xbox with me. He endlessly asked me girl advice, and I kept my irritation locked in as much as possible. Part of me hoped my suggestions would work, and Phil would get a girlfriend to save my sanity.

Phil moved his body in swift movements to copy his avatar on the screen in front of us. "Are you sure about holding doors open for girls? I once got shoved for holding a door open for a girl."

"I'm going to let you in on a secret. Although, it really shouldn't be a secret at this point, since I have told you quite a few times."

He paused the game and leaned toward me. "Okay. I'm ready this time. You have my full attention."

"Not all the girls are the same. What one girl likes another might hate."

"How can you tell the difference?"

"You pay attention and don't assume you know what she likes. If you aren't sure about something, ask her."

He gasped. "Talk to her?"

I narrowed my eyes. "Why would you not talk to her?"

"As soon as my mouth opens, girls run. That's why your

letters always worked well. I'd hand them the letter. It made them love me, and I'd ask them to pizza."

"Okay, so you talked to them. At what point did they run?"

He started our game back up. "When we sat down to eat and started a conversation."

"What do you tell them?"

He shrugged one shoulder. "I gave them interesting facts."

My eyebrows shot up. "What facts? Give me an example."

"My favorite is to point out that Lego people live in houses made of the same things as their flesh."

My head jerked to the side. "What?"

"Lego people live in houses of their own skin. They are what their houses are."

"Alright. Give me another example."

"Flamingos bend their ankles and are standing on their tiptoes. You can't see their knees because they are close to their bodies and covered by feathers. Another is that roller coasters were invented to distract Americans from their sins. When I tell the girls that one, I grin and ask them if they would like me to distract them from their sins at the amusement park when it opens for the season."

My character died, and I put my controller up. "You can't see how any of that might be problematic?"

"No, why wouldn't they like to learn those things?"

"On your next date, try letting her tell you about herself, and then you tell her about you. Not in too much detail. Surface things like how many siblings you have and about your pet turtle. Small talk and give her a chance to speak. Save your facts for the second or third date and don't overdo it."

"You think that will work?"

"Yeah, I do." I answered my ringing phone. "Hey, hot stuff, how's it going?"

Ivy giggled. "What are your plans for New Year's?"

226

"I was hoping to be with you."

"We've been invited to a party, and we really need to go."

I stretched my leg out and gave it a rub. "Okay. Why?"

"It's Becca's party. I'm not sure anyone else is going to show up."

"Alright. Let's go then. Is it okay if I bring Phil?"

"Yeah, the more, the better."

We hung up, and Phil seemed a little too excited about the entire thing. He insisted he knew a lot of people who he could convince to come.

Chapter Thirty-Four

I wore a silver, flowing dress with a sweetheart neckline. The sleeves tipped to the edge of my shoulders, and the hem reached my knees. Nude tights kept my legs warm, and I completed the entire look with matching flats. I curled my hair, and Chloe did my makeup at her house.

"Boaz is going to love the smoky eye look." Chloe turned me around to face the mirror.

"He's not going to recognize me. I've never worn dramatic makeup in front of him before." I swished my dress, watching it move in the mirror. "It's great you're coming with me. I miss going to things with you."

Effie came out from the bathroom. "Do you think the ponytail is weird for the party?" She turned around.

"It's cute. I like it."

"Yep, it elongates your face in a good way," Chloe agreed.

Effie drove us in her red jeep, and I braced myself for us to be the only ones. Becca tried really hard to get people to like her, but it was excessive. It scared people away. We had to park a block away because of the abundant cars lining the streets, which made sense on New Year's Eve. There were probably a lot of parties happening in the neighborhood. Music flowed from Becca's brick two-story house. It looked like a dollhouse with double white doors that each had matching Christmas wreaths on them.

Several kids from school chatted on the lawn, holding red cups and beer cans. Chloe, Effie, and I made it inside, where Becca stood next to an entry closet, smiling.

She waved. "Welcome to my party! Can I take your coats? Get you a drink? The bathrooms are down the hall to your left. It might be full. If it is, just follow the blue footprints on the ground that will take you to the basement one. Red ones lead to refreshments. We have spin the bottle and other games happening in the family room. Follow the green and yellow for all the activities. Purple will take you to dancing."

I glanced at the floor to see construction paper feet going in all directions. "Don't you want to join the fun?"

"No, I just want to make sure everyone else is having fun. Tell your boyfriend thank you, by the way. He got his friend Phil to invite all these people."

Effie laughed. "Oh, that explains it."

I gave her an elbow nudge. "I'll let him know, Becca. Thank you for inviting us."

"You're welcome! Let me know if you need anything at all. I'm here to help." Becca hung up our coats and returned to her spot by her front door to greet the next guests.

I considered staying to convince her to enjoy her own party, but she strangely seemed to be by what she was doing. I glanced at my phone again to see if Boaz had texted me. He said they were at the pool table in the basement.

Chloe and Effie told me they wanted drinks and would meet me downstairs. I followed the blue footprints since Chloe said they led to the basement and found Boaz, Phil, and about five others gathered around the pool table.

Boaz leaned against the wall with a pool stick in his right

hand. His hair had its wild look, and I took a minute to enjoy the fact he was mine. It did things to me that propelled me forward.

His eyes widened at my approach, and his lips parted. It took him a few seconds to find words. "Wow!"

"Is it too much?"

He shook his head and pulled me to him by my waist. "You look perfect. Always perfect."

We kissed until everyone shouted at him to take his turn. He followed through, knocking in three solids. I slipped away to the bathroom, but as I opened the door, I slammed right into someone. Todd, the jerk that hurt Chloe, stood in front of me.

"Sorry. Excuse me," he said.

I kicked his shin as he moved past. "I'm not the one you owe an apology to."

He squinted and went on his way while I went into the bathroom and fumed. I closed my eyes to calm myself and avoid the urge to run back out to punch him. After I returned from the bathroom, Boaz studied me.

He squeezed my hand. "Are you alright?"

"Todd is here."

"Oh, and Chloe is too."

My eyes widened. "Oh, no!" I shot upstairs and pushed through the crowd that seemed to have doubled since I'd left the upstairs. I shoved through tightly spaced bodies into the kitchen. Effie sat on a counter, talking to a girl I thought was in my chem class.

"Effie, where is Chloe?" I asked.

"She went outside with Todd." She took a sip of her drink.

"She what?"

Effie pointed at the sliding glass doors. "Out there."

I rushed outside. Chloe and Todd stood under a black pergola next to a hot tub. It was freezing, and no one else was in the backyard. Chloe had her arms crossed as she glared at Todd. His back was turned, making it impossible to see his facial expressions. He touched her arm, and she jerked back.

"Look, I'm sorry, baby. That was stupid of me. I'll make it up to you." He took a step forward.

"How are you going to make it up to me? You convinced me to sleep with you. You said you loved me. I believed you. I believed all your words. Then one day later, you publicly humiliated me. Do you have any idea what that did to me? How that made me feel?"

"Why don't we get in the hot tub? I'll make it up to you."

"Did you hear anything I just said?"

"I heard." He stepped inches from her. "I said I'd make it up to you."

"You can't."

He grabbed her wrist and pinned her against a post. "Sure, I can."

I jumped out of my hiding spot. "Back off, Todd!"

He whirled around and glared. "We're having a private moment here."

"Let her go, or I'm going to give you a real private moment. Think about what I did to your shin elsewhere."

Tears fell down Chloe's cheeks. "Todd, just go!"

He snorted, releasing a sharp laugh. "No, this is between you and me. Your friend can make her way back into the party before I force her inside."

"Todd! Stop!" Chloe tried to yank her arm free. "You're hurting me."

I marched over. "Let her go."

"Get lost." He shoved me to the ground.

I jumped up to smack him when a shadow moved in front of me, and a cracking sound halted me.

"Ever touch Ivy or Chloe again, and you'll get more than a

broken nose." Boaz stood over Todd, looking the angriest I'd ever seen him.

It stunned me as I hadn't known that level of fury lived inside Boaz. Todd slammed into Boaz. They rolled around on the grass. The ruckus had drawn a crowd from inside. Punches landed back and forth.

Becca ran out, covering her mouth. "Oh, no! Let's talk about this, guys. We need to all use our words. It's important."

Todd got to his feet, and I screamed as he slammed his boot into Boaz's leg. My boyfriend cried out and crumpled into a heap. Todd moved toward him with wrath in his eyes. He slammed his boot into Boaz's head, and Boaz went limp.

Phil charged into the yard with a sword outstretched toward Todd. "Stand down before I enact the ancient ways of the samurai."

Todd cocked his head at Phil. "Like you really would."

Phil let out a battle cry and charged toward Todd. Todd's eyes grew, and he bolted. Phil chased him so that Todd had to climb over the privacy fence to escape.

I dropped to the ground. "Boaz!" Tears warmed my icy cheeks. "Boaz, answer me!" A black eye was forming on his left eye, and he didn't move an inch. "Someone, help!"

Becca stood next to me. "An ambulance is on the way." She looked up at Phil. "That was one of the hottest things I've ever seen."

Phil broke his stare at Boaz to meet Becca's eyes. "You think so?"

She smiled. "Yeah."

I held Boaz until the paramedics arrived and let me ride with him to the hospital.

He stirred in the ambulance and smiled. "You're the best thing to wake up to," he mumbled.

I cuddled next to Boaz in his ER bed, and we watched the Times Square ball about to drop on the TV. We counted down, and when it struck midnight, our lips met as he sweetly kissed me.

I gently touched by his back eye. "I'm sorry this happened. It shouldn't have happened. Thank you for stepping in like that."

"There's no universe in which I won't protect you."

My chest did flips. "You've always been good at that."

Our breathing steadied as we stared ourselves into another kiss. Throat clearing broke us apart.

The ER doctor stood at the foot of the bed. "Your parents are on their way."

Boaz tried to sit up. "What? No, that's not necessary."

"You're still a minor, which means we have to inform your parents, and they need to sign for your treatment. Is there a reason you don't want your parents here? Would you like to talk to a social worker?"

Boaz shook his head. "No, they work a lot, and I didn't want to bother them."

"I'm sure this is something they would want you to bother them over."

"Right."

The doctor left, and my mom texted me she'd arrived.

I kissed him and slid off the bed. "Call me if you need me at all."

"I'll be fine." He held my hand until I stepped too far away.

He sunk into his bed, and I disappeared out the door. I called Chloe as soon as I got home, but it went to her voice-mail. I called Effie next, and she picked up right away.

"Hey, Effie, did Chloe get home okay?"

"Yeah, I'm with her now, but she's sleeping. How's Boaz?"

I crawled under my covers. "He's okay. Has a mild concussion. They're going to do an MRI on his leg to see why he's still having so much pain. Other than that, he's okay."

"Todd got arrested. A few people gave witness statements against him."

"Good. I hope something comes of it."

We hung up, and I called Boaz. "Hey, are you still okay?"

"Yeah, they're going to keep me overnight and do the MRI when the tech gets here in the morning."

"Alright. I miss you."

"I miss you too." He sighed as we hung up.

Now that I was in my own bed, all the events exhausted me and led to fast sleep. It had been a crazy New Year's, but hopefully, now, Todd would get some of what he deserved.

Chapter Thirty-Five

The techs woke me up early for my MRI, and then I got taken back to my room for breakfast. Despite the doctor saying my parents were on their way, I had yet to see them. It didn't shock me because it was the one thing I could count on from them.

Police interrupted my breakfast and took my statement. I was angry and hadn't realized how much rage had boiled inside me until the moment I'd broken Todd's nose. He'd used my words to hurt my friend. I was angry at myself for writing Chloe such a personal letter and violating our friendship in that way. My rage was strong against Todd. He used words I wrote to bring Chloe happiness to hurt her in one of the worst possible ways.

I'd followed Ivy out of the basement and lost her in the crowd. When Effie directed me outside, what I'd seen released my built-up rage. Todd had Chloe pinned, and then he shoved Ivy. I'd punched him in a blur. The entire fight had blurred. Todd pinpointed the general area of my gunshot wound some-how, which shot the nerve pain through me. It disarmed me enough to let him stomp on my head. I pushed my empty tray to the side and reached for my TV remote. The door swung open, and my dad stood on the other side.

He stopped in the doorway. "Is it okay if I come in?"

"Yeah, have a seat if you want."

He scooted a purple plastic chair over to my bed. "I don't like seeing you here again, bud."

"Sure."

"Did the doctor say anything? Like if you can go home?"

"Yeah, I have a minor concussion and had an MRI on my leg to make sure it's healing okay."

Dad's jaw looked tight, and he nodded, staring at the floor. "Your mom and I came to see you last night, but you were sleeping."

"You had to sign consents, right?"

"I wanted to make sure you were okay. I'm worried about you, Boaz."

I snickered. "Sure, you are."

"They said you got in a fight."

"The guy deserved it."

Dad met my eyes. "I have no doubt he did. Do you want to talk about it?"

"Not with you. You didn't have to come back. I'm not sure why you did."

"For starters, I've been worried about you. The police also want to know if we want to press charges."

I furrowed my brow. "I hit him first."

Dad looked around as though to see if anyone heard. "I was told it was self-defense."

"Not self. I was defending Ivy and Chloe. The guy wouldn't let go of Chloe's arm, and he shoved Ivy to the ground."

"Then the guy has everything he gets coming to him. I'm proud of you. You turned into such a great kid. I know that wasn't because of your mom and me. I know we failed, Boaz.

Like I told you on Christmas, I depended on your responsible behavior too much and let the years go by without a second thought. I can't change that, but I'd like to see if we can build a relationship from here on out."

I picked at the fuzz on my blanket. "Why now? If my disappearance and memorial service didn't wake you up to all of this, why now?"

His shoulders slumped. "I don't know."

"That clears it all up, then. I'm not going home."

"I'm not going to ask you to come home. It's not something I feel I should ask at this point. My thoughts were we could spend time together once a week for now. Whatever you want to do."

I shrugged. "Maybe if you'll bring Noah with you. I'll do it for him."

"Okay." He pulled a phone from his pocket. "Here's a new phone, so I can call you about it. Since your old one will be shutting off in the next day or so."

"What about Mom?"

"She doesn't need to know." My dad signed my discharge papers while he was there.

The doctor released me and said they saw nerve damage on the MRI and to continue with physical therapy. I didn't mention that wasn't possible anymore since I'd moved out on my own. He also suggested I could get some injections that might help. For now, I'd have to not worry about it.

Phil picked me up from the hospital. "I got a date!"

I glanced at a text from Ivy. "On your own?"

"Yeah, I'm surprised too."

"Who is it?"

"Becca."

My eyes shifted to the left. "Becca Summers?"

"Yeah! She thought my samurai sword act was hot."

"I'm not sure I want to know."

He pulled into his driveway. "It's great too because we already talked for hours, and she still wanted to go on a date with me."

"How did that happen?"

"After all that excitement happened with you, everyone left. No one stayed to help her clean up. She said it was okay because she loves to clean up after people, but it still didn't seem right. I told her so many facts, and she told me they were all interesting. She liked that I knew so much and called me smart. She's so pretty too. I'm not sure how I got so lucky."

"That's great, Phil. I'm happy for you."

❦

My mom had blocked me from seeing Noah and took me off the pickup list at his school. She was doing it to punish me, but that didn't anger me. The fact it hurt Noah angered me. To get around her rules, I brought him lunch and waited on a bench inside the cafeteria. He walked in with his arm around one of his friends.

"Noah! Noah!" I called.

His head whipped around until his eyes landed on me. He ran across the room, threw himself against me, and shook. "I missed you, Bo! I missed you so much! You left for so long. I don't like that."

"I don't like it either. We can eat lunch together." I wiggled the paper bag next to him. "How does subs sound?"

"I love it! Thank you, Bo!"

For the next two weeks, I brought Noah lunch every day. My dad had texted and called me, but so far, I'd turned down his requests. One day, he sent me a text, pleading with me to meet him at a café, and I finally agreed. I met him for dinner and found him in a corner booth. We stayed quiet until after we ordered our food.

My dad fidgeted with his fork. "Your mom left."

"Left where?"

"She left me. Packed up and moved out."

I gaped and stared for a few seconds. "Why?"

"Things haven't been good for a while. Years, really. I threw myself into work, and it made everything seem good. If I could work, I could deny reality. I've been thinking about what you asked me about how I acted when you were found. I kept working because I had an important meeting. I should have rushed home, but I didn't. That's something I will regret. It made me realize I've been using work to tell myself things are fine while my family falls apart."

"So, because you were in denial, you kept working instead of dropping everything after you found out your missing son was actually alive."

His gaze dropped to the table. "I have no excuse. All I know is that when you said you were moving out, and then you did, the thought of losing you again woke me up. The idea of experiencing that pain again became real. There's nothing I can do about the past, but I hope you will give me a chance to prove myself and that you'll come home."

I folded a napkin into a swan, thinking over his words. "I don't know. There's less stress where I am now. Less conflict. You and Mom are always fighting. She may have moved out. What if she comes right back, and the fights start right back up?"

"Noah misses you. If you can't come back for me, can you for him?"

I started on my second napkin swan. He had me there. If the conflict was gone, there was no reason to stay away. There was no reason to further traumatize Noah with my absence.

"Okay. But I'm not going east for college. I don't expect you to pay for any of it, but I'm not going."

He nodded. "We can talk about it as it gets closer."

"Don't expect me to change my mind."

"Okay."

The waitress brought our food, and we ate most of it in silence.

♥

"You sure this is a good idea?" Noah stared at Mandy, who was eating one of the cookies I'd help him make for karaoke night at the playhouse.

Kids were enjoying snacks, and the songs were set to start in fifteen minutes. It gave him plenty of time to ask her if she would sit with him at the ice cream social next week.

I plugged in the sound system and made sure the lights came on. "The worst thing that will happen is she'll tell you no. If you don't ask her, it's the same thing. She won't sit with you if you don't ask her. You might as well see if she will."

"How do I look?" He grinned with his hands in the pockets of his Ninja Turtle hoodie.

"You look great. Go for it."

He let out a loud breath. "Okay. Okay. I'm doing this. It's happening. It's happening."

I watched as he went over to her and said something that made her gawk at him. My chest sunk a little as she shook her head. Noah laughed, and I narrowed my eyes to determine what was really happening. She laughed and nodded. Then it happened.

She gave him a kiss on the cheek and winked dramatically before walking away.

Noah pumped his fist in the air and ran back over to me.

"Did you see that, Bo?"

I gave him a fist bump. "I take it that it went well."

"She said she would sit by me at the ice cream social if I pick a new song tonight."

"Are you going to?"

He scrunched his nose. "Duh. I'd pick a new song every week for her. It's true love."

I turned away to avoid him seeing me laugh. "You might want to take it a bit slower. True love takes time."

"I've known her for so many years." He threw his hand up and down like he always did when he wanted to point out something he thought I'd gotten wrong.

"Okay. You better get to thinking of a song."

He hurried over to the song list and studied it intently. By the time it was his turn to sing, he'd picked one he never had before, and Mandy gave him thumbs up. When we got in the car to head home, he asked if we could listen to "Stand by Me" through my phone.

The song concluded, and he smiled. "That's still my song to you, Bo. Mandy doesn't have to know I still played it for you."

"My lips are sealed," I said.

"I'm glad you're back home. I miss Mom. Do you think she'll visit soon?"

"I'm not sure. She seems to really like work." As much as it hurt to be honest with Noah, I always would be in the gentlest way possible.

I'd moved back in with my dad and Noah two weeks ago, and so far, things were going well. Dad took Saturdays and Sundays off, and we did something both days each week. To my surprise, Dad had volunteered to help with the junior cooking classes at the playhouse, and he was teaching Noah how to cook some of his mother's recipes. Two weeks was too soon to know if it would be permanent, but it was a start.

Chapter Thirty-Six

I'd arrived extra early to find that Phil, Becca, Chloe, and Effie had gotten the decorations set up. Red, pink, and white burst everywhere. The tablecloths had hearts all over them and joined all the other testaments of love, like cupids and roses. The cupids had their golden arrows pointed at chairs as though our guests would be unable to escape love's impalement.

Rose petals blanketed the ground in front of an archway made of red heart balloons where people could get their picture taken in front of a beach sunset backdrop. Romance had exploded all over the banquet hall. Caterers brought in food that Boaz had talked a local Italian place into donating.

On the far wall was a silent auction with gift baskets put together by local businesses. They contained gift cards and other merchandise from each place. Boaz and I had gone around for a few weeks to collect the donations, and Boaz had done an excellent job of promoting it as a great way for the businesses to market.

The most important feature was the children's wall, where people could donate to a specific child or place a general contribution in the box at the end. The kids were the entire reason this was happening. Chloe was placing the preordered cards on the tables.

I laid my coat on our supply table and looked through the cards. "Are these what's left?"

"Yeah, two baskets, and we'll have them all in their spots," Chloe said.

Boaz had worked endlessly for weeks making cards to sell, and people preordered them from a website Phil had set up. Guests also had pre-purchased seats, so their cards and other gifts they'd bought for tonight could be laid out beforehand. Boaz had written a note on each item with buyer requests and where they needed to be placed. I finished the last bit and went down the hall to see if catering needed any help.

Becca turned bright red and pulled away from Phil, who she'd been kissing before I walked in. "Sorry. We should be helping. We're slacking, Phil, and shouldn't be making out when there is work to be done." She yanked him out of the room before I could assure her it was fine.

They had been dating for almost two months now, and things were going well. Both seemed happy and perfect for each other. I found Boaz directing where to put everything in the large commercial kitchen. The staff was cooking things fresh and serving it like in a restaurant.

I loved how his brow furrowed as he tried to solve the dilemma of whether to have the salad dressings on the tables in boats or serve them on each plate in tiny ceramic bowls. His hair looked controlled but didn't disappoint with the way it spiked up slightly from the gel he'd used to keep it in place. His lopsided smile that appeared when he noticed me made my stomach tumble. People had accumulated in the hall, and the kitchen was a buzz with staff. Boaz yanked me into the walk-in freezer.

I tugged on his tie to pull him to me. "This suit looks good on you. Like you're a spy or bodyguard."

He looked over my plum, knee-length dress. "Well, your dress is killing me in the best possible way."

We became lost in our kiss, pressing closer and quickening our pace. I screeched as my back bumped into the freezer wall. Boaz removed his jacket and put it around my shoulders while laughing.

After giving his suit jacket a delightful sniff, I gave him a playful shove. "You think it's funny that I now have back frostbite."

"With the way it made your face scrunch up, absolutely." He took a deep breath, and his mouth tightened.

"Hey, what's wrong?"

"My nerves were part of why I dragged you in here. You are the best distraction."

"You mean this?" I kissed him slowly until his shoulders relaxed.

"Yeah, that's exactly what I mean."

"This is your big night, but it's going to go perfectly. You've planned it well. It'll be great."

He rested his forehead against mine. "You're right. No matter what, it'll be good. Any amount of money raised will help. It'll be a good night. I guess we better get back out there."

"Tell me how I can help. That's what I reserved my entire night for. Support my boyfriend night."

He squeezed my hand and led me back out of the freezer. "Can you greet people and direct them to their seats? I'm going to make sure everything else is coming together."

"On it." I went to the entrance and spent the next thirty minutes giving people brochures and telling them where everything was.

The music started, and I slipped into the banquet room in time to see Boaz step onto the stage.

He picked up the microphone and paused a second to take in the very full room. "Thank you, everyone, for coming tonight. A little over a year ago, I found out something terrible was happening in the world. I discovered orphans were dying alone in terrible ways. When I found the extent of this horror, I grew furious. I yelled at my computer screen. I wanted to know why no one had done anything about this. Why no one had stopped this from happening. After the anger cooled, something inside me woke up. Instead of being mad that the world overlooked this, maybe I should do something. Maybe I needed to help fix this thing that enraged me.

"I started out by saying if I could fund one child's adoption, that would be my something. That happened, and it still felt empty. It wasn't enough. I sold handwritten love letters for students in my high school to give to those they liked. The business did well, and I was able to top off the accounts of twenty kids. It still wasn't enough because there are still children out there who need to get out. They need families so they can have lives to thrive in. A life where they won't die alone, chained to a bed on the floor of an institution. I have a video that explains things more thoroughly. A few families who have adopted helped me put this together." Boaz pushed a button on a remote, and the screen behind him played several families talking about adoption and the things they experienced at the orphanages.

After the presentation, dinner was served, and I ate next to Boaz at one of the tables where he answered questions from some of the biggest donors. Once bellies were full, the room opened up for dancing. The music started out fast and joyful. We jumped around in celebration until my feet ached. I removed my heels and swayed against Boaz's chest. He twirled me in and out, guiding me to the flow of the soft music.

Phil and Becca had made a Conga line and were circling the room. They picked up people as they went around.

Phill tapped Boaz on the shoulder. "Come on, man, let's go."

Boaz shook his head. "Nope, I gotta dance with my girl for a while."

Boaz put the final amount in the calculator. "Are you ready for the total?"

"What do you think, Jackson? Spill it!" I barely held back from ripping the paper from his hands.

"We raised $30,456.42."

I scrunched my nose. "Someone donated forty-two cents?"

He squinted. "That's your first thought?"

"It was actually, but yay! This is amazing, Boaz!" I flung myself at him, knocking him off his desk chair.

He brought me with him, and we landed with a thud on the floor.

Phil walked in and peered down at us. "Don't mind me. Carry on."

Boaz gave me a quick kiss and helped me off the floor.

The amount raised would be enough for startup costs for Boaz's greeting card business as well as top off the accounts of several kids. I smiled at the handsome profile of my boyfriend as he explained that after the cost of supplies, a hundred percent of the proceeds made from his business would go to the kids and families.

He'd never keep a penny for himself despite all the work he was putting into the entire thing. He offered to pay me for my help, and I told him he'd lost his mind. The time spent making the cards together was our time. It usually ended with kisses and a game of hide and seek.

I left to use the bathroom and returned to find Boaz gone. "Phil, where is Boaz?"

Phil tipped back in his chair and pointed to the night-stand. "He said to direct you there."

I picked up the note and read. *Today's clue is the best place to watch the stars.*

I bolted out the door and drove back to my house. A spring breeze filled the air with the scent of the honeysuckle and roses my mom grew along the sides of our house. I tore through my house toward the backyard.

"Ivy! Door," Mom shouted.

"No time! I can't handle the suspense."

"Ivy!"

I stomped to the front door to shut it and then bolted out the sliding glass.

"Ivy!" Mom stood in the doorway, moving her hand back and forth across the opening.

"You're right there! Can't you close it?"

"So you can continue your barbaric ways of not closing doors? No way!"

"Fine!" I closed the sliding door and huffed to the tree.

Boaz sat on the exact branch he'd rescued me from when we were kids. "Hey, beautiful. Are you ready for today's letter?"

I jumped up, grabbed the lowest branch, and hoisted myself next to him. "What do you think? It took a lot of effort to be here today. I had endless obstacles and burdens to make it to this branch."

He handed over the love letter of the day and leaned back against the tree. "Maybe this will make all that trouble worth it."

I unfolded the red heart.

Dear Ivy,

A year ago, you hated me, and it took us losing ourselves to find each other again. I thought it would be fun to return to the place where a bear and a winter storm shoved us together while we fought fate, kicking and screaming. Feel free to tell me I'm crazy, but I found our shack and thought a camping trip was in order.

My eyes snapped to him. "You found the shack?"

"Yeah, with Phil's help. We used the location we were found and backtracked through Google Earth. It took a few weeks of searching, but we found it and the owner."

My mouth dropped open. "You found the owner? Is it the guy who shot you?"

"Nope, but I arranged with them to let us camp there sometime this summer." He yanked on my arm and helped me to his branch.

I leaned back against him and stared at a robin hopping along the fence that used to divide me from a terrifying dog. "There's an irony to us willingly returning to the place we tried to escape for weeks. I can appreciate it."

He kissed my temple. "You always did love irony."

The sun had started its dip into the horizon, splashing the sky with splatters of color. A light breeze chilled my arms that Boaz rectified by draping his jacket in front of us. We cuddled in the branch of the tree to watch another day fade into a starry night. I tucked today's letter in my pocket, excited to return to the place fate had laughed at us—the place I'd fallen in love with Boaz Jackson.

Epilogue

Noah bounded out of the house, waving his Ninja Turtle figurine. "You have to take this with you, so I know you'll come back."

I accepted his gift and set it on my dash. "There's no question I'm coming back, but see, I put it right here where I'll see it as I'm driving. It'll remind me you need it back."

He threw his arms around me. "And you."

"And me."

"I love you, Bo!"

"I love you too, Noah."

Ivy and I would be gone a week, camping at our shack. Summer had started a week ago, and I'd graduated early as planned. I was in no rush and decided community college on the other side of town would suffice while I figured things out. My dad no longer argued with me about it and had kept his word for months to spend his weekends with Noah and me. Our relationship felt like it was finally headed to a salvageable place.

My mom had left and never looked back. It had been one small thing that severed the tiny thread she'd battled for years.

She'd found out my dad had given me the phone and threw in the towel on her family like she'd wanted to for years. Of course, it really wasn't about the phone. It just gave her the excuse she'd desperately wanted to shed the weight of her family. I did my best not to think about her.

Ivy ran out of my house and leaped into my arms as she wrapped her legs around my waist. "I'm so excited!"

I grinned and kissed her. "I couldn't tell. Not in the slightest bit. You showing up at four am to remind me we were leaving didn't clue me in at all." I plopped her into the passenger side of my truck and got in to drive.

We drove for hours, which gave a clear picture of how far Ivy and I had traveled during our wandering. It had been so easy to get turned around, and we'd found ourselves lucky to have survived. The odds hadn't looked good for us, but we'd beaten them. Now we were back to take on the wilderness on our terms.

On the way, we sang to the radio and talked. At one point, Ivy fell asleep with her head on my lap. It became a battle between looking at her beautiful face and the road. However, that was a struggle anytime I drove with her in my truck.

We vibrated as we ventured onto a gravel road. Blue snowy mountains surrounded the area, and the yellow grass backed up to hundreds of trees full of bright green summer foliage. A lake glistened under the sun in a cloudless sky.

Ivy stirred and sat straight up. "There it is! There it is!" She clapped and jumped out of the vehicle as soon as I threw it in park.

The shack door creaked open, and we stared at the bed and small area around it that we'd somehow lived in for weeks. It brought nostalgia more than trauma. It was a place of fond memories that had seemed devastating at the time. We set up camp and spent the afternoon fishing. I cooked our dinner on a battery-operated grill, and we sat on logs enjoying a properly seasoned meal.

We hiked back up to the abandoned mine and cloud watched in the field where the grass concealed our make-out session. As the sun set, we went back to the shed and fed each other cake Noah had made.

I leaned back against the wall, facing her. She reached over and squished cake in my face, which meant I had to return the favor. She pressed frosting into my hair, and I leaped forward, smearing a good portion on her collarbone. We made ourselves a giant mess and went swimming in the lake to get clean. The moonlight made her visible enough to find and pull to me. We twirled and danced in the water. I locked my palms together, and she stepped on them to launch herself farther into the lake.

She flung a ton of water at me, and I chased her. She squealed as I caught her and dunked us both. Her hair stuck against her face, framing it in deeper shadows than the low light of the moon brought. I stared at her to appreciate each perfect line that made up her expressions and awakened me. I carried her out of the water and brought her over to a log, drying her legs and moving upward. She wrapped a towel around me, which cocooned us against each other. We changed into dry clothes in the shed and cuddled under the blankets, watching the stars through the tiny window that we'd watched snow fall from months ago.

♥

I used a fishing line to dangle today's letter in front of the door. I laid on my stomach on the shack roof and knocked to wake Ivy. She stepped outside, read the letter, and glanced up as I'd directed on the note.

Her shirt had slipped off one shoulder, and her brown hair looked rumpled from sleep. Her newly awake eyes peered at me, and I took in a sharp breath at how gorgeous she appeared, silhouetted by the almost risen sun. My love for her simmered until it boiled up through my throat in demand to have her close.

I pointed to the side of the shack. "Get up here!"

She scrunched her nose in a way that always left me amused. "What?"

"Climb the ladder over there and get in my arms already."

She complied, and I yanked her to me as we fell back on the blankets and pillows I'd placed for us. We rolled under a blanket to snuggle close, and I indulged in the pressure of her lips against mine. I held her as we took in the sunrise. The colors brought promise and warmth.

"I think fate is pretty pleased with herself," Ivy said.

"You think so?"

"Definitely. She turned my enemy back into my best friend and took it a step further by making him my love."

I kissed down her neck to enjoy the way it made her shudder. "We got pretty lucky she took such an interest in us."

"We're the luckiest. The most ironic thing about all of this is that the love letters I despised became what I treasure more than anything. The love letters of Boaz Jackson are pretty powerful." She turned over and touched her nose to mine.

"Are they now?"

"They are. They restored the lives of orphans and captured my heart. I'm not sure there's anything much more powerful than that."

"You might be right. It was pretty difficult winning your heart." I tickled her, and she giggled and squirmed. "I'm holding on to it pretty tight."

"Fortunately for you, I freely give it."

She buried her face in my chest and hummed as she

smelled my shirt. I kissed her head and savored the way we curved together. Orange painted the sky, fanning out from the pinks and purples. She smelled like fresh rain and strawberries. It worked to dull my senses to anything else but her. My love for her flowed through me, made strong from all the things we'd endured together since childhood.

Ivy Carter and I would live our lives together in an imperfect world and wake up each day to make it a little better. We wouldn't turn a blind eye to the voiceless, and we would give the innocent who others ignored a chance to thrive. That's what I had been doing all along, lending my voice to those who couldn't fight for themselves. In doing that, I'd been blessed to fall in love with my best friend—the girl I would never stop writing love letters to.

Coming Soon by Dani K. West

The Summer of Fireflies

Chapter One

My mother, Ester Boone, believed in magical things despite never bearing witness to a single one. She believed in the Fae, good luck charms, and terrible omens. She kept her head in the clouds filled with dreams that held no place in the studio apartment we crammed ourselves inside. We lived in the worst part of Brandle. They called it the Alleys because most everyone lived down a too-narrow street as the city had built too many apartments to hide away the poor. Even after all my mother's mucky misfortune, she still believed the fireflies of summer brought magic from faraway lands—lands she wanted to escape to.

Mom had given me the little window cove as mine, making it the closest thing to a bedroom she could provide for me. It consisted of a blue cushioned window seat with two small shelves carved into the wall at my feet. Drawers underneath the seat contained all my clothes, and purple fairy curtains gave me privacy. I kept books and school supplies on the shelves, all lined up in organized piles. Above the shelves were my board and calendar, where everything could be written to maintain my schedule and appointments to perfection.

She flung back my curtains and waved the ticket in her hand. "This is it, Harlow! We'll get out of this dump and have a better life. They're letting ten families from the Alleys move into the newly built houses on the west side."

I wrote the answer to my latest equation and set down my pencil . "There are thousands of families in the Alleys. The odds aren't good for us. Would you like me to calculate them?"

She laughed. "Statistics don't count magic."

"How would we even afford to live over there? Just because they let us move in doesn't mean it's sustainable."

"They set you up. The home is furnished. We could have beds, Harlow. Real beds and maybe one of those soaking tubs. They give living expenses for two years and help provide jobs. It's about really bringing people out of being poor."

I sighed, not liking that this contest would bring her disappointment. "Mom, it's a really long shot. They aren't going to pick us."

"I rubbed my rabbit's foot all over it."

I closed my eyes, not to roll them, clinging to my respect for my mother. "Don't you think that foot is bad luck? It came from your beloved Cherry. He didn't have the greatest end for a bunny."

"The entire thing was full of good luck. The hawk carried him away, but my father found the body and gave me the foot. That seems pretty lucky he could locate it, and the magic part was still intact."

"But your rabbit was dead."

"Pretty lucky for that hawk," she said.

"Not if it didn't get to eat it as a meal. I have homework to do."

She stuck her ticket in her pocket. "Maybe we could sneak up on the roof later and check on the garden."

"Maybe. If I can get ahead in math and my history presentation."

She tied her frizzy black hair into a ponytail. My mother had chaotic hair that had a life of its own, and she only tried to tame it when she cooked. It hung free to carry out its will the rest of the time. She was young, as she'd had me at fifteen and found a way for us ever since her parents kicked her out of the house. She always claimed their disappointment in her pregnancy was understandable, as they believed she'd transgressed against God.

She avoided questions about my father like they were the Egyptian plagues in her Bible. Though immensely creative and resourceful, my mother often seemed childlike with her carefree spirit. She claimed a head injury when she was five had left her unsmart, as she put it. She seemed like one of the most intelligent people I knew, but not in the way of math and science that most people valued.

Her vibrant green eyes always filled with a light she pulled from somewhere in the darkest times. My brown ones seemed appropriately ordinary as the mundane kept me safe. Responsibility meant I'd get us both out of Brandle. My mother was rainbows and dancing while I stabilized with black and white and stringent routines.

She left me to do my homework, and I pushed away thoughts of how disappointed she'd be when that ticket didn't work out. Between math and history, I took a break to look down at the smokey streets four stories down. Few people went out after dark, and the scarce flicker of streetlights lit up empty sidewalks and rusted, dented cars parked along the curb. The city-owned grass remained yellow, not because it hadn't recovered from winter but because it suffered neglect along with the litter-infested flower boxes.

Windows on apartments and storefronts had bars to defend against frequent thievery. Crime was why everything shut down after the sunset. Store hours changed dependent on the sun's seasonal behavior. A man smoked a cigarette and leaned against a boarded-up shop. Another man walked by him, and they exchanged something in a passing handshake.

"Low! Dinner is ready!" Mom called from the kitchen that rested a few feet from my cove. Everything in our apartment rested a few feet from my cove.

"Canned green beans and bread and butter again?" I took my seat at our wobbly metal table.

"Yeah, it's pretty great that Mr. Gallinger let me take the butter home."

"Yeah, very nice of him."

My mom did odd jobs around town as work was difficult to come by in the Alleys. It was worse for my mother because she had never gone to school or learned to read. I'd tried to teach her, but it only confused her. Mr. Gallinger was a man whose house she cleaned twice a month. He often gave her food to take home as part of his payment. Otherwise, we had nights I went to bed early to avoid hunger. That was the importance of school to me. I'd find opportunities for us both.

I helped her clean up dinner and glanced at the clock. "I'm not sure I can go up to the roof tonight. My history presentation is only two weeks away."

"You told me it was almost done."

"That's true, but I need to make sure it's up to standards."

"Give me an hour, Low. One hour."

I sighed, unable to take her pleading eyes and tight mouth. "Okay, Mama. One hour."

She grabbed the lantern from our tiny pantry that only held three canned goods, the lantern, and backup batteries. I unlocked the window and stepped onto the rickety fire escape platform. My sneakers kept the grooves from pressing into my feet, but Mom climbed the five stories barefoot like it wasn't hazardous.

Her garden comprised of three flower boxes I'd made in shop class. I unzipped my backpack and unscrewed the jars of water I'd collected in my school bathroom. She watered two, and I took care of the last one. The tulips had finally bloomed along with the daisies and sunflowers. They brightened the lifeless grey roof that looked over the smoggy alleys. Her flowers were like her, a bright spot in a world of dismal grey.

She laid back on the blanket and pillow she kept up there. "Did you bring a new book since we finished the last one already?"

I sat cross-legged in front of her, leaning against one of the boxes. "Yeah, *Little Women* or *The Secret Garden*?"

She propped herself up with her arms behind her. "The garden one."

I opened the book and started into the first chapter. My mother stared at the stars as she listened like she had since I'd first learned to read. I owed her the skill because she walked miles with me every day to get me to school, even in the winter. She'd bundle me in blankets and a coat she'd found in the dumpster. She layered all the clothes she owned for herself and carried me on her back to the better school across town. Someone had told her the ones in our neighborhood had a high rate of violence and poor test scores. So, every day she sacrificed to take me to the school she thought would teach me to read and keep me safe. I repaid her by reading her books whenever she asked.

**

Even all these years later, I walked miles to school to go to the better one. Mom and I walked together until we got out of the Alleys and into the better neighborhoods. From there, she went to find odd jobs for the day, and I headed to school.

As usual, I arrived early and took my spot under the willow tree at the back of the school. The timer on my phone gave me an hour to study before I needed to go in to get breakfast. I went through my alphabetized folders and found my history presentation. My mom had enjoyed the story so much last night that I'd read to her much longer than I should have. Sleep was important for function, and it needed to be kept at the same time each night.

"Help! Help!" a voice shouted from somewhere in the woods to my left.

The large four-story high school to my right would have made more sense for a voice to be coming from. The pine trees grew close and gave little space to trek through. Kids often journeyed inside to play odd games and make out. The numbers on the timer decreasing tempted me to ignore the continued pleas for help.

Integrity mattered more than routine, so I packed my bag and headed into the woods with reluctance and sighing. The green scents of moss and pine needles overwhelmed the earthy aromas of rich black soil that sunk a little as I walked. Birds scattered at my approach, filling the air with chirping and the wisp of flapping wings. The cries led me to a tall oak tree hiding among the evergreens. Its leaves had yet to recover from winter's hostility.

A boy dangled by his feet from a rope that wrapped around his ankles. His brown hair flew about like wild grass caught in the wind and occasionally gave a view of his reddened face. "Hey! Help!"

"I heard. You disturbed my homework."

"Sorry for the inconvenience, but could you cut me loose?"

"Maybe. It depends."

He tossed his hand to the side. "On what?"

"Why did someone capture you?"

"Because I'm an idiot."

"That seems clear, so why should I set an idiot free?"

"Does it matter? It's the right thing to do."

I circled around him to get a better look at his face. "Is it?"

"Yes!"

"How would I even get you down?"

He pointed to the ground. "I dropped my hunting knife a little bit ago. It should be somewhere on the ground."

"You expect me to climb the tree and cut you down? That sounds dangerous. We should call the fire department."

"No! I'd rather live in this tree. The game is sacred, and I'm not willing to ruin it for everyone."

"The game?"

"Survival. All the high schools start them randomly throughout the year."

I crinkled my nose. "On a school night?"

He snickered. "Yeah, come on. Help a guy out."

I searched the ground until I located his knife. It seemed dangerous to climb a tree with the knife but leaving him wasn't right either. I stuck the weapon in my backpack and scaled the tree. He hung from the middle of the branch, and I scooted along on my belly until I made it to the knot in the rope.

I sawed until it started to give. "It's about to break." With a few more knife swipes, the rope loosened and snapped.

He plummeted toward the ground but flipped himself enough to land on his bottom.

I scaled down and reached out my hand to help him up. "Are you alright?"

He accepted my hand and stood up. "Fine. Thank you!" He kept a hold of my hand and shook it. "Trace Viotto. It's nice to meet you."

"You don't go to my school."

"You're right. The west side is more my area."

I rolled my eyes. "Figures you get yourself in trouble. You

have time to waste because your future is set. The disparity is appalling. You could use your time to help the world instead of wasting it on games."

"Who says I don't help the world other times? Because I have fun and come from means, you assume I waste all my time."

"I'd bet on it."

He sent me a crooked smile. "Are you going to tell me your name since I gave you mine?"

"No." I turned and walked out of the woods, leaving a smirking Trace behind.